Mr Prendergast's
Fantastic Find

John Brassey

Mr Prendergast's Fantastic Find

A novel

by John Brassey

Best

John

Chapter One

Dave

Only a day and seventeen hours remain when I spot it. I stop scrolling and scroll back up again. Are they what I think they are? I've done this a thousand times and, okay, once or twice I've had a winner like the 'pottery man on wall' for a tenner who turned out to be a fabulous antique German gnome tobacco box and sold for a hundred and fifty pounds, and the 'golf pitcher' for eight pounds that was a rare original watercolour caricature by a famous illustrator and ended up in a Floridian golf academy and paid for a holiday in the Caribbean. But those are the exceptions and I've lost count of the 'amazing' finds that have turned up on the doorstep in scrappy cardboard boxes padded out with screwed up pages from *The Sun,* reeking of stale cigarettes and bearing no resemblance to the treasure I'd imagined when I looked at the blurry photos and clicked the bid button.

My best ever find could have netted me a very hefty profit but I could tell that my luck was out the moment the courier handed me the ominously rattling box. I knew immediately that my beautiful ten thousand pound William De Morgan ceramic charger was going to be a one thousand piece William De Morgan jigsaw puzzle.

I spend hours every week on eBay. You might call me an addict but I see myself as a bargain hunter. For me it's one enormous antiques fair, or car boot sale perhaps. Here the whole world is setting out its wares and, instead of me having to get up at six in the morning and drive miles to some muddy field or cold village hall and hope that I spot the treasure before the twenty antique dealers and fellow eBayers who got there before me see it, I can scroll at leisure page after page after page until my fingers (and my eyes) can't take any more.

So how do I feel about paying eight pounds (I did bid a hundred but nobody else was bidding) for that two thousand pound caricature? Should I feel bad about it, taking a huge profit from some poor bloke who couldn't recognise fine artistry or spell 'picture'? I don't think I'm quite as bad as the smug idiots with their knowing grins who you see on *Antiques Roadshow* telling the expert that they bought, what now turns out to be a fifteen grand Faberge piece, in a charity shop... for a fiver. I'm still waiting for the day when the valuer, instead of joining in the smuggery of it all, says "Oh, and which charity shop was that?" and when the punter replies "Oxfam" the expert turns to the camera and says "Well I am sure that Oxfam will be delighted to hear about your windfall. How much do you think you'll be donating?" It will never happen of course.

Antique dealers are fair game. If they don't know that their 'Edwardian' cup is two hundred years older, that's their problem. Car boot sales are debatable. Many of the sellers are running a little business as part of the black economy. Who is to know if the black metal candlestick for one pound fifty really did come from clearing out their dead granny's flat or was simply something that they picked up from a charity shop whose manager was equally unable to identify tarnished Georgian silver if it socked him in the mouth.

I'm not going to reveal my methods, but let's just say that if a magnificent and rare coffee service by Clarice Cliff is listed in the 'Televisions' section as 'Six Old Cups And Saucers And A Pot', or, even better, 'Old Crockery' with just one poorly focused image, things start to look up. Why on earth would it be in the 'tellies' category? Happens all the time. You put your TV for sale, click on 'List Another Item' and forget to change categories. 'Simples', as the Russian meerkat would say.

I almost fall downstairs in my hurry to give Sheila the news. She's at the table writing.

"Careful" she says, "you're going to kill yourself one day"

"I'm okay. Just in a rush to show you this"

"What now?'

I place the MacBook Pro down in front of her.

"Hmmm."

"They're worth thousands," I say. "Thousands. Just one sold in Lenhams New York last year for eighty-five thousand dollars and this is a pair – a hundred grand at least. You never see a pair. They'll set a new record for Yabu."

"Hmmm. How many times have I heard this? How many?"

Sheila opens the cupboard behind where she is sitting.

"Isn't this the rare Swansea porcelain worth five thousand pounds?" She hands me the gaudily decorated cup and saucer that I'd be lucky to sell for fifty pence.

"I know. I know. I got that one wrong. It looked right. It was worth the gamble. It was only a fiver."

"Plus the shipping. You always forget to mention the shipping"

"Okay so ten maybe. That's nothing. The price of a decent steak at the butchers."

"Ten pounds might be nothing but when it happens a hundred times it starts adding up to a hell of a lot of prime beef. We could have our own blinking bull grazing in the garden."

"Don't exaggerate. Remember the caricature."

"Yes. One caricature and a nice holiday in ten years is not what I'd call a worthwhile use of your time. And this?" Another dismal mistake is held in front of me. I feel like the accused hoping for a friendly jury. "You told me we'd be off to Venice when you sold it. We didn't even get to Blackpool... It's still here."

"Okay. I was wrong then too."

She reaches back into the crammed cupboard.

"Don't get any more out. You've made your point, but look, just have a look."

I click on the zoom-photo option. There's only one photo and it looks as if somebody with a bad hangover took it through a net curtain.

"How do you know they're what you think they are?"

"I can just tell."

"You can just tell?"

Sheila makes to open the cupboard again. "You can't see anything from that photo."

"Yes but read the description."

She reads from the screen. "*Two Flower Pots With Frogs On.* That's a catchy heading. *These two flower pots are from my Grandad's house. They are quite nice but I have no place to put them so they need to find a new home.* It's not exactly marketing genius. What's the seller's user name? Saatchi & Saatchi?"

"Actually, I think there *is* a clue in the title and the user's name. Go into that translation website. What's it called? Babel Fish or something and type in 'Flower Pots'."

"What language am I translating into?"

"Try Spanish. I've only been searching for stuff within fifteen miles of our post code but that user name doesn't look English."

"In Spanish it says 'Flower pot' is 'florero'"

"Okay. Now do them back the other way round."

"What do you mean?"

"Type in 'florero' and translate Spanish to English"

"Vase...Ah. Lost in translation, eh? They've used an Internet translator."

I reach over Sheila's shoulder and open a new tab. I click on Lenhams' site and type Yabu Meizan into the search box. Hundreds of items flash onto the screen so I filter them down to prices over ten thousand and list in price descending order and there it is.

"It's not the same."

"It couldn't be the same. All his pieces are unique. If they were the same I'd be worried that they were wrong but the shape makes me wonder if they once formed part of a garniture with the other."

"So you better start asking the seller some questions then."

"You must be joking. And start them thinking they've got something valuable when someone with two thousand feedbacks gets in touch. They might look closely at the listing and realise they've listed them under Pots And Pans and before you know it it's cancelled and we've lost our big chance."

"Well you can't just bid on them. What if they're chipped or cracked they won't be worth a hundred grand then."

"They'll still be worth what I bid"

Sheila looks back in the direction of the cupboard.

"Look at the listing again" I say, "It's been running for nine days and nobody has seen it. Look at the hit counter."

"Three. That's not nobody."

"One's me, the seller is almost certainly another and that leaves just one more and if they were at all interested they would have been back time and again. I'm telling you. This is the one."

"So how much are you going to bid?"

We hear the front door open and slam shut.

"Hi, love. Good day?', Sheila calls.

A muffled "okay" reaches us from the hallway before the door opens for our son to make his usual two second appearance before disappearing into his room and slowing the Internet speed for the entire neighbourhood for the night.

"What's up?" he asks.

"Oh it's your dad. He's just found our fortune on eBay."

"Really?" he pauses, "Again?" He turns to leave.

"Wait," I say. "Don't just make fun without looking. That Philip Mould found a Gainsborough on eBay a few years ago. Just have a look."

Simon towers over me. I was happy with my average 5'10" until a growing spurt took him six inches beyond me.

He looks me up and down. "Ah yes. The suave, debonair, handsome and probably very rich Philip Mould. Perhaps *you'll* be in line for a series with 'Rear Of The Year' Fiona Bruce after this." He peers at the screen with the same air of dismissal. "So what are they then? Chinese vases like that one in Ruislip that sold for fifty million?"

"Not quite in that league, son, but good money. Something that might help you to get onto the housing ladder."

"So *that's* why you're always scrolling through eBay. You want to get rid of me."

Sheila looks dotingly on the love of her life, "Of course we don't"

"I just thought that perhaps *you* might want to get away from us. Thirty and still with your parents isn't ideal."

I feel a solid punch in my back.

It's time to shut up before we get into the same old argument. Maybe I'm selfish but I can see the clock running down and our lives still revolving around the kids just before the dementia sets in or the heart gives out. I thought it would have ended soon after I drove that last long journey back from Oxford, helped him get his CV sorted and looked forward to the empty nest lifestyle we'd enjoyed during term times for the previous three years. Things like having a good Internet signal, watching what we wanted on TV, eating what we felt like (and when we felt like it) and yes, I am embarrassed to admit it, the sex. At sixty-two I'm not expecting to be at it like a couple of rabbits but it was nice once in a while to be able to enjoy a bit of lovemaking at the time we wanted without worrying about the bedroom noises. It doesn't seem to worry him mind. We have to put up with a hell of a racket from his visitors. I yearn for the days of sleepovers and of pillow fights reverberating around the house. Even the later years of Limp Bizkit and Marilyn Manson were preferable to the soundtrack of that scene from *When Harry Met Sally*. Now the pillows are firmly over my ears.

"So. Are they by that Yabu Whatsit you're always going on about?"

"There you go Sheila. Even Simon can see they're by Yabu Meizan."

"I didn't say that Dad. It's just that half the stuff in that cupboard was *supposed* to be by him. And wasn't."

"Oh ye of little faith. Just you wait. This time next week you'll be laughing on the other sides of your faces."

Chapter Two

Maria

I check out the eBay auctions again. They finish tomorrow night and most are doing okay. I hope that bidders are not too put off by my English or by the lousy photos. I just cannot get the focus right on this old iPhone.

It is sad that nobody seems to want the floreros. No bids and only three views and they start at just thirty pounds. It will take me ages to pack them up and get them to the post office. Poor old Abuelo would not be happy. I remember he told me he brought them back from San Francisco at the end of the war. He explained how all the Japanese people had been taken away from the city, how their houses were looted and how their belongings ended up in auctions and second hand shops. He found these pots in one of those shops. He said that they were almost new then so they are not antiques and will not be very valuable. I loved them when I was little. I used to spend ages looking at all the tiny frogs and marveling at the borders filled with miniature delicate flowers. They are only small but there is nowhere to put them in this bedsit and I need some money.

Should I cancel the sale and save me that packing? Nobody would mind. Nobody is watching them, nobody has bid. Nobody will care.

I flip open the phone cover and tap on the eBay app. Just as I am about to tap on 'cancel sale' the phone gives a trill notification ring.

'Question About eBay Item Two Flower Pots With Frogs On'

Good timing. So, somebody *is* interested.

I open the message. It's from SimonOxford1985. I wonder if Oxford is his surname or that is where he lives. I love that place. I worked there as an au pair when I first came to England. I check what he has to say.

> 'Hi MuchachaBonita are these pots in good
> condition or are they cracked or chipped? Can you
> tell me any more about them? I see that your
> location is not far from me. Would you be happy
> for me to collect them if I win the auction?

I am not sure that it is sensible to allow a man to come
to my bedsit to collect them. I think carefully before I start
my reply.

> 'Hello SimonOxford1985. The pots are in very good
> condition but there are lots of tiny cracks or
> crackles in the surface. They are not chipped. Also,
> on the bottom there is a gold square with squiggles
> inside also in gold that I think is Japanese. I cannot
> translate it and this phone does not let me take
> good photos. They are very nice and I think you
> will be happy if you win the auction. I am not sure
> that you can collect them.'

I press send, close up the phone and head to the fridge.

It is only five minutes later and I am chopping an onion
and trying to resist rubbing my eyes and making the
soreness even worse when the familiar trill rings out again.

> 'Question About eBay Item Two Flower Pots With
> Frogs On'

Is another bidder interested? Will more bids come in or
is it SimonOxford1985 again?

I wipe my oniony fingers on my apron and flip open the
phone. I tap on the question.

> 'Hi again MuchachaBonita thanks for your speedy
> response to my question. I know that you may not
> want a stranger coming to your house but I assure
> you that I am quite harmless. I promise to ring the
> bell and stand a few paces back so you can just put
> them down and shut the door if you are worried.
> Think of all that packing time and the trip to the

post office you will save.'

I smile. He is a little 'descarado', or cheeky as the English might say, but in a nice way.

'Hello SimonOxford1985. I suppose that if you stand a few paces back I might let you collect them. Will they be long paces?'

I wait to see if he responds before I have to get back to cooking. The trill is almost instant.

'Question About eBay Item Two Flower Pots With Frogs On' 'I'm six foot four so they'll be very long paces ☺*'*

I reply, '☺'
The phone comes back to life.

'Question About eBay Item Two Flower Pots With Frogs On' 'By the way. Final question. What does your user name mean?'

I tap into the phone

'It is Spanish. It is what my grandfather used to call me. It means pretty girl but of course all grandfathers think that their granddaughters are pretty.'

I am getting hungry but I wonder about the six foot four SimonOxford1985. Is he a single man?
He replies again.

'Question About eBay Item Two Flower Pots With Frogs On' 'Final, final message I promise. If you let me collect them I will see if Grandad was right ☺*'*

I hope he is single with that message. I would not want my man (if I had one) sending flirty messages to anonymous strangers on the Internet. Whatever next? Sexting? No thank you.

My stomach has been waiting too long. I send a final speedy '☺'.

Chapter Three

Dave

I'm relaxing over breakfast when Simon joins me in the kitchen.

"Well Dad. It looks like you might be right for once."

"What do you mean?" I'm never right as far as my son is involved.

"Yabu Whatsit's vases."

Why does he always call him 'Yabu Whatsit'? He knows exactly who he is. He studied fine art at uni and I know he's extremely knowledgeable on all sorts of works of art and antiques.

"What do you mean? Been checking out the world record vase on Lenhams' website?"

"No. Better than that. I asked the pretty girl about them."

I splutter into my Earl Grey. "You what?"

"The pretty girl 'MuchachaBonita', the seller on eBay."

"But I didn't want to approach her."

"I know but I didn't think you'd mind me doing some asking for you. After all I know how much you'd like to get rid of me."

"Yes... But you might have got her thinking. No—I don't mean yes— I'd like to get rid of you. Of course I don't." Was that convincing? I somehow doubt it.

"No. Don't worry I haven't stirred up any hornets' nests for you. I just asked her a few things about the vases?"

"Like what?"

"Would she cancel the sale and sell them to me for twenty grand?"

I've no idea where my son got his sense of humour.

"Ha bloody ha. I suppose she said yes but if she did she's a liar because I looked five minutes ago and they're still there."

"Nah. She said she'd only stop it if I make it thirty grand."

"Stop trying to wind me up, because you're doing a very good job of it so far."

"There you go," he hands me his iPhone open on the eBay app.

I scroll through the messages, my spirits rising as I read about the all-over crackle (absolutely right for this type of Satsuma ware). The gold seal too in a square box - Yabu Meizan's signature can be best described as a series of squiggles in a gilded square. And she might consider letting him collect. Perfect. No chance of another costly jigsaw puzzle.

"Well I raise my hat to you, son. Well done. I was pretty sure but now I'm certain. But when you collect them it's just a quick hello and goodbye I don't want to fleece someone for a hundred grand and discover she's not a dealer."

"You know she's not a dealer. You can tell from the other stuff she's selling. Dresses, a kettle, some saucepans just the usual household stuff."

"Lah lah lah. Don't want to hear any more. Maybe collecting them is not such a great idea. Don't antique dealers wear dresses and own kettles?"

"So you're willing to risk two precious vases packed by an inexperienced packer with the Post Office?"

"No. But I can just tell that this is going to cause problems"

"You and your conscience Dad. Most people wouldn't care less. They'd say 'Look. She's listed them for thirty pounds, which means that she will be happy to get thirty pounds.' They'd probably even ask for a discount for collecting them and saving her the hassle of packing. They wouldn't give it a second thought."

"But I'm not *most people*. I *do* care. And what happens when they sell and set a world record? She'll see it in the papers."

"It won't merit more than a paragraph in the local free sheet."

"And the *Antiques Trade Gazette*."

"Yes I'm sure she'll subscribe to that. We may even get a sexy junior reporter round here to interview you. You'll be the hero who found them for thirty quid on eBay."

"Until the sexy junior reporter follows up her story and discovers that the original seller was a disabled cancer survivor selflessly raising money to fund an orphanage in Ethiopia."

"I wouldn't worry for now, Dad. Sort your conscience out when you've got them. How many times have we heard we're all going to be rich and you're going to see Mum and me and Susie right? Even if you might just have a chance this time there's a long way to go."

"There's only a few hours left."

"I'm off to work now so good luck."

Chapter Four

Dave

I'm sitting at the dining table in the open plan kitchen-diner. The radio's on and I'm enjoying a listener's favourite tracks. For the past hour I've been in the West Indies. I started with an all inclusive multi–roomed cheap and cheerful place in Antigua but forty minutes later I was browsing Princess Diana's favourite Montpelier Plantation in Nevis researching the price of a fortnight in a suite followed by a chartered yacht around the Caribbean. Sheila keeps muttering about counting my chickens but I've told her that when we are rich she'll be downing Killer Bees at Sunshine's and checking out if Travolta and Beyoncé have got beach bodies as good as hers.

When we are rich! This might be our last (and best) chance. I've been retired for four years and the mortgage is still not paid off. There's only sixty K to go and the house is supposed to be worth almost a million. So, theoretically, I *am* rich. Yes I'm almost a millionaire but I don't feel like one. The bank pension isn't exactly keeping us in the lap of luxury and I can't believe that I find myself wishing our sixty-fifth birthdays would hurry up so that we can draw our Government pensions. What a sad case -wishing our lives away for a bit of cash. Perhaps we can sell the semi and head up north where I read that you can buy a mansion for a few hundred thousand.

One hour to go. I keep refreshing the listing. Still no bids. Still only half a dozen views. I refresh again. Two more viewers. That's a bit worrying.

I usually snipe my finds. That means that, even if I am out, a computer will put my bid in during the final ten seconds and nobody will be able to react and outbid me (if I put a big enough bid in). But what if I type my password incorrectly into the snipe program? What if the snipe program's server goes down? Well I could put in snipes on two or three different sniper websites. What if they all fail? Don't be stupid they won't all fail.

Sheila comes in from the garden.

"How long to go before we're rich then?"

"Forty-seven minutes and twenty seconds."

"You're not going to just sit there for another forty-seven minutes pressing that blinking refresh button are you. There's a pile of ironing needs doing and the kitchen looks a mess."

"Okay. If you tidy the kitchen, I'll get on with the ironing."

I pull the ironing board out from the cupboard beneath the stairs and set it up near the table so that I can see the laptop and refresh it regularly to save the screensaver coming up. I run upstairs and collect the pile of ironing. I run back down and take the iron to the tap to fill it up with water.

Refresh, iron, refresh, iron, refresh, iron. The pile of creased clothing is quickly diminished and replaced by a pile of crisply pressed garments. I finish and there's ten minutes to go. I grab the pile of clothes and run upstairs with them. I put everything in its proper place and hurry back downstairs.

Six minutes to go. I move the computer to the opposite side of the table and draw up a chair.

"You've left the iron plugged in."

"Sshhh. I'll sort it in a minute."

Sheila moves towards the iron.

"Don't worry, love. I told you, I'll sort it in a minute there's only five minutes left."

"That's plenty of time for you to do it and get back to your precious eBay."

"Okay, Okay I'll do it." I hesitate and press refresh yet again. Another viewer but still no bids.

"I don't like the room looking a mess with an ironing board in the middle of it. I'll tidy it. Did you remember to put something down on the floorboards to catch all the drips from the iron?"

"Sorry... I forgot." I'm hardly listening. Refresh. Still no bids. Four minutes left. Refresh.

Sheila yanks open a kitchen drawer with a force that

almost pulls it off its runners. She grabs a thick tea towel from the drawer. She crosses the polished floor towards the ironing board. "How many times do I need to tell you —" the words are barely out of her mouth when she blurs into a flailing flash of white cardigan and blue jeans. Crash.

"Sheila!"

I panic. Three minutes twenty seconds. That was quite a slip. I leap from my seat and see that she's shaken but there looks to be no damage done.

"Don't come and help me then."

I move towards her. Two minutes and fifty seconds. She struggles to pull herself upright using the ironing board for support. Too late I realise that I didn't click it properly into position when I put it up. It starts to fold shut sending the heavy, hissing and scalding hot appliance flying into the air like Smaug on his way to Rivendell. I watch helplessly as a liquid parabola arcs from its reservoir. Bang. The room goes silent. Ed Sheeran stops telling his girl he will still love her when he's seventy and the gentle and comforting hum of the wine fridge drones to a halt.

I reach in panic to the laptop. I press refresh.

'You are not connected to the Internet.'

Refresh.

'You are not connected to the Internet'

"For God's sake!"

I rush to the wall socket and pull the plug from the wall. I pick up the tea towel and carefully mop up the iron's spewed contents. I gingerly wipe dry the socket and all around it. There's a searing pain in my left hand and I recoil. "Bloody iron."

"What about me?" Sheila is now standing. Her face is the colour of chalk and she's not just shaking like a leaf she's trembling like a whole blinking forest.

I ignore her and swing open the door to the under stairs cupboard. I open the fuse box, searching for the trip that's in the opposite position to all the others. I find it and flip it. Ed Sheeran's back on and he's found love. The wine is starting to cool down again and I press refresh.

'You are not connected to the Internet'

I look at the wireless router. One of the lights is flashing orange. Come on. Come on. Still flashing orange. Please. Pleeease.

The broadband light goes steady orange. The long strip at the bottom is still orange. Orange, orange, orange. Come on. Come on. Blue.

I leap out of the cupboard.

I press refresh.

'Sale ended.'

I slump into my seat.

"Have you forgotten me?" Sheila has stopped her quivering now and the colour is returning to her cheeks. "Well? Did you get them?"

I shake my head. "No."

"No? No? *NO*? I nearly died and you *DIDN'T* get them!" She grabs the tea towel and flicks it...hard.

I recoil as the wet material catches my glasses and wrenches them from my face taking one of my hearing aids with it.

"Careful," I say.

"Careful. I'll give you careful. Killer Bees at Sunshines. Chartered bloody yachts."

I reel from another blow from the tea towel. I put my arms over my head preparing for an onslaught.

The muffled sound of the front door opening comes from the hall.

The kitchen-diner's door opens and Simon's head peers around it, "What's going on?"

"Nothing."

"It doesn't look like nothing to me. There's a pair of broken glasses on the kitchen tiles, one of your hearing aids is dangling from the light fitting and the iron's burning a hole in the floorboards."

"Your mum's just had a little accident."

"That's why *you* look like you've been punched in the face by Tyson Fury."

"Don't be daft. Your mum slipped on the floor, I went to

help her up" –Sheila shoots me a Gorgon stare – "and I went down with her."

"Good job you weren't going down *on* her with me coming home from work early, eh Dad?"

"Christ son, If I'd made a joke like that in front of your Nana and Grandad at your age I'd have been out on my ear with my case packed before you could say 'Jack Robinson'."

"I don't think Nana and Grandad would have got it, and anyway, as you keep telling me, you were in your own place when you were twenty-two."

Sheila flushes "What's brought you home at this time, darling?"

"I just wanted to see how Dad got on with Yabu Whatsit. I had a free period at three and managed to get away early. Should I be shouting "Yabu Dabba Doo" and pouring us all a glass of champagne?"

"He didn't."

"Didn't what?"

"Get anywhere with them."

"You're kidding me. I thought this was the find of a lifetime. Did someone else spot the sale and outbid him?"

"He didn't get his bid in."

"What about his failsafe sniper program?"

"Ask your father."

I refresh the computer page and turn it towards Simon. "Aw Dad. Ya Boo Sucks."

Chapter Five

Maria

That did not go too badly. Twenty-five pounds for the backless dress, ten for the kettle, thirty for the pans, forty for the dressing gown (I do not think I paid that much for it when it was new) but no bids for the frogs. Perhaps it is a message from Abuelo. He did not want me to get rid of them. I wonder what happened to SimonOxford1985. He seemed to be really interested. I think I will keep them for now and try again some time in the future.

My phone starts trilling at regular intervals as the payments begin to come in. I quite enjoy the mix of trilling and 'ker-ching' sounds as I get ready to go to work.

I have got my uniform on and have another look at the phone. Brilliant. They have all paid already. That is a few hundred pounds towards next month's rent. I click on the screen to transfer the money to my bank account. There is another trill.

'Question About eBay Item Two Flower Pots With Frogs On'.

SimonOxford1985: *Hi MuchachaBonita. Or can I just call you Bonita? I'm so, so sorry. I really wanted to get your two pots with frogs on but I missed my bus on the way home and when I got to my computer I was too late.*

Has he not heard of smart phones? I was sure he was using a smart phone app yesterday.

MuchachaBonita: *What happened to your cell phone?*

SimonOxford1985: *No signal on the bus.*

MuchachaBonita: I get that sometimes on the 82.

SimonOxford1985: *The 82 to Golders Green?*

MuchachaBonita:*That is the one. You know it?*

SimonOxford1985: *On it every day. I live in Finchley. Don't tell me you're the tall dark girl who gets off at the railway arches stop by the Spanish restaurant at six o'clock. Now she IS mucho bonita.*

MuchachaBonita: *It is not me. But I do know that restaurant. I work there. And, as you English say, BY THE WAY, it is Muy Bonita.*

I press send and realise that I have just told a flirty stranger where I work. At least I have not told him where I live.

SimonOxford1985: *So what is going to happen about the pots? Can I buy them privately without bothering going through eBay? It will save you some fees.*

MuchachaBonita: *I am not sure. They belonged to my grandfather and it is possibly him that made you miss your bus. He may have wanted me to keep them for MY grandchildren.*

SimonOxford1985: *Ooh spooky. I think I did catch a whiff of Rioja and Marlboros on my way to the bus stop. But that might just have been from the Tapas Bar by Boots. I'm sure your grandad's ghost would want me to have them. I'm a frog collector you see.*

MuchachaBonita: *I have heard of stamp collectors and coin collectors but what is a frog collector?*

SimonOxford1985: *I collect anything to do with*

frogs. You name it. I collect it. Pictures, mugs, t-shirts, computer games, toys. I'm a frog fanatic. They would look great in my collection.

MuchachaBonita: *I am late for work. I will think about it. Good night SimonOxford1985.*

SimonOxford1985: *Goodnight, MuchachaBonita. Please think about the pots. If you want to get in touch without using eBay, my mobile is – he lists a number in words instead of figures. (Can't put number in in numbers as I don't think swapping numbers is allowed on this app). P.S I'm feeling a bit hungry. I might see you later at Casa Nuestra.*

I flip the phone cover closed and put on my coat. I hope that last part of the message is only a joke. I do not have time for a six-foot-four frog collector in my life.

Chapter Six

Dave

"What are we eating tonight, love?"

"You say that as if nothing has happened. You think I feel like eating after what I've been through?"

"I know it shook you up but there was no damage done."

"No damage! Those glasses cost nine hundred pounds. There's an iron-shaped burn in the floorboards, my knee is killing me and you dangled a luxury yacht in the Caribbean in front of me and then snatched it away."

I want to say 'and whose fault is it that the glasses are broken?' or 'if you could have waited five minutes to tidy your precious house we might now be rich' but I know whose fault it is that she slipped. I've never managed perfection in forty years. I'm not going to start now.

I say nothing.

"You get something to eat. Don't let me stop you eating. I suppose nothing has happened as far as you are concerned. Eat. But don't you dare mess up that kitchen."

"I thought we might go out. There's not much in the fridge."

"And where are we going to get the money to go out to eat?"

"I was only thinking of the Spanish place by the railway arches"

"Why there? It's miles away."

"It's not too bad on the bus."

"Why the bus? You could go in the car."

"I thought I might have a few beers or a couple of glasses of wine."

"So why go all that way? You could go to the Italian on the High St."

"I just fancied Spanish tonight and..."

"And what?"

"Nothing. It's just... Simon reckons the seller of the Yabu vases works there and—"

"So that's it. It's nothing to do with wanting a paella. I don't want to hear another word about those bloody vases after what you've put me through."

"Sorry. But I really want to try and put things right."

"Well you go then. I told you I'm not hungry."

"But you've eaten nothing all day. You must be hungry."

"I'm not hungry and I've got a splitting headache. Don't let me stop *you* going and spending what little money we've got .You go out and enjoy yourself. Leave me here checking all the pages in your Internet history and looking at where you were going to take me. You spend all day telling me about the West Indies, then you half kill me and *then* you expect me to relish the prospect of walking to the bus stop in the pouring rain to eat a meal in a Spanish restaurant half an hour away. I sometimes wonder if you know me at all."

"It *is* a very good Spanish restaurant—"

"I don't care if it's got three Michelin stars. You just don't get it."

"I'm sorry, love."

"So that makes it all alright then. Let's forget the glasses and the floorboards and probably a new iron. You're sorry. So that makes everything better."

Sheila slams the door and heads upstairs.

I pull on my hat and scarf and then think again. I'm not sure my bladder will hold out for the time it takes to get to Casa Nuestra. For the last couple of months, when I need to go, I need to go fast and the number 82 bus is not the best place to get caught short. I envisage rushing into the restaurant, past the hostess and straight to the gents all the while fiddling with my fly and quietly thanking God that it's a zip and not buttons. That's hardly going to endear me to the girl who Simon tells me works there. 'Ah yes Señor certainly I will sell you my pots' she'll say surveying me in my malodorous pee-stained trousers.

I take off the hat and scarf and go into the toilet. I pull down the loo seat and my trousers in a coordinated well-practiced movement and take a seat. No standing for me.

No standing means no drips, no dirty seat, no sticky floor and a much quieter and more peaceful life. I don't know why all men don't do it – the divorce rate would plummet.

After flushing and straightening my clothes I go to wash my hands. I look in the mirror. 'Suave and debonair', Simon's words ring in my ear. Expensive titanium rimmed designer spectacles don't have the same impact with two Elastoplasts holding the lenses in place. My grey hair gets thinner every day and I struggle to fasten the elasticated chinos despite them being two sizes bigger than the last pair.

And then there's the bloody hearing aids. I'm not really deaf it's just that odd things kept happening. The waitress in the local pub would tell me the day's special was steak and chips. I'd say "Great I'll have the special then," and then she'd bring me hake and chips. I kept getting drivers hanging onto my taillights and flashing me before overtaking and making up and down hand gestures that indicated that I was regularly using my right thumb and forefinger inappropriately. "Your *indicators*." Sheila would say, "Are you going deaf? Can't you hear them?" And I would always say "Of course not. You've got the radio on too loud. How could I hear that click?"

It all came to a head when old friends came to stay and I demonstrated the new curved Ultra High Definition TV. Both bounced off the sofa, as if performing a synchronised trampoline move, shouting in unison "TURN IT DOWN."

The audiologist in Boots showed me a graph that indicated that I had 'partial hearing loss' – as I said, I'm not *deaf* – and went on to show me the remedies available. I went for a pair from the 'invisible' range that fit snugly behind the arms of my specs and are invisible to everyone. A short length of what looks like transparent nylon fishing line with a miniature cone on the end goes from each aid into the orifices.

"You can't see them," Sheila said.

"You really can't," said the audiologist handing me a mirror.

I'd left the treatment room door open and a woman sitting outside in the waiting area shook her head and added, "You really, really can't." I wondered if this was my *Emperor's New Clothes* moment. Was I the little boy who saw that the Emperor was in the altogether? I could see the aids as clearly as I could see the sign across my forehead that read *OLD MAN*. "I'm sure the *optician* won't be long," I said as I pulled the treatment door to.

"Just you wait," said Sheila shortly after we completed the paperwork for the sixty-day free trial before a three thousand pound commitment "nobody will notice." We were driving north to meet Susie. She lives in Suffolk and we'd arranged to take her to lunch on Southwold Pier with the grandkids. Nobody had flashed or made inappropriate signs on the two-hour journey.

We parked near the pier and strolled towards the beach.

"There they are on the sand" Sheila said waving down to our daughter who was struggling to keep two little bundles of energy from a soaking in the waves. We walked down to meet them and, as soon as they saw us, Sally and Emily ran towards us. We both crouched down with arms wide open for a hug. It was two-year old Sally who picked me. I clutched her to my chest, stood up and swung her around. I turned to look at her but instead of her usual adoring gaze I saw her eyes transfixed and felt a stubby and sandy little finger pulling at one of the fishing lines. "Yep, bloody invisible," I muttered.

As the aid popped from my ear and the sound of the waves immediately diminished Sally waved it and said "Gra Gra's got mousies." Emily leaned across from her nanny's arms and more gritty little digits started to find their way to my other ear.

"Careful darling. Careful sweetie. Grandad's mousies are very expensive mousies," I said.

The girls stopped their investigations instantly.

Sheila was still holding Emily and carefully lowered her back onto her feet, "Sally, give the mouse to Mummy, darling."

Sally held the aid by its cone and directed her hand towards her mum. She made a couple of squeaky sounds and shook the 'mouse' by the tail. "Oh! Gone" she said and fifteen hundred quid's worth of miniature audio technology flew into the soft sand near our feet.

"Don't anyone move."

For a minute we were like a group of Anthony Gormley's sculptures on Crosby beach. Then Susie bent down and started sifting the sand through her fingers.

"It won't be far," she said, but with each handful of shifting sand the chances of recovering it diminished.

"Lost something mate?" A local man had seen Susie's frantic hunt going on.

"Hearing aid," I said, "A very tiny one."

"Any metal in it?"

"Only the battery."

"That's okay. This thing will pick up a five pee at fifteen inches. So where did you drop it?"

I saw that he was holding a metal detector and told him that it should be right beneath our feet.

"Move away then, everybody."

By now a small crowd had gathered to see what was going on. The dectectorist was clearly enjoying his audience and swung his machine with an extravagant flourish, a look of concentration on his face. He found two pound coins, three ring pulls and a fifty-pence right where we had been standing. I made a mental note that this was not a bad return for five minutes work.

"You sure it was just here?" he said. "This is the XP DEUS. The Merc of metal detectors. It's infallible for tiny finds."

He moved away, swinging the detector over a wider circle. My heart sank, but then...

"There we go, mate. This what you're looking for?" he handed me my sand-coated mousie together with a business card printed with *FRED'LL FIND IT- FREE RECOVERY SERVICE* above a mobile number in bold capitals and a cartoon of a pirate waving a metal detector and resting his peg leg on a treasure chest.

"How on earth did it move over there?"

"You'll be amazed how sand shifts, mate. Good job you didn't budge."

"What do I owe you?"

"Read the card mate. Free recovery service."

"A pint at least," I said.

"Nah. Don't drink. All part of promoting the hobby. Keep hold of the card mate. Might be something valuable next time."

Chapter Seven

Dave

I keep looking over my shoulder as I head to the bus stop. Sheila will be following, I'm sure of it. We have our fallouts from time to time but she always comes around after a cooling off period. I know I'm a pain to live with, with all my obsessions and spending all of our money on gadgets and fripperies but after forty years she knows what I'm like. Christ! What am I like? I've just told her we're going to come into enough cash to pay off the mortgage with plenty to spare and then whipped it away from her. No wonder she's hating me. I turn to head back home.

But, the vases. There's still a chance of the vases. Perhaps, for once, I will prove her wrong and get back in favour. I check my watch. The bus is due in a few minutes. I turn back into the rain and get to the shelter as the 82 pulls into the kerb.

It's nine when I reach the oddly named Casa Nuestra. It opened when *The Godfather* was all the rage and I think the Spanish owners wanted to cash in on Brando's Mafiosi popularity with a pun on the Cosa Nostra. I open the door and am amazed to find it packed on a Monday night. A middle-aged woman in a smart black trouser suit and white blouse greets me.

"Buenos noches Señor. Have you a reservation?"

"No. Sorry I didn't think. Monday night, you know."

"A table for one?"

I nod.

"I think I can find one for you. Please wait here a moment."

She directs me to a couple of comfy armchairs alongside her reception desk, hands me a menu and makes her way into the crammed dining room.

I start to shift in my seat and do my usual restaurant arrival procedure of spotting the loos in case there's a need for my Usain Bolt impersonation. I don't have to look far. They are just across from where I am sitting.

"Ah Señor, follow me, please."

Before I have time to interrupt, the señora leads me deep into the lowly lit room and directs me to a table close to one of the two kitchen doors.

I sit and fidget with the menu.

"A drink Señor?" a beautiful young woman is standing above me, she wears a white blouse like her manager but a short black skirt replaces the smart black trousers and showcases a well-toned and long pair of suntanned legs. I imagine that every time she sees the sign in the kitchen that reads 'Think Tips' she hitches that skirt a centimetre higher.

I order a beer and then leave the table for a quick comfort break.

My ice-cold San Miguel is waiting as I return to my seat.

I order several tapas from the enormous menu. While waiting for them to arrive from the kitchen I look around the place. It's clean and simple – gingham tablecloths and paper napkins, nothing special but they're thick paper napkins and smart gingham tablecloths. There are three or four waitresses and a couple of waiters. All are most certainly Spanish.

The walls are filled with photographs. Each portrays the same ageing, smiling Spanish guitarist in the full black gear, his guitar standing alongside him. A beautiful young woman in a variety of flamboyant flamenco costumes accompanies him in most. There's always a third (and sometimes a fourth) party in the picture. I lose count of the famous faces whose arms are around the Spanish couple. Every star who has appeared on the London stage seems to have found their way to this Spanish backwater; most of the best known Arsenal and Spurs footballers are there and I can tell, from where the photos hang, which team held the Señor's allegiance. Sadly the famous faces are faces of the eighties and nineties and I guess that the guitarist is no longer with us. I look more closely at the photo nearest to me and look again at the manager, leading a couple of late arrivals to join their friends. Great posture. That's what dancing does for you.

The room is buzzing with conversation, the cheerful patter of the waiting staff, the clatter of dishes and the swinging to and fro of the doors in and out of the kitchen. The buzz is occasionally drowned out by the thunderous roar of a Northern Line tube train rattling above us on its journey to or from central London.

One of the waiters has delivered most of my orders. I'm not massively hungry although I've enjoyed my second San Miguel; bocadillos, olives; a salad of marinated peppers, radish and cucumber; anchovies; patatas bravas and chicken skewers. In between (and during) each course I've been guessing who MuchachaBonita might be. I don't want the waitresses to think I'm ogling them and do my best to look away whenever one catches me looking her way.

I wonder if it could be the waitress with the long legs. She took delivery of an extravagant present earlier in the evening. A motorcycle courier arrived with a box festooned with ribbons. The manager summoned her from the floor and I watched as she opened the gift and looked in amazement at, what I can only imagine must be, a designer handbag with a name that transformed it from a mere bag to an extremely valuable accessory. The other girls looked envious as she took it through to the kitchen. I saw it was embossed with a tree design.

Maybe MuchachaBonita works in the kitchen. I can hear plenty of female voices each time the doors swing open. All the waitresses are young and pretty all could be described as *bonita*. How do I approach this? If I open my mouth and utter the words 'Muchacha Bonita' I could be inviting a slap round the face.

I'm going to go home disappointed, fifty quid worse off and with a very cold bed to welcome me. The restaurant is starting to empty and the staff are clearing the tables. I ask my waiter for the bill. It's not long before he brings it to the table before disappearing back into the kitchen.

I take out my credit card and try to catch the eye of one of the waiting staff. The handbag girl spots me and comes to the table with her portable card machine. I hand her the card and she pauses as she notices the name.

"Mr. D J Prendergast! Dave Prendergast?"

"That's right." I'm flattered. Has my fame as a retired bank clerk gone before me?

"But we were supposed to meet outside when I finished."

What on earth has Simon fitted me up with?

"Don't worry," She continues " It's only ten minutes to closing time. I will be back soon."

She smiles and hands me back my card and receipt.

I leave a generous tip on the tray in cash and she takes it with another, slightly puzzled smile.

I look around the rapidly emptying restaurant.

"On the house, Señor," my waiter is back at the table handing me another ice cold San Miguel.

"Why thank you," I say. I raise the bottle towards him and start to sip the beer. I take out my mobile and check for messages from Simon. There's no signal so I have no idea what hare-brained plan he's got me involved in.

The tables are all empty now and I look towards the toilets and decide that a pre-departure pee might be advisable. I stand and prepare to head towards the gents when I feel someone linking my arm.

"Okay Dave. I'm ready now. Where are you taking me?"

A tall, beautiful, dark-eyed and dark-haired young woman, forty years my junior is linking my arm. 'Where am I taking her?' What sort of question is that?

I pause to compose myself as we pass the reception and out into the street. I look briefly back towards the safety of the loos feeling like a child being dragged reluctantly past a toyshop but the door slams shut and we are outside. After the warmth of the lively restaurant, the dark cold of a London suburban street hits us both and she presses in close to me.

A very large and very new silver Mercedes is slowing traffic down outside the restaurant. It's half on the pavement and its hazard lights are flashing as if its owner is saying 'I've got a very big and very expensive car. My hazard lights are flashing so that entitles me to block one of the main routes into the city'. There's no sign of the driver.

'Wanker,' I think.

"So where are you parked, Dave?"

"Sorry. I mumble. I came in a taxi."

Her face falls, "You said we'd be riding in luxury."

"Some of the newer black cabs are quite well fitted out," I half-heartedly offer.

It's still raining. I step off the kerb to flag down a cab, and feel an icy-cold surge around my ankles. I look down to see the rushing rivulets of water filling the gutters. My once smart pair of brogues are now one tan and the other a soggy, dark brown. The dark-brown matches one leg of my chinos, which is now two-tone and flapping icily against my shin.

I open the taxi door and guide the young woman in, respectfully avoiding looking at her calves (and thighs).

The cabbie flicks his meter, "Where to, guv?"

A feeling of panic sets in. What arrangements have been made? Surely if I am to complete the transaction we need to do it at her place.

"Your place?" I ask.

My partner looks down at her feet. "If you say so, Dave. But you did mention dinner at your club."

I pat my stomach. "A bit late for that now. Those tapas are more filling than they look."

She gives the driver her address. It's three or four miles in the opposite direction to home.

I'm sitting on one of the little fold-down seats and she has the whole of the back seat to herself. She leans back into a corner; her legs are stretched out so that they almost touch the opposite door. She starts to fumble with her new toy. It's a very good-looking handbag. Sheila would love a bag like that.

"It's beautiful, Dave, isn't it?"

"Oh yes it certainly is... I'm sorry I've just realised I only know your online name."

She smiles shyly, "I know that's not true. Your present found me at work."

My present? Simon is spending the profits before we've even got the vases but I suppose a few hundred pounds is a small price in the grand scheme of things.

I laugh nervously.

"I've never done this before," I say.

She blushes, "Neither have I."

"So," I say "what do we do? The website says we shouldn't carry out any transactions privately but now that we are getting to know each other I hope that you'll be able to trust me."

"I'm not sure Dave. The bag is beautiful – really beautiful and more than I could ever have wished for but we haven't agreed anything yet. And..."

She hesitates.

"And what?" I ask.

"Well, Dave, I do not want to be rude but you do not look very much like you do in your photo."

My photo. I set up my eBay 'About Me' page over fifteen years ago when I weighed eleven stone and had all my own hair. Why on earth has Simon given her my user name? She will have read all that stuff about me collecting valuable Japanese Satsuma wares. No wonder the price has risen from thirty pounds to an expensive couturier bag plus whatever else we negotiate.

"I am sorry about that photo. I suppose I just wanted to show myself in best possible light."

"But *my* photo is up to date Dave."

If her photo had been taken at the same time as mine she'd be wearing her nursery school uniform in it.

"If we are going to trust each other, we must be honest with each other."

"Of course we must. Honesty is the best policy. That's what I always said when I was in the bank."

"Yes and that is probably why you were a chief executive when you retired."

Simon has gone overboard with the bullshit but I go along with it.

"As I used to say to my millionaire clients, 'shall we go ahead with the transaction?'"

She looks me up and down once more.

"Not tonight, Dave. I am tired and I have a busy morning of exercise classes tomorrow."

I try to keep the conversation going. "Exercise classes? Where do you do them?"

"You know the old synagogue they converted into a gym?"

"Know it? I've been a member for years." I can sense her incredulity but I am telling the truth. Simon paid my enrolment fee and first six months membership as a retirement present. Inertia meant that seventy-five pounds a month has disappeared into the fitness centre's coffers for the past five years for precisely nothing.

I steer the conversation back to the vases, "And our deal?"

"I need to think about it, Dave. Let me contact you tomorrow." She taps on the cabbie's screen. "It's just here."

"But can I just come inside and have a quick look at the goods now that we are here – we can get down to business another day?"

She looks slightly shocked. "No, Dave. I promise I will contact you tomorrow..." she pushes the bag towards me "and I think it is better if you keep this for now."

The cabbie pulls in to the kerb. He asks me to pay before he unlocks the doors.

"But I'll be going on," I say.

"Alright. You don't look the sort to do a runner."

I help my companion out of the cab. We're in a pleasant suburban street full of semi-detached houses built in the early twentieth century. There's a welcoming light in the hallway and she runs quickly to the front door.

"Goodnight then," I wave.

She turns briefly and waves back. "Goodnight Dave." She unlocks the door and she's gone. I get back into the taxi.

"Bit of a cracker, eh?" The driver moves off. "Where to now, boss?"

I tell him my address and sit back. Her scent envelops me. I study the handbag. Sheila will give me the third degree if I try and pass it off as a peace offering.

"No luck then mate?'

"She's just a friend."

"Of your granddaughter?"

The effects of the third San Miguel are starting to make themselves felt and I start moving to alleviate the urge. We're still a couple of miles from home and it's going to be touch and go. I need to be prepared for the second I open the front door and make the dash to the loo.

My bladder is pushing and pushing. I put my hand inside my coat. I unzip, my fly and adjust my boxers in readiness.

I'm rocking and shifting up and down in my seat.

"You dirty... I've got CCTV in here! Just because you didn't go in for a coffee you're not doing that in my cab."

The taxi slams to a halt. The driver pulls back his screen. "Fifty quid."

"But it only says forty on your meter."

"Plus ten for cleaning up anything nasty on the seat," he says.

I haven't got time to argue. I pass the notes through the screen.

"No tip then?"

He unlocks the door and I stagger onto the pavement. I've no idea where I am but as soon as the cold hits me I can't hold out any longer. It's a suburban street. There's a tree a few yards ahead. I run to the tree, fumbling at my clothes. I rest my forehead on the bark and do what's necessary.

I'm nearly finished when a strong-white light illuminates the tree.

It's followed by flashing blue.

Chapter Eight

Dave

The car pulls alongside and draws to a halt as I finish straightening my clothes. The front passenger door opens and an officer steps out. She's young, very dark skinned and about my height.

"Good evening, sir." The night has turned decidedly colder and, whilst her rich Caribbean accent brings a little warmth, the small cloud of steam that accompanies her words makes me wonder what sort of hellish situation I have got myself into.

"Good evening, officer."

She shines a torch. She begins at my head and, as my eyes screw up from the temporary blindness, she starts a full body scan.

Her torch focuses downwards to my feet. "That was not a very good aim sir."

"It's not what you think, officer."

"So what should I think sir? This is a very quiet suburban street. It is well past midnight and I find a gentleman propped against a tree, relieving himself in public whilst clutching a purple handbag. Should I throw the book at him? Indecent exposure? Committing a public nuisance? Drunk and disorderly?"

I'm getting cold and start to shiver. My teeth chatter as I respond.

"NNnnnnone of those, constable."

"It's sergeant, sir. Would you like to get out of the cold and into the car"

I love the lilt of her accent. I half expect her to announce that *The Archers* will shortly be following the news. She opens a rear door and helps me inside. She gets back into the front passenger seat. Her male colleague at the wheel turns to her.

"What's the situation, sarge?"

"I'm thinking, indecent exposure, committing a public

nuisance and drunk and disorderly."

"That's the least of it, sarge. A purple bag with that coat is criminal."

I can't see their faces from my seat in the back but I can imagine this episode as a little light relief from their regular world of drugs and knife crimes.

"Name, address and date of birth please and... any form of identification?"

I give the sergeant the information she asks for together with my Two Together photo rail card.

"Is this Mrs Prendergast?" she says inspecting the pictures on the card?

"Yes."

She taps my details into a screen.

"You won't find anything on me on there, Sergeant. Not even a speeding ticket...Not even a *parking* ticket. Sixty-two years of clean living, that's me."

After scrolling through my computer record for a minute she says "But you've been living dangerously tonight Mr. Prendergast. What have you had to drink?"

"Three small bottles of San Miguel. That's all."

"So that's why I found you leaning against a tree, urinating all over your trousers."

"It's not urine. I stepped in a puddle. I seem to be developing some sort of bladder problem officer. I couldn't hold on until I got home. I am sorry. It's very late I didn't think I'd be noticed."

Now that I am no longer cold, my speech is clear and lucid. There's no way that they will think I've had too much.

"May I see the bag please sir?"

I hand the bag to the male officer.

He inspects it closely.

"These bags aren't cheap, sarge."

"I could never afford one," she says, "Don't see the point mind. I could get twenty bags in Top Shop for the price of one of these."

Her colleague opens the clasp and looks inside. He pulls out a card and reads.

"To my lovely sugar baby, Señorita M. From your sugar daddy, DP."

He turns around in his seat and looks me firmly in the eye. "So you're someone's sugar daddy are you Mr. Prendergast? Who's the lucky girl then?"

"I can explain. It's not my bag—"

"Not your bag? The card inside has your initials – DP."

This could become extremely complicated. "Okay," I say, "It *is* my bag but it's not *my* bag. I was going to give it to somebody."

The sergeant interjects, "The lovely Señorita M?"

"Yes."

Her once warm voice becomes decidedly colder. "Does Mrs. Prendergast approve of your little señorita?"

"It's not like that."

The driver hands the bag firmly back to me and adds, "Okay Mr. 'Sugar Daddy'. Were you on your way home?"

"Yes." I'm not going to say a word more than is needed.

"We're headed that way aren't we, sarge?"

The sergeant turns to him and smiles.

It's only a few minutes before we are pulling into my street.

"You can drop me off here, officers. This will be fine," I say.

"No. We insist on taking you to your door. All part of the service."

"Okay but my wife will be asleep. I don't want to wake her."

"We're sure that you don't," the sergeant adds. She turns in her seat and looks at me. "We won't let that happen, sir."

We pull up outside my house. No lights.

The driver unlocks the passenger door.

Both officers speak in unison, "Goodnight, sir."

I open the door as softly as I can. I get out of the car and close the door without slamming it. I walk quietly to the front door, put the key in the lock and turn to look at the officers. I see the sergeant smiling as I turn the key. I wave.

With a brief flash of blue light and four blasts of their siren they wait a few seconds and then drive away.

Chapter Nine

Dave

'Bastards' I think as I close the door quietly behind me and bend to remove my shoes in preparation to tiptoe up to bed. There's not much point as the house is already lit like Blackpool illuminations. Simon is at the top of the stairs in his Armani pants with Sheila peering over his shoulder in her facepack looking like Marcel Marceau.

I try to hide the handbag beneath my coat.

"What's that?" Sheila shouts down.

"Nothing."

"Nothing? I can see it's not nothing. What is it, and why have you come home in a police car?"

She pushes past Simon and flies down the stairs two at a time descending upon me like one of the skeletons in *Jason And The Argonauts*.

She pulls open my coat. "What is it? Give it to me."

There's no point trying to escape my fate. I reveal the bag.

"But Dave... for me? You know how much I've wanted one of these. We could never afford one. What's going on?"

She's got the bag at arms length and is looking at it with the look she gave the children when they were babies, but hasn't given me for a very long time. "It's beautiful."

She goes to open the clasp.

"Wait I say. Just wait. I was going to wrap it." I try to take it back.

"No need now." She pulls it back to her chest and again moves to open it.

"But don't you want to hear about the police car?"

She hesitates. Simon is now beside her. "Yeah Dad. What've you been up to?"

I'm still watching Sheila's hand on the clasp. "I foiled an armed robbery."

"You *WHAT*?"

They both look at me in disbelief.

"Dad! The only thing you've foiled in your life is a roasting tray."

"No," I say "just listen."

"I'm not standing listening here in the hall," says Sheila, "The heating's gone off and it's flipping freezing. Simon go and get me my dressing gown please, love."

Simon goes upstairs for his mum's gown. While he's away Sheila looks at me. Her eyes are screwed up in puzzlement. She shakes her head, "This had better be good."

Simon returns and hands her the gown. She puts it on and we head into the lounge.

I've only had three beers but they are working wonders for my imagination and soon I'm describing how I'm waiting for the bus home after my dinner; there's no bus due for ten minutes so I decide to head into the all night News & Booze near the restaurant for some mints to freshen my breath. Two seedy characters follow me into the store. Suddenly one leaps over the counter, smashes open the cigarette cabinet and starts to pile the packs into a large holdall while his accomplice holds Mr Ali, the shopkeeper, at knifepoint.

I fearlessly rush at the armed robber and snatch his knife from him. He releases the dazed shopkeeper who staggers to the till and, coming round, presses an alarm button and grabs a cricket bat. He whacks the accomplice firmly across the shoulders. Cigarettes scatter across the floor as the thwarted robbers try to make a dash for it.

Sheila and Simon's jaws have dropped. They look like a couple of goldfish as they listen to my tale.

Encouraged by their incredulity, I become more immersed in my storytelling.

Instead of giving the criminals their freedom I stick out a leg and both tumble to the ground. Each is at least six foot six and built like a brick outhouse; bald like one of the Mitchell brothers; scars everywhere; 'DEATH' tattooed across the forehead and 'HATE' across the knuckles.

Three squad cars arrive outside and six police officers enter the shop to find the shopkeeper and me, each sitting on a prisoner. The robbers are handcuffed and led away and, after I give my statement, I'm given a lift home.

"Hmmm," is Sheila's reaction.

"Wow Dad. You'll be in the news tomorrow."

"I doubt it son. It was too late to make the papers."

"No I mean the radio and TV news. They'll be queuing down the road. We'll have satellite vans parked on the pavement."

"I asked for anonymity."

"Why?" says Sheila. "Who do you think you are? Batman?"

"I just thought they might have friends. You know."

"Who? The Mitchell brothers?"

"Yeah."

Sheila yawns. "I'm going to bed."

She stands up leaving the handbag on the sofa. She has her back to me so I take my chance. I move towards the sofa, open the bag and take out the card. Sheila turns back, snatches the bag and walks away. "Bag or no bag, *you're* still sleeping here."

"So what's on the card, Dad?"

"Nothing, son."

"Come on, Dad. What's going on? You go out to try and meet MuchachaBonita and get hold of two vases that are going to make your fortune and you come home in a police car holding a very expensive handbag, having saved Mr. Ali from the clutches of violent robbers. What about the vases? Did you meet her?"

"Yes. I met our MuchcachaBonita alright. There were lots of pretty girls working there and if I had started mentioning Muchacha Bonita I might have got a slap around the face and escorted to the door but thanks to you – and I've no idea what you told her but well done – I somehow ended up in a taxi with her and that flipping handbag, and then she had a change of heart and said that she'd think about it."

"I don't know where the handbag fits in all this. That's got absolutely nothing to do with me."

"Honestly?"

"Honestly."

"God knows what's going on. I just thought I would get there, it would be obvious who she was, I'd get chatting and, Bob's your uncle, the vases would be mine and your mum would be happy again."

I'm not going to complicate things further by telling him she's going to the gym in the morning.

"It's going to take some effort for Mum to be happy again Dad. You've done it big time with this one. Why didn't you just wait until you had the vases before mentioning them? You know how many times you get it wrong. Do you want me to try and send another question to MuchachaBonita?"

"No. Leave this to me. I've dug this hole. I'll get myself out of it."

Simon moves to leave. "I'll get you a couple of blankets."

He leaves the room. I hear him call "Goodnight Dad.". Two blankets land at the foot of the stairs with a thump.

I get onto the sofa, pull the blankets around me and try to sleep. My head is spinning with the events of the night and my plans for the morning. What time does that gym open? Six 'clock if I remember correctly. I'm counting on MuchachaBonita needing a lie-in after the night's adventure and set my phone's alarm to six-thirty.

Chapter Ten

Maria

I asked the girls to look out for a very tall customer but I have heard nothing as service starts to die down. So it appears that Simon's comment about feeling hungry and coming to Casa Nuestra *was* a joke.

Margarita swings open the 'in' door as I am preparing a couple of salads. She rushes to the pass. She shakes her head. "Still no show," she says.

I finish the salads and go to the 'out' door and look through the round porthole. I scan the restaurant for anyone of above average height. Most of the tables I can see are starting to empty. I open the door and walk slowly around the room just to make sure that Simon is not hidden behind a pillar or in a dark corner. A young couple are standing. The man is helping his partner with her coat as I pass.

"Are you the chef?" he asks.

I blush and nod, "Si Señor. But only one of them."

'Well, that was delicious. Thank you."

I smile. It is good to be appreciated. The couple leave and soon there will be only a middle-aged man on his own and the table of four whose order I need to finish.

Miguel shouts to me "Maria! Service! You have two salads and a patatas bravas to plate."

I return to my station. I finish the dishes and wait for Margarita to collect them.

As my shift ends and I leave the restaurant there is a huge traffic jam outside News & Booze. A lorry is blocking the road as a big silver car is lifted onto it. My favourite police officer, the one I call Sergeant Marley, is controlling the situation. I see her arguing with a silver haired man dressed in an elegant, grey suit. I cannot see his face but he seems familiar.

I get back to the bedsit. I take off my whites and pick up my phone. No messages. No questions from eBay. I scroll back to SimonOxford1985's questions and write down the number he gave me. If I send a text now he will probably be asleep and will not see it. I decide to wait until the morning.

~

It is well past eight when I tap into the phone.

> *Hello Simon. Were you not hungry? You did not visit the restaurant.*
>
> *The phone pings back almost instantly ?????*
>
> *Last night at Casa Nuestra*
>
> *Is this MuchachaBonita?*
>
> *You can call me Maria.*
>
> *Sorry Maria. I couldn't make it. But I heard there was a lot of excitement.*
>
> *It was a busy night but nothing exciting happened.*
>
> *Did you not hear about the incident with the police nearby at News And Booze?*
>
> *I saw the police talking to a man.*
>
> *You were a witness?*
>
> *No. I just saw a man talking to the police.*
>
> *That was my dad. The hero.*
>
> *The police did not seem very happy with him*
>
> *I'm sorry Maria. I have to go into school now. Can I phone you later?*

School and frog collecting. I am beginning to understand.

> *You are a kid?*

No. Teacher!

Okay. I will be free at about five.

Don't do anything with the frogs.

I will not.

I put the phone into my bag and go into the bathroom. I shower and, after drying off, I put on my gym outfit and head out to the old synagogue.

Chapter Eleven

Dave

I didn't need to set the alarm. The sofa is not the comfiest of beds and I've been tossing and turning for hours trying to keep warm. My head's been spinning with thoughts of the vases and how surprised Sheila will be when I come home later in the day and show them to her. Maybe it will help us get things back to how they used to be when Simon was at uni. She may be enjoying her second bout of motherhood but I'm certainly not. I sometimes wonder if we are going to become yet another statistic in the divorce figures.

I throw off the blankets at six and, shivering, climb the stairs and tiptoe through our bedroom into the en-suite. I daren't turn on the lights or run a shower for fear of waking the household so I settle for a good wash in the dark. I try to shave by the light of my cell phone. It's not my brightest idea and I leave the bathroom with three bits of toilet paper stuck to my face.

I creep back into our bedroom and, encouraged by Sheila's rhythmic breathing reach into the cupboard above the fitted wardrobes for my gym outfit. Clump! A heavy trainer hits the floor. I gingerly pick it up and listen. The breathing, though still mostly rhythmic, is now intermittently interspersed with what sounds like a navvy clearing his throat. I allow myself a smile as I imagine the hefty kick that would have brought if I were the one making that noise.

My smile dissolves instantly when trainer number two follows its pair. Instead of thumping onto the carpet it bounces off my shoulder and, as if I've scored a strike at ten-pin bowling, clatters into the perfume bottles and beauty products on Sheila's dressing table before smashing into the mirror. No need to tiptoe now. The lights are on.

"What the hell is going on? What time is it?"

"Shhh," I say. I play my trump card. "You'll wake Simon."

Her voice lowers instantly, she whispers, "What are you doing?"

I shrug my shoulders and point to the side of my head to show her that her words are falling upon deaf ears. "Just off to the gym."

"Why aren't you wearing them? What's the point of spending three thousand pounds if you're not going to wear them? And why the hell are you going to the gym? You haven't been for years."

I walk to the bed and bend over. My lips almost touch her ear.

"Sorry darling. Go back to sleep. I just woke up early sleeping on the sofa and thought I'd get out of your hair for a few hours."

"You can get back in bed. I've been freezing cold all night."

'You've been cold!' I think. Try sleeping on the bloody sofa with no central heating on. "No. No. It's okay. I'm up now."

I go back downstairs quickly and bring the blankets up from the lounge. I put them over Sheila and tuck them firmly under the mattress.

"That better?' I ask.

She pulls the covers up to her nose and closes her eyes.

By turning down the olive branch she offered inviting me back into bed I've missed an opportunity to get back into her good books, but the vases will be more than an olive branch – they'll be a whole forest of olive trees with a dove smoking a peace pipe perched on every branch.

I roll on plenty of deodorant and spray on my aftershave. I put on my shorts, socks, gym vest and trainers, grab a towel and go back downstairs. I put the hearing aids in, take my anorak off the coat stand, put it on, pocket my wallet and head out of the front door.

The cold hits me immediately, so I zip the anorak up and tie the hood tightly under my chin. It's a crisp morning. Last night's rain has gone but it has left a layer of ice underfoot. I was going to jog but, after my brush with the law, I don't fancy a brush with another emergency service this morning so I walk, very carefully.

It's about seven when I approach the gym and I'm surprised to see it has changed. There's a new name '*We Can Work It Out*'. It sounds as if it has been taken over by a hairdresser. It always amuses me to see the names that hairdressers come up with. I love *Jack The Snipper* but *Curl Up And Dye* is my very favourite. As I walk towards the steps, I start to think that the world would be a far happier place if hairdressers were allowed to name all the shops on the high street. The butcher would be *Well Hung*, obviously; the greengrocer, *The Plum Centre*; the plumbers, *Let It Flow*. We could even extend it to the public sector with *Cop Shop*, for the police station, *A Stitch In Time* for A&E and the local GP would be, wait for it – no, that's it - *Wait For It*. There could even be a Spanish restaurant called Casa Nuestra.

I reach the main door, go through and look for the card swipe machine to allow me into the inner sanctum. It's gone. I push on the glass door but it is firmly locked. I cup my hands to my forehead and press my nose against the glass. I can see plenty of activity at the reception desk so I knock on the glass. A young man in a dark blue tracksuit spots me. I wave my membership card and he pushes a button to open the door.

"Under new management, sir. The old card reader's gone. We're using biometrics now. Too many non-members *borrowing* cards. How can I help you?"

I look closely at the young man and remember him from four years back when he took me through the initial initiation rites of gym membership and gave me my fitness assessment.

"It's Djimi isn't it?"

"That's right." He looks at me but I imagine that in four years he's inducted hundreds of people, "I'm sorry, you are?"

I hand him my membership card.

"Ah yes. Mr. Prendergast."

"Dave. Please."

"How can I help you, Dave?"

While we are talking, I'm aware of a number of members entering through the glass doors, giving Djimi a friendly greeting and moving off in the direction of the changing rooms or the various studios that I was shown around on my previous visit.

"I was thinking of a couple of exercise classes."

He looks down at his screen and starts to tap on the keyboard. He looks up "Well Dave, your membership is certainly in order. You've paid us over three thousand pounds and, as far as I can see you've only been to that one induction visit. As you have kept up your membership without being the most regular of attendees, I think I can perhaps offer you a few *free* classes today. I'll just need a fingerprint and you'll have to sign a disclaimer as it's been four years."

"Fingerprints?"

"For the biometric admission system."

"Of course."

He hands me a device and asks me to insert my right index finger. I look over the desk at his screen and, seeing my print, think of last night's encounter.

"That's it, Dave. Painless eh?" He hands me a sheet of A4. It's closely printed and headed 'HEALTH WAIVER'. "Just sign here please," he points to a small box at the foot of the page.

I don't read the small print. Who does? Every day some website or other asks me to confirm that I've read and agree to their terms and conditions but, as those terms and conditions often run to the length of a short novel, how can I ever read them, especially when I am only looking to buy a train ticket or perhaps a book? No doubt one day somebody from Southern Rail or Amazon will knock on the front door and demand my firstborn and the keys to the car. When I protest, they'll cite clause 352. Maybe they will both arrive at the same time and have to fight over it. I'd take the car. I sign and hand the form back to Djimi.

He thanks me and says, "And here's something for you."

"What's this?" I ask, inspecting the large sealed plastic bag.

"A *We Can Work It Out* members' pack. Part of the new image."

"Thanks," I tuck the bag under my arm.

"So Dave, which classes do you fancy?"

I hesitate, "Do you have many Spanish members?"

"It's the United Nations here, Dave. Why do you ask?"

"It's just I met someone at a Spanish Restaurant last night who said they come to your classes."

"If it was Casa Nuestra, they all come. Their boss fixed up a corporate membership for them. Two or three come here most days. Now let's see what I can offer you." He looks down at his screen. "You're in luck, Dave. We've had a couple of cancellations. You know what it's like when winter starts to draw in. It sorts out the men from the boys. I can offer you HITT, LBT, Core and Spinning—"

"Hit?" I ask, "Does that involve punch bags?"

"Nah. High Intensity. A bit like Boot Camp."

"Don't tell me I have to sing in front of Simon Cowell and Sinita."

He smiles generously at my feeble joke. "Nah. We're more Louis Walsh here. Shall I put you down? You'll like Sam."

"Sure," I say, "When does it start?"

"You've got fifteen minutes. Do you want to book any more?"

"What's that lesbian, gay, bisexual, transgender one?"

"It's LBT. Not LGBT."

"Lettuce, bacon and tomato?"

"*That's* a BLT. *This* is Legs, Bums And Tums."

"Sounds a bit girly."

"Well most of the class members are women but..." From where he is sitting, my gut is at his eye level.

"You don't need to say it. It might do me some good."

I'm trying to get in touch with my Spanish waitress. Her legs bum and tum are all in extremely good order and that may be as a result of LBT. "Put me down," I say.

"That clashes with pure core but you could fit in spinning at the end. That will give you a pretty exhausting return to *We Can Work It Out.*"

"At this rate, I'll have had my money's worth in about ten months. So? Spinning? What's that about?"

He tells me but I refrain from attempting any jokes about spindles, bobbins or wheels.

It's time for HITT in Studio One with Sam.

Chapter Twelve

Dave

"Good morning everybody."

I wonder who this particularly confident young woman may be. We're still waiting for Sam. Perhaps he's running late – not a good start.

"I see we've got a newcomer." It's Little Miss Over-Confident again. "Would you like to introduce yourself?"

I look meekly around at my mixed bunch of companions. They range in age from sixteen to, well sixty-two I suppose if I count myself. They're a rainbow nation both in skin tone and in their choice of outfits, in which tight, Lycra leggings in jazzy patterns topped by colourful, cotton tops are in the majority. Designer trainers are *de rigueur* and I look down at my own which are, at best, reinforced plimsolls. Most of my classmates are female but there are two other men. Neither, regrettably, is rocking my pregnant look.

"Hi. I'm Dave," I resist the impulse to add 'and I'm an alcoholic'. "First time for a while I'm afraid," I pat my stomach.

"Don't worry, Dave. We'll ease you in slowly. Take a break and grab some water whenever you feel the need."

It dawns on me that this slight, bespectacled young woman, whose own outfit looks to have been sprayed onto her amazingly taught body, is Sam, and the boot camp sergeant major I'd been dreading was just a cruel figment of my imagination. I joked about Simon Cowell and Sinita but we've got Kylie. I should be so lucky.

Sam checks her watch. Bang on time she switches on some loud music and starts us off with a few warm up exercises. I can manage these but I've been lulled into a false sense of security as, from there, we move straight on to knees ups. There's no Mother Brown involved but it's otherwise quite similar to the old East End dance. We have to pump our knees up and down as high as we can for a minute. That doesn't sound much I know, but that's a whole sixty seconds and after twenty of those seconds my steamed up specs are slipping down my nose. After half a minute my top has become untucked from my shorts revealing my belly which seems to be the only part of me that has got the hang of the up and down rhythm. Fifty seconds in and I take my first water break. I towel myself down. How long did Djimi say this class was? He didn't.

Knees ups are followed by shuttle runs, or in my case, shuttle jogs. Okay, shuttle fast(ish) walks. Sam barks her orders and the class responds instantly.

We're now on star jumps and I start to question my sanity. MuchachaBonita is not in this class so why am I doing this?

Lunges, leg raises, sit ups, press-ups all blur into one.

"And now it's time for the plank."

Sam is looking directly at me. She's certainly got my measure. Is she asking me to perform solo? But the whole class has dropped to a mat on the floor and each member is resting on their elbows with their feet stretched out behind them, toes pointing to the floor. I think that this looks a bit easier than what came before, but I soon discover that it isn't.

"Keep your bum down, Dave." This makes it even harder.

Sam encourages us, "Come on everyone. Try and beat last week's times." It's been about twenty seconds and my body is shaking as I try to maintain the pose. I don't want to be the first to give in, but thirty seconds is my limit and I collapse onto the mat. Thirty seconds later the other members begin to drop but one woman, who can't be much younger than me, is still going for it. Her face is contorted with effort but one minute passes and then another.

"That's it, Caroline. You're over two minutes. That's your best yet."

It's two and three quarter minutes when Caroline finishes to a wild round of applause from everyone else. One thing's for sure, Caroline won't be having a midriff like mine any time soon.

The class ends with a cool down routine. I towel myself down, drain most of my water bottle and mop up the puddle on the floor around where I've been exercising. Sam comes across to me.

"Well Dave, how did you enjoy HIIT?"

"I'm not sure that enjoy is the right word, Sam but ..." I point at my gut, " I've got to do something about this."

"You'll be surprised how soon you'll get your fitness back. But don't overdo it. Take things slowly."

"I'm doing legs and bums with Charlie next, and then spinning with Clare."

"Tomorrow and Thursday?"

"No. Today."

"I'm not sure that's wise. Have you done a fitness assessment with Djimi?"

"Yes... but it was four years ago."

"So you've signed a disclaimer."

"Yes."

"Let's hope we don't need it, Dave. Remember what I said. Take things slowly."

I head back into the reception and ask Djimi where to go for Legs Bums and Tums. He directs me to Studio Three upstairs. It's only one flight of stairs but I'm panting when I reach the top. I open the door to Studio Three. Lively chatter stops briefly as the occupants check over their new colleague whose sparrow legs, lardy bum and beer gut tum are certainly in need of a workout. I feel like screaming 'it's not a beer belly. I bloody hate beer.' But then they might think that the new member is not only a fat slob but also a demented fat slob.

These members are all female and mostly middle-aged. Most offer me a weak smile by way of a greeting although I fear that my presence will spoil their women's talk.

I look around for a familiar face. I find one. Yes! It's not MuchachaBonita but I've definitely seen the youngest in the class, a young woman of about thirty, before. She's about five foot six tall. She's slim with long black hair tied back in a ponytail. She has a pretty face and olive complexion. I nod towards her. "Casa Nuestra?" I say.

"Si," She smiles.

I try to think when I saw her last night. She wasn't one of the waiting staff. Then I remember her coming out of the kitchen and walking around the tables as if looking for somebody.

"I saw you last night," I say, "You spoke to the guy on the next table to me."

"Ah yes. He was very nice."

Our conversation is interrupted as our instructor enters the studio. This time there's no surprise and Charlie is exactly how I would expect a gym instructor to look. I notice that he gets plenty of appreciative glances from my classmates. He's not some body-building, knuckle scraping, Neanderthal type. He's tall, slim, tanned and about twenty-five. He has a public school air about him that's emphasised by his blonde, floppy hair.

He addresses the class, "Good morning everybody." He turns to me, "You must be Dave."

I wonder if Djimi and Sam have warned him of what the cat dragged into *We Can Work It Out* this morning.

"That's right, Charlie. As you can see my LB&T are pretty desperately in need of some TLC."

"Sam said that you managed okay with HIIT but please don't overdo it. I don't want any casualties on my watch."

Charlie asks us all to pick up a mat and lay it on the floor facing him. I drag mine alongside the young Spanish woman.

"I'm Dave," I say, "and you are?"

"I am Maria. Pleased to meet you Dave"

"You cook at Casa Nuestra?"

"Yes."

"You're a very good cook. My meal last night was delicious."

No time to converse any more. Charlie has us starting our routine. More loud pop music signals the start of the class. Same old warm up exercises as last time. I'm already getting into the hang of this stretching. It's just a pity about what follows.

It's not as exhausting as HIIT but the exercises are reaching parts that haven't been used for years. We do Russian twists followed by Bulgarian split squats. As we move onto Romanian lifts I start to worry that we are going to do the entire Eastern Bloc. We've done press-ups, sit-ups, jump ups, and enough planks to keep Bluebeard in business for years.

My abdominal muscles don't know what's hit them as we end with an exercise that involves leaping into the air, hands straight up, before crouching down onto all fours, kicking the legs backwards, bringing them forwards again and repeating over and over. I feel last night's dinner digesting and do my utmost to keep control of my guts. With my final leap upward, trapped wind that's been brewing for half an hour makes its getaway in the second most embarrassing way possible. I don't know what to say. Perhaps the rest of the class's grunts and groans of exhaustion drowned it out. Nobody says anything. I think I've got away with it.

"That's it," Charlie signals for us to stop. "Well done, Dave. Now you know why we call those exercises *Burpees*."

I flush and attempt to make light of my digression. "I hope we're not doing *Fartees* next."

Charlie laughs. "It's rather too confined a space for those."

As we finish the customary cool down I take the chance to speak to Maria again.

"I'm sorry to bother you Maria. But I'm trying to get in touch with a young lady who works at Casa Nuestra. She said that she was going to be here this morning."

"Margarita perhaps? She usually does spinning. What does she look like?"

I worry that a simple description, which might be 'Phwoaar', will make me sound like an old lech. So I tone it down a little. "A little taller than you. Long dark hair. Very pretty."

"Yes that is Margarita. She may not come today. She told me that she was going out on a very important date last night."

"Oh that's a pity."

"Can I give her a message? I will see her this evening at work."

"Don't worry. Perhaps if she's not in spinning."

I mop up again, clean my mat with antiseptic wipes handed out by Charlie, hang the mat up and go back downstairs to reception.

Chapter Thirteen

Dave

"You survived LBT then, Dave?"

"Thank you, Djimi. Yes. I surprised myself."

"So you're all set for spinning now?"

"Sure," I'm not sure that my voice has the confident ring I was attempting.

"Upstairs again. Studio Five."

This time it's two flights and I'm more than puffed when I reach the top. I open the door to find that I'm the first to arrive. It's a bright airy room with floor to ceiling windows around three walls. About sixteen exercise bikes are positioned in a horseshoe that has its open end facing the completely mirrored fourth wall. In the middle of the horseshoe's opening is a further bike facing the others.

I choose the first bike in the arc. I sit on it and put my water bottle into the bottle holder. I can't reach the pedals so I jump off and make adjustments to the various levers that control the height of the saddle, its distance from the handlebars and the height of the handlebars. Happy with my fine-tuning I jump back on and start to pedal. Easy peasy. I'd been given the impression that this was going to be my nemesis but the pedals spin with ease. I hardly need to push.

The studio starts to fill and it's like a pit stop on the Tour De France as thirteen busy bodies bend over and twiddle with levers to personalise their machines to their optimum settings.

At the other end of the horseshoe a woman in her thirties is adjusting the bike exactly opposite me. She's wearing the customary jazzy leggings. They cling to her shapely legs. I've seen such a variety of leggings this morning that I now realise there seems to be some sort of leggings pecking order - the fitter the wearer the jazzier the outfit. This pair is grey with white flashes – by far the smartest I've seen so far. She's wearing an equally snazzy pair of trainers with turquoise laces and diamante panels. Her top is a simple extremely low cut t-shirt with a tiny designer logo on the breast. She completes her adjustments and climbs aboard. As she leans forwards and starts to pedal, from where I am sitting, it appears that two bald men are fighting to get out of her t-shirt. The faster she pedals the more they struggle to stay confined. She's right in my line of sight. I don't know where to look.

I start to fiddle with the straps on my pedals. I make tutting noises, and shrug with what I hope looks like spinning bike expertise. I climb off the bike and go to the last remaining machine. This one is positioned dead centre of the horseshoe facing the front. I'm next to Maria again. Now, instead of watching a pair of heaving breasts, I am confronted by a florid, grossly overweight old man in a sweat-drenched top wearing glasses stuck together with plasters. I think that the mirror is like one of those fairground ones that exaggerate your features until I see that everyone else in the group's reflection looks completely normal.

The class is due to start any minute. I do a couple of final adjustments to the new bike and look out of the window. A big silver car glides into the car park. Its driver jumps out. I catch a glimpse of silver hair as he runs towards the gym entrance.

Seconds later the studio door flies open.

"What time do you call this?" shouts the woman in the low cut t-shirt.

"Car problems. Long story," comes the reply as the driver heads towards the horseshoe. "Brrr," he gives an exaggerated shiver. "I love these chilly mornings. An hour of this and I'll feel rosy all over." He nods in the direction of the young woman to my left – a strapping coffee skinned Amazon. "You up for it Rosie?"

My neighbour doesn't laugh. "The only bit of me you'll be feeling is these," she says brandishing her fists in a seriously menacing way.

"Calm down dear. Only a joke. Wow. I can't believe my luck. How did this happen? The best seat in the house is still here. Thought I'd missed it this week." Mr. Grey Hair starts to adjust the levers. He's about my age, a bit taller but a fraction of my weight. The Sunday supplements would have him down as a silver fox.

Miss Fancy Leggings laughs. "That gentleman appeared to have a problem with it," she says nodding in my direction.

He looks towards me. "My gain is your loss, sir. This bike's like Viagra. Gives me an extra lift if you know what I mean." He hesitates a moment. "Bloody hell. If it isn't Dave! Dave Prendergast? Well I never... never thought I'd see *you* here."

My heart sinks as I realise who has joined us.

Chapter Fourteen

Dave

"Hello Martin."

I can't say any more, as Clare enters the studio. She runs through the operation of the bikes' gears and explains the different seating and standing positions we'll be using in the next forty-five minutes for the newcomers. We do a few warm up exercises and then – we're off.

We've got more of the latest music to accompany us. Before this morning, Radio 2 pop was just the background noise to our time at home but after two hours of it blasting my eardrums I'm getting to know one or two of the tunes and the words that go with them. The words are mostly irrelevant but I find that if I pedal in time to the beat it's a big help to my spinning efforts.

Clare soon tells us to adjust the gear lever to a higher number and my hoped for hour of the pedals spinning effortlessly dissolves in a flash. We're only on level three (of twenty) and I'm panting.

"Stand up," is the instruction.

It's easier than sitting down but then Clare adds "Another two gears."

I follow her instruction and my pedals slow. I look around at my fellow classmates and see their legs and wheels flying round in a blur. Martin hasn't even broken sweat yet his legs are pumping like those of a silver-haired Bradley Wiggins. I'm not sure that I can cope with forty-five minutes. At least I have the excuse of HIIT and LBT.

By the time our gears are into double figures my shirt and shorts looks like they have just come out of the washing machine. Clare tells us that we are on a hill climb and that we'll soon be freewheeling down the other side The song is telling us 'it's all about the bass' but for me it's all about keeping face. It's bad enough failing in front of a class of young, fit people, but to fail in front of bloody

Martin Hetherington would be, as Simon would say, an "EPIC FAIL". He's humiliated me so many times I don't think that I can cope with another.

I check the time on the large wall clock. It can't be too much longer before that downhill but now Clare wants us to set the gears so that we feel as if we are "wading through treacle". I was wading through treacle in third gear. I've waded through sand, and through mud and now I'm wading through flipping concrete that's not quite set. There can't be much more. Even Martin has rivulets of sweat running down his brow although they won't reach his eyes as he's wearing a trendy headband. He looks across at his pal whose boobs are rising and falling so vigorously with the music that I worry she'll give herself a black eye.

"Come on Helen," he shouts, "One last push before we go down." He's straining now, but the music track changes and it's Queen's *Don't Stop Me Now*.

"Okay everyone. Reduce your resistance, sit down and let's fly back down."

There's a flurry of activity as the class adjusts gears, sits down and pedals furiously towards an imaginary finishing line with Freddy Mercury spurring them on.

I'm over the moon that I've not humiliated myself. I take the gear down to number two and my legs are spinning quickly. "Yessss," I say to myself silently.

And then it happens.

Chapter Fifteen

Dave

The pain starts slowly but builds up fast and, oh boy, is it bad. I know exactly what it is but I also know exactly what a class of fit and healthy exercise fanatics looking at a sweaty and exhausted old man clutching his chest must be thinking and, sure enough, panic soon sets in.

"Call an ambulance."

"Can anyone do CPR?"

I picture that Vinnie Jones heart charity ad and the whole spinning class doing Travolta moves and singing *Stayin Alive* while Martin pounds on my chest.

"What about mouth to mouth?"

I try to indicate that I will be okay but my protests are ignored and I find myself lying on my back with Maria leaning over me administering, or attempting to administer, a kiss of life. It's not exactly an unpleasant experience, and would be quite enjoyable if not accompanied by the excruciating pain.

"It'll be ages before an ambulance gets here," I hear Martin's voice and see him looking down at me in between Maria's kisses. "My car is in the car park. I'll get him to A&E."

Together, the group gets me to my feet. I have one arm draped over Martin's shoulder as he half walks me - half carries me towards the door. The pain is so strong I'm clutching my chest with my spare arm and, unable to speak, I simply go with the flow. The door opens and we're onto the landing. I'm sure that I sense Martin waiting for an audience and the rest of the class to reach the door before he puts me over his shoulder in a fireman's lift and carries me quickly down two flights.

As we reach reception I'm helped back into an upright position and, with one arm draped around Martin's shoulders, I soon find myself being dragged out of the doors and into the car park. Martin props me up against the back door of the car whilst he opens the front passenger door and drapes the luxurious leather upholstery with towels. Considering that the entire membership and staff of the gym is watching from the steps, thinking that I am in the throes of a heart attack, he takes an inordinate amount of time to ensure that his precious seating is not tainted by my sweat. He throws my free gift from the gym onto the back seat.

He props me into place and fastens my seatbelt before heading round to the driver's side and getting ready to set off. He reverses from his parking space, slams the car into drive and the Merc purrs out of the car park and into the London traffic. If I'd been in an ambulance the blue lights would have cleared a path to the hospital but in Martin's limo it's likely to be a long ride.

"I'd use the bus lane," says Martin "but after what happened last night I'm not sure that's such a good idea."

I'm still clutching my chest but I can feel it easing. I take a sip from the water bottle that someone remembered to return to me as I was dragged from the studio and, as the now lukewarm water hits my gullet, it's as if it releases an airlock in my chest and a gush of trapped wind belches from me. I appear to be performing a very long and very bad impersonation of a sheep giving birth.

"Marinated peppers," I say when the noise finally subsides. "Sheila always tells me not to order them."

"So why did you order them?" Martin's waving his hand under his nose. I don't blame him as the strangulated sound had disguised the noise of more trapped wind making its getaway via the alternative route. He winds down his window.

"So that's all it was? Indigestion. Christ, we all thought you were a goner back there."

"I could have told you but I couldn't, if you know what I mean."

"So. I'd better stand down the paramedics in A&E. Djimi will have phoned to tell them to be ready for your emergency arrival." Martin presses a button on the steering wheel and speaks loudly, "Telephone."

"Please say the contact name or number" a disembodied voice from the dashboard states, flatly.

After a long conversation with the car's voice controller and numerous false starts, each of which diminishes his attempts to impress me with the poshness and German efficiency of his car I leap in,"Ve vant ze number of ze hospital. Scnhell. Dumkoff."

I so want the car's response to be "Of course sir. Why didn't you say so?" but at least "Did you say Hospital?" is an improvement on what Martin has elicited from the thing.

By now the hospital is in view.

"I might as well just jump out and tell them," I say.

"Okay, but I'll wait for you and give you a lift home."

I get out of the car, cross the busy road and head into the crowded A&E department. Fortunately the receptionist deals with me straight away and I'm relived that I won't be joining the throng filling every seat in the waiting area. I explain the situation and leave. I'm not convinced that any paramedics had been awaiting my arrival as, looking at the severity of some of those waiting, there are plenty of more important cases to deal with.

As I leave the hospital there's no sign of Martin's Mercedes at first but I eventually see it weaving through traffic towards me. I run back across the road and try to open the door only to find it locked. Martin presses a button and I'm able to get in.

"Security locks," he says. "You don't want to be driving in a rough neighbourhood like this with the doors unlocked. Someone could lean in and snatch a handbag off the front seat and be gone in a flash." He pauses "So Dave, where to? Are you still in the semi?" There's an emphasis on *semi* which I am sure is a precursor to me hearing about a luxury apartment or detached property of immeasurable grandeur and opulence. It'll only be a matter of minutes.

"Yes same old same old, you know."

"Still with Sheila?"

"Of course. And Jane?" I ask.

"Jane's history."

"Sorry to hear that Martin."

"Oh don't be sorry Dave. There's plenty of life in the old dog you know. She took me to the cleaners mind. Had to sell the Bentley. *And* she got the mews in Chelsea and now I'm stuck with this," he pats the leather steering wheel, "and one of those new penthouses on the river."

"Oh dear."

"But it does have three bedrooms and a roof garden designed by a Chelsea gold medalist and a double garage so I can keep the Porsche out of the rain."

Martin joined me as a fellow rookie on the first day of our banking careers and we'd followed each other's progress (or lack of progress, in my case). As his charm and guile took him into the stratosphere of head office and board meetings, my bluntness had the opposite effect on the powers that be and my working life developed into a series of mundane clerical appointments culminating in the role of Head Of Securities in a big city branch. It sounds important but it wasn't. I lost count of the number of times Martin was promoted. Whenever our paths crossed it would be, "Well done on your getting that Chief Cashier" from him and "Local Director eh! Do I have to call you sir now?" from me.

We weren't friends but we bumped into each other at the bank's social and sporting events from time to time, and it was part of his charm and success that he never forgot a face and never forgot a name. "You never know when they might come in useful" he would say.

It was difficult to imagine Martin without a woman in his life. Jane had put up with a long string of his affairs. She had once been friendly with Sheila and had confessed to her that she was quite happy for him to fulfill his urges outside of the marital bed as long as she was enjoying the lifestyle to which she had become accustomed.

"So, did Jane catch you cheating?" I ask.

"Only twenty times or so."

"She was a very tolerant woman. So what made her push for a divorce?"

"I reckon she just did her sums. She worked out that my retirement was around the corner, I'd reached the top, the gravy train was about to pull into the sidings and the days of the high life on expenses were coming to an end. Best take me to the cleaners while there was still plenty to get her claws into, and boy, did she get her claws in. She even used a private detective to investigate the affairs and hired the most expensive lawyers in town."

"So, is there a new partner on the horizon?"

"What's the point, when you can get laid so easily nowadays with no strings attached?"

"I wouldn't know anything about that. Not that I'd want to."

"You don't know what you're missing. There are hundreds of web sites packed with gorgeous, young hotties looking for guys our age."

"I'm not sure that any gorgeous young hotty would be looking for me."

"She would if you were a millionaire. And your house *must* make *you* a millionaire, at least on paper. I can give you the address of a website full of girls looking for sugar daddies."

"I think I'll pass on that."

"You don't know what you're missing. You should see my latest."

We pull to a halt at traffic lights and he hands his iPhone to me.

"Legs up to her armpits and boy what legs!"

"I know."

"You know her?"

"Uh huh,' I nod.

"You're kidding me. How do you know her?"

"Because *somebody*," I glare at him "on a sugar daddy website, told her *his* name was Dave Prendergast."

"Oops."

Chapter Sixteen

Dave

Martin laughs as he pulls away from the lights.

"You think it's something to laugh about? You've no idea what sort of trouble you could have got me into."

"*Trouble?* That's the last thing I'd call a night of hot sex with a twenty-something Mediterranean beauty. *I* buy a designer handbag and *you* get laid! Serves me right for being unoriginal in my choice of names."

"*Me? Laid?* Don't be absurd. I would never cheat on Sheila. If Sheila caught me even *looking* at another woman I'd be dead."

"The slaughter of the innocent eh? Come on Dave. Don't tell me you weren't tempted by a girl like Margarita. I've had my eye on her for a while at spinning. When she popped up on that site I couldn't believe my luck. She has no idea it was me."

"Weren't you playing a bit close to home? As soon as she saw it was you picking her up wouldn't she have run a mile?"

"Of course not. They all love me in that class."

"That's not the impression that that Rosie gave when you said you were going to feel her all over."

"That's just banter. She loves it really. Margarita's the same. Always rolling her eyes and muttering under her breath in Spanish but I can tell it's just an act. She's loving every minute of it. You missed your chance Dave."

"I shared a taxi ride with her and, if I were thirty years younger **and** single I'd certainly be tempted. But I'm not sure that she's the sort to sleep with anyone for a lousy handbag."

"Of course she is. Why do you think she signed up to the website? What was she expecting in return for evenings of luxury and elaborate gifts? A peck on the cheek?"

"Possibly. What does it say on the site? Does it say there's sex involved?"

"Of course not. It's far more discreet that that."

"If my name is on that site Sheila might find out. How will I explain *that* to her?"

"There's no way that will ever happen. I use a nickname. Margarita asked me my real name when we were arranging to meet up."

"So, why did you use Dave Prendergast?"

"The pensioners' magazine had just arrived in the post. I was flicking through it when her message arrived and there was one of those *Training Class Of Seventy-Five: Where Are They Now?* photographs."

"And I was smack bang in he middle of the front row."

"You saw it."

"Too true I saw it. Sheila and Simon had a field day with the kipper tie and the Oscar Wilde hair."

"That's why I picked you. Such a looker."

"I wished you'd picked Steve Haworth or Mark Jones."

"Not in your league Dave."

"So I'm supposed to be flattered?"

"Of course. And anyway your initials fitted nicely into my" he taps the side of his nose, "online strategy."

I have no idea what he is talking about and am not really interested in finding out.

"And there's no way that Sheila could possibly think this has anything whatsoever to do with me? She has open access to my computer and checks what I've been up to regularly—what about photos? You haven't used *my* photo?"

Martin gives me a quick glance up and down. "I'm wanting hot sex not looking for someone to take me to the shops in my wheelchair."

"You cheeky bastard! Margarita and I hit it off very well together last night."

"Yeah. While I was trying to persuade that bloody copper not to take my car to the pound. Cost me two hundred pounds to get it back this morning. Two hundred plus fifteen hundred for that handbag made it a pretty expensive night out and I didn't even touch first base."

Good Lord, I think to myself. One thousand, five hundred for that handbag. How do I get myself out of this one?

"She seems pretty sensible to me," I say, "I didn't even get past the front door."

"Well, she certainly owes me big time."

"I wouldn't count on it Martin. She doesn't seem like that kind of girl to me. How long has she been on the website?"

"She said I was her first contact. She said she liked my profile and my photo which, *okay*, wasn't my photo – and what I said I wanted."

"Which was?"

"Company for nights at the theatre, Michelin starred restaurants, opera you know, that sort of thing."

"What young woman wouldn't like that? I'd like a couple of fancy dinners and to see a show or two myself. There's no mention of having to sleep over in return. I still think you've got her wrong. Her English isn't that perfect and you were, I assume, fully dressed in your photo and not waving anything inappropriate around."

"The guy in the photo was perfectly dressed Dave - immaculate in fact. Paul Smith, Armani you know, the full works. Don't worry. I save *those* photos until at least the third or fourth contact."

'Well can I suggest that when you send any of *those* to anyone in the future they're clearly labeled as Martin Hetherington and *not* Dave Prendergast."

"You sure, Dave? They might enhance your reputation with the ladies. There's no face in them."

"Quite sure thank you, Martin. I think my reputation with the ladies - and everyone else for that matter - is just fine as it is. I've no plans to reinvent myself as a sixty-two year old Dirk Diggler."

We're almost at our road and my indigestion has, thank goodness, receded. "You can drop me off now, Martin. I can walk from here."

"No. I insist on taking you to your door. What would

Sheila say if I let you off here and you collapsed with a stroke?"

"Well done, probably," I mutter under my breath.

Martin pulls into the kerb.

"This is it isn't it? I never forget a place with good taste."

We're outside our neighbours' and Martin is studying their group of garishly painted gnomes in various poses on the small waterfall beneath their front bay window.

"Next door," I say.

I get out of the car, lean in and thank him for his help. I take my water bottle, towel and anorak, and move to shut the door.

"Hang on, Dave. I can't come round here without saying hello to Sheila. Old times sake and all that."

My heart sinks as I shut the car door. I'm about to open the door again to mention the resident's parking rules but he pulls away and manoeuvres the car into a space a short way down the road.

Chapter Seventeen

Dave

It's one o'clock when I turn the key in the front door. As soon as I open it Sheila is in my face.

"Have you been standing there all day?" I ask.

Her hands are on her hips and her lips are tightly clenched.

"What do *you* think? Where have you been? I've been worried sick. You go out at some ungodly hour to a gym you haven't been to in years and I don't have sight or sound of you for hours. All this, the day after you come home after midnight in a police car and give me a handbag that sells on Selfridges website at one thousand, five hundred pounds. One thousand, five hundred pounds we haven't got. What's going on Dave?"

"I can explain. Just let me in. I need a wee and then I'll need a shower."

Sheila holds her ground at first but seeing me hopping from foot to foot, she moves aside to let me hurry past her and up the stairs to the bathroom. "Won't be long," I shout down, "and by the way..."

My voice trails off as the doorbell rings. Sheila answers it and I hear her surprise.

"Martin? What on earth brings you here?"

I spend longer than necessary in the bathroom, in an attempt to gather my thoughts but they are no clearer when I've finished my shower and got myself dressed. I feel better as I put on my best chinos and smartest shirt. I comb my hair as neatly as I can and splash on a bit of my favourite after-shave. I head downstairs. I may hate Martin but at least he's taken the sting out of the situation with Sheila.

"As I said to Sir Allan," I can hear Martin from the stairs, "Theresa May would be delighted if you were to go ahead. I think we could get Kylie involved and Elton...and

Sadiq will let us use the park..." His voice tails off as I come into the dining room.

He and Sheila are standing at the table peering at the laptop screen. He has a hand lightly brushing her backside. He looks up and says "Ah. Here he is. The warrior returns"

Sheila laughs as if it's the best joke she's ever heard.

"Sheila's just about to show me your latest fabulous find on eBay." He says removing his hand from her posterior without the slightest hint of embarrassment.

"Pfftttbb..." I somehow can't get the words out. I rush across to the table and slam the screen shut.

"Just Sheila's little joke I say. No interest to you. They were a mistake anyway. Not what I thought they were. No definitely not. I'll have to keep looking. No. No luck this time." I pick up the MacBook and put it under my arm just to be sure.

"That's not what you told *me*," says Sheila.

I shoot her my nastiest look. I really can do some nasty looks if I try. She gets the message.

Martin looks at his watch, "Er I think it's time I made myself scarce, you two. Been great to see you both again. Really must fly now."

I lead him to the door, open it and show him out. As he leaves he pauses and turns back, "Remember Sheila. Look me up if you ever come round my way. I'll give Dave my card."

He hands me a card. God, he's even carrying personalised calling cards in his gym shorts pockets. As I take it, I notice a familiar vehicle drawing up outside.

"Hang on Martin," I say, "Let me give you one of our cards too. Come back inside for a minute."

He steps back inside and I shut the door.

I start scrabbling through drawers in the sideboard. I take as long as I can, and then a bit longer looking for cards that don't exist.

"Sorry Martin. Must have given the last one out. Never mind I'll write the details down." I scribble our phone number and email addresses on a piece of notepaper and hand it to him. We move back to the front door.

As I open the door and he steps outside, Martin momentarily turns into the guy in that Edvard Munch painting before letting out an enormous bellow and charging down the path.

"Oh Martin," I call after him, "*So* sorry, mate. Did I forget to mention the residents' parking scheme?"

Chapter Eighteen

Dave

It's a couple of hours later when I drive back from the car pound after dropping Martin there. I bring back Djimi's gift bag that I'd left on Martin's back seat. After I pull up to the house, I open the bag and have a look at the contents. There's a nice range of *We Can Work It Out* goodies.

I go in and find Sheila in the dining room sitting at the table tapping away on the laptop. She closes it up and I sit down next to her. "How was poor Martin? Why didn't you offer him our pass? You know that you only have to be here ten minutes before you risk the pound."

"I was about to tell him but it slipped my mind. There are plenty of signs outside he should have checked. He's lived in London long enough."

"He always was a risk taker was Martin. Hasn't done too bad for it though has he?"

"He's done alright."

"Alright? If you call a penthouse on the river alright. They start at six million."

"He's probably got a massive mortgage. He worked in a bank remember."

"Yeah. And I suppose the Merc and the Porsche are on HP, he's borrowed the Damien Hirst he was telling me about and the Yoji Yamamoto trainers he's wearing for the gym came from the charity shop."

"Okay," I grudgingly accept, "He's done *quite* well but he's not got what we've got."

Sheila looks around the room. "So what have *we* got that Martin hasn't got? An IKEA sideboard perhaps? A print of the haywain that your gran left you? A vase from John Lewis?"

"I don't mean *things*. I mean a *relationship*. Look at us. We've been together all these years. Martin's on his own and you know, from Jane, that his marriage was a disaster."

"Maybe we'd be better off on our own. You could spend all your time on eBay and wouldn't have to worry about me and my impossible demands for attention and the need for maybe a holiday one day. I'd get myself a little flat in town and do all the stuff I want to do."

"You don't really mean that do you? We're good together. Everyone says 'Look at Dave and Sheila' when they're talking about solid relationships."

"Yeah. Look at Dave and Sheila. Solid as concrete... and about as interesting."

"That's what I love about you."

"What?"

"That sense of humour," I move towards her and kiss her gently on the cheek, "I really do love you, you know. And I really am going to get us some money and get you the holiday of a lifetime. There's still a chance with those vases. Simon's following up a lead for me. Just wait a day or two. You'll see. And please... don't talk about us splitting up."

Chapter Nineteen

Maria

What a morning it has been. I really hope the old man at the gym recovered okay. After that mouth-to-mouth I think I will cut back on the garlic in the patatas bravas in future.

I am worried about Margarita too. She was not at the gym this morning and she almost never misses. She was going on a date last night with a complete stranger who must be at least twice her age. She told me it was all fine and there was nothing to worry about but... I try her mobile. It goes to voicemail. I leave a message in Spanish "Margarita, llámame pronto."

I hope she calls me back soon but I cannot sit around waiting for her. I have got six parcels to pack and take down to the Post Office counter in News & Booze before I get ready for work. Packing really is the downside of eBay. All the listing, the photos, the emails, the questions, the auctions, the feedback and the money of course are fun but when the sales are over you are left with a pile of stuff and wondering what you can find to pack it in without spending all your takings on Jiffy bags, bubble wrap and postage.

I pack the easiest pieces first. The dress, the dressing gown and the rest of the clothes I can wrap in brown paper. I bought a roll on eBay and it has been brilliant. It is not long before they are done, neatly labeled and ready for Royal Mail. The toaster and the set of pans are not so easy. What was I thinking of, quoting ten pounds for shipping? The pans weigh kilos and I find myself searching the bedsit for something strong enough to box them in. If only the handles were removable I could manage with a smaller box.

I finally remember the new vacuum cleaner. It is sitting in the cupboard packed in its original packing. I am so short of space that it makes sense to keep it like that so I can pack other stuff on top but I will have to do a balancing act in future as it is all I can find. I cut the box down as much as I dare to keep the weight down and after half an hour the pans are ready for the post office.

The toaster is packed with a mixture of taped together cereal, washing powder and biscuit boxes covered with brown paper. It looks like a piece of modern art when I've finished.

And I look like a piece of performance art when I try to carry them to News & Booze. I have got the clothes parcels in big carrier bags hung from each arm. I am wearing my handbag like a rucksack on my back and the package with the pans is held at chest level with the toaster balanced on top as I edge carefully down the stairs. At least I do not have the floreros to carry as well.

My journey to the post office is like an assault course. I cannot see over the toaster unless I clamp it into place using my chin and walk like a hunchback. The pavements are as packed as always. I worry that I will not make it to the counter before it closes and I will have to repeat the journey back looking like Coco The Clown performing in the Big Top.

I feel my phone vibrating in my handbag and hear the muffled *La Bamba* ringtone. I should not even think about trying to answer it. But what if it is Margarita? I am near the doorway to a closed down shop. I step off the pavement and, struggling, put my parcels onto a bundle of rags covering an old sleeping bag. The phone stops ringing.

"Oi. What's going on?" I am startled to hear a voice from the sleeping bag and look in horror as a straggly, grey shock of hair emerges from under the rags.

"Oh sir. I am so sorry. I did not see you there."

"I'll let you off, love. You've made my day. First time I've been called *sir* in twenty years but I'm not going to sleep with this weight on me."

I move my parcels and check in my handbag to see if I have anything to offer to make up for my clumsiness, but I have only got enough cash to pay for the postage.

"I am so sorry, I do not have any change I can offer you."

"That's alright. I take cards."

I fumble back into my bag.

"Only kidding, love. But it won't be long, you know. My mate Charlie is setting up Apple Pay so the yuppies can swipe his cardboard box with their iPhones on the way to Starbucks and salve their conscience with a bit of charity before their Fairtrade frappuccinos."

My phone rings again. I take it out of my bag. 'SimonOxford' is flashing on the screen. I look at the time. Five o'clock. I swipe the answer button.

"Hello... Hello. Is that Simon? Hello?"

I turn away from the road and look down at the old man. He's singing *La Bamba* and appears to be dancing in his sleeping bag.

"Hi.Yes, It's Simon. I promised to call about the frogs. What are you up to now? Any chance of me calling on you to see them?"

"I am sorry Simon. I cannot at the moment. I am on my way to the post office. I have to be there for half past five. I have some urgent post. I am on duty tonight at Casa Nuestra but I usually get a ten-minute break. I could bring them in. "

There's a slight panic in Simon's voice, "I wouldn't do that. You might risk breaking them. I would rather see them at your place."

"I am sorry Simon. I do not know you. I cannot give you my address."

"Well. Can I meet you quickly when you've finished at the post office? I'm walking down the High St now. I just got off the bus. You can't be far away."

"I am sorry, I am in a hurry. I have your number. I will phone or text when I have had time to think. I have to go or I will miss the final post."

I put the phone back into my bag and start to reload my burden. I am struggling to balance everything but I manage with difficulty and walk as quickly as I can. I am not far from the post office when I hear a voice behind me.

"Excuse me but you look like you could do with a bit of help with that lot."

I turn and see a tall figure towering over me.

"I've just finished a phone call," he says. " The person I was speaking to was in a hurry to get to the post office and it doesn't exactly take Sherlock Holmes to deduce that you are possibly on your way to the post office. My call was to a Spanish woman and, please forgive me if I am being rude, you certainly have an Iberian look. My caller goes by the name of MuchachaBonita and, again please forgive my forwardness, you are certainly very bonita. So, Maria, I'm Simon. Delighted to meet you." He holds out a hand.

Chapter Twenty

Maria

Thanks to Simon I make the post office counter with five minutes to spare. Mr. Ali is on duty and handles my parcels with his usual efficiency.

As he takes the final one Simon starts to chat with him.

"I didn't expect to see you here today, Mr. Ali."

"Why is that? We open twenty-four seven. I hardly get an hour off. "

"You know..,after all the excitement last night."

"Ah. The *excitement*. You mean the police and the old man?"

"Yes. But not just them. Your bit too. You know. The cricket bat." Simon makes an imaginary stroke but before he can continue there's a panting sound behind me.

"Am I still in time to post this lot?"

I turn around and see a man struggling with a big pile of packages that look like they have been wrapped by a three year old with two left hands.

Mr. Ali raises his eyebrows. "Behold the joy of eBay," he says as the parcels spill onto the counter.

I leave the shop with Simon and we stop on the pavement outside. "So, Maria, do you trust me enough to let me come and see your vases?"

He has been a gentleman. He is tall and quite good-looking. He is polite. I know some people who jump into bed with complete strangers after seeing one photo they chose to swipe right on Tinder. Surely I can trust him. Another thirty pounds would be very useful especially as the pans cost ten pounds more to ship than I charged the buyer. But what is the rush? Can I trust someone who claims to be a frog collector? Is that not a bit weird? The pots are safe at home and I have got to be ready for work in a couple of hours.

"I do trust you Simon." I say "But now is really not the

best time. I have a night off on Thursday. How about we arrange to meet then?"

"Okay Maria. I won't push you. Thursday? Let me check my phone and make sure I'm free. I've got a parents' evening at school coming up but I'm pretty sure that's a week on Thursday and the Frog Convention isn't for a few weeks yet, if I can still get a ticket..."

He has a smile on his face as he says this.

"Just kidding," he continues, "We could hold our convention in a phone box and there would still be room for a few more. It's not exactly mainstream, you know." He scrolls through his phone and says," Thursday is absolutely fine. How about meeting here at seven?"

"Seven is fine for me."

"And don't make dinner plans. I know a couple of decent places."

Chapter Twenty-One

Dave

Simon told me that he was following up on the vases and I'm struggling to concentrate. I'm half-heartedly scrolling through screen after screen on the Internet but I've found nothing to come close to matching the excitement of the Yabu Meizan pieces. There may be a Minton Majolica jardinière hiding behind a description of 'ornate plant stand' but that stuff had its heyday twenty years ago when the Americans were snapping up the most mediocre pieces for hundreds. And how would a seller get such a big item to me from Inverness in one piece?

The front door opens. Simon kicks off his shoes in the hall, comes into the dining room and sits down at the table opposite me.

"Hi Dad. Good day?"

"Not bad, son. You?"

"Great. I met our muchacha."

"You did? And?"

"She wasn't wrong with her description. She's quite a stunner."

"I'm not interested what she looks like. She can look like Quasimodo for all I care. What about the vases?"

"Hmm. No luck as yet but—"

"But what?"

"Definite progress to report."

"Go on."

"She won't tell me where she lives. But I'm meeting her on Thursday night and taking her out for a bite to eat."

I groan. "You call that progress? I know what you're like with women. You'll be inviting her to stay the night here and we won't even get to see the vases."

"Oh Dad, ye of little faith. Do you really think I would mess up your 'find of a lifetime', your one big chance to get a few quid in the bank?"

I don't reply.

"You do don't you? You think I'll mess up. You think I'll upset MuchachaBonita and we'll never see her again. Don't worry. I'm not stupid. I will be charm personified and, even if she's the most fanciable girl I'm ever likely to find myself on a date with, I promise to behave impeccably and be back here with the vases before you know it."

"Promise?"

"I promise. Mind you. Once I've got the vases the rules may change."

"Well let's cross that bridge when we get to it."

Simon leaves the table and goes upstairs to change out of his work clothes. I've got to wait two days before I find out if I've got the vases. The suspense is going to be unbearable.

I hear Simon and Sheila exchange greetings on the landing before Sheila's light footsteps on the stairs. As she reaches the bottom the doorbell rings.

"I'll get it," she shouts. I see her open the door from my seat in the dining room. It's dark outside. Sheila's been telling me to replace that light bulb for months but when I hear the rich deep tones of, "Good evening madam. Is Mr Prendergast in the house" I don't need light to know who is there.

"Yes officer."

"May we have just a couple of words with him?"

I close the laptop, get up and walk into the hall to stand beside Sheila.

"Why sergeant. Constable. How nice to see you again."

I turn to Sheila, "The officers will be following up on last night. I'll deal with them."

"Not without me you won't." Sheila beckons the couple inside. "Do come in officers."

She leads them into the lounge and tells them to take a seat. They both take off their hats and sink into a sofa. Suddenly our sitting room seems infinitely smaller than it did five minutes ago.

"I'm sorry. We haven't been introduced," Sheila says.

"I'm Sergeant Clarke and this is PC Stevens."

"Cup of tea officers?" Sheila asks.

"That would be lovely. Two sugars for PC Stevens and three for me."

As Sheila goes to make the tea, Simon, now in jeans and jumper comes into the room to join us.

"Wow. May the force be with us. Hi officers. Come for another statement from our hero? Or are you here with his medal? No? Please don't tell me there's been another fire at the school."

"All is quiet at the school Mr Prendergast. No problems there. We are here to talk with your dad."

"Should I make myself scarce then?

"Probably best," I say. "This room is cramped enough."

Simon leaves and Sheila returns carrying three cups of tea and a plateful of custard creams on a tray that she puts down on the coffee table in front of the officers. She serves the police and sits in an armchair resting the third cup on her knees. I move across and perch on the arm of the chair.

"So errr Sergeant, how can I help you," I say, in trepidation.

" I'll let PC Stevens explain."

PC Stevens takes out his notebook. He turns over a few pages, reads some scribbled notes and begins.

"Plainclothes have told us to be on the lookout for some very distinctive handbags and we believe that the handbag that you, Mr. Prendergast, had upon your person last night may fit the description. May we see the bag again?"

Sheila shoots me a furious look, puts her cup and saucer down on the coffee table and stomps noisily out of the room into the hall.

"Don't mind Sheila, officers." I mouth the word 'menopause' and regret it straight away as Sheila, returning, flings the bag and scores a direct hit on my cheek.

"I knew you were up to no good with that bag. When did you ever buy me expensive gifts likes that? What's he been up to?"

I hand the bag towards the PC who is busy putting on a pair or thin rubber gloves.

He takes it and starts to examine it carefully. "Does it

check with the notes Stevens?" the sergeant asks.

He turns it around, checks the stitching, the lining, the interior zipper, the clasp. He consults his notes and checks the bag again.

"Everything checks out, sarge. Fits the bill exactly."

Sergeant Clarke takes the bag back. "I am afraid that I am going to have to take this bag back to CID at the station, Mr. Prendergast."

"Wait a second. I can explain," I say.

"Don't explain to us," says Stevens, "it's not our investigation but expect a call from our colleagues in plainclothes." He writes a receipt for the bag and hands it to me but Sheila snatches it away.

"He's got *plenty* of explaining to do," she says. She reads the receipt, "'Received from Mr. D Prendergast: one Mulberry handbag.' What's this? 'Reference 'Sugar D'?"

"Just a case reference for our records, Maam. I forgot to write the case number down in my notebook so I just used that as a reminder."

Sergeant Clarke stands up. "That will be all from us for now, Mr. Prendergast. What is the best number for my colleagues to contact you on?"

I give her my mobile number before showing her and Stevens to the front door. I watch them walk down the path together and then close the door and steel myself.

Simon comes bounding back down the stairs and earns me a brief respite. "So what was all that about then? Where's your medal?"

"Your father won't be getting any medals," Sheila says, "but when I find out exactly what murky business he's been *meddling* in he'll wish he'd never been born."

"Ouch," Says Simon, "I think I'll just nip back upstairs and leave you two to it." He strides onto the stairs shouting behind him, "Lights blue touch paper and retires." As he reaches his room he adds, "Seconds Away. Round One."

"I can explain," I begin, "Genuinely. It's all a misunderstanding. It's quite straightforward really. A simple misunderstanding."

As Sheila's silence continues I try to extricate myself from the deeper and deeper chasm I am digging for myself.

"It's Martin's fault." It's the best I can come up with and it's sure to bring a response.

"Martin? Martin? What on earth has it got to do with Martin? No. Don't tell me. After you went to the Casa last night you bumped into Martin who you haven't seen for years and he gave you a fifteen hundred pound handbag. Just like that. Well I'll tell *you* something. Martin invited me round for a cup of coffee at his place tomorrow. I turned him down but now you're blaming him I've changed my mind. Where's that card he gave us?"

I shrug. "Don't know," I say, "I might have put it in the bin."

"You did not put it in the bin. Now where is it?"

Sheila goes to the cupboard under the stairs. She keeps a calendar that has compartments for vouchers, appointments and that sort of thing on the back of its door and it only takes a second for her to find it right where I had left it.

Within a minute she's on the phone. "Martin? Are you still on for that coffee? You are? Great. Eleven o'clock? See you tomorrow then." She rings off. "If it's got anything to do with Martin I'll hear his side of things tomorrow. You can get back to your precious eBay. I'm watching TV."

Chapter Twenty-Two

Dave

It's eight in the evening and I'm sitting at the dining table scrolling through page after page of junk on the laptop when the mobile rings.

"Mr. Prendergast?" says a warm, female, Scottish voice.

"Yes."

"Mr. David Prendergast?"

"Yes that's me. I don't want to claim for PPI. I haven't had an accident that wasn't my fault. There's no sun here so solar panels would be a waste of time. I've got double glazing, cheap energy, Sky TV, superfast broadband and, charming as you sound, I haven't got time to hear about what you're selling even if it will change my life forever. So thank you very much, and good night."

"CID here. DC MacIntosh."

"Oh."

"I think you were expecting my call, after Sergeant Clarke's visit today."

"Of course. Sorry. What can I do for you, Constable?"

"Detective Constable."

There's a short silence. We aren't exactly getting off to the best of starts. "Sorry, Detective Constable MacIntosh. How can I help?"

"I need you to tell me more about the purple Mulberry handbag I've got here."

"Er... I can't say much, apart from it's purple, leather and very smart."

"I can see that, Mr. Prendergast."

"Call me Dave."

"I can see that, Mr. Prendergast but I need to know more about the circumstances surrounding how it came to be in your possession."

"I can explain that. I was in a cab with a woman and..."

"Not now. I would like you to come down to the station

and tell me all about it.   Can you be here for eight tomorrow morning? "

"Eight? Of course. Where do I meet you? Finchley Police Station?'

"No. That office closed. We operate out of Barnet at thirty-two High Street. Get the tube to High Barnet. The office will be closed when you get here but use the intercom, tell them you're seeing me and I'll come down for you."

"Will do, DC MacIntosh. Thirty-two High Street let me write that down. I look forward to meeting you. It's a very simple explanation. Should take no time at all."

"I'm sure it will. Good evening Mr. Prendergast."

"Good evening."

I press the red end call button and sit back in my chair.

Sheila shouts from the living room, "Who was that?"

"Just the police following up their visit."

"And?"

"They want me to go down to the station in the morning."

"What time?"

"Eight o'clock."

"You'll have to change that."

"It's the police. How can I change it? And why?"

"I need you to drop me off at the hairdresser at nine."

"How was I supposed to know that? It's not on the calendar."

"I only made the appointment today."

"After you arranged coffee with bloody Martin I suppose. You'll have to go in a taxi or on the tube."

"No. *You* will have to get back onto the police and change the appointment."

"I'm sure that will work. 'Of course, Mr Ripper. Mrs. Ripper has an appointment for a perm? We understand. Could happen to anyone. What time can you make it? No problem at all, sir. Have a nice day'— I don't think so. You could try an Uber. "

The volume on the TV increases by several decibels and I hear this week's *Radio Times* hit the wall.

Chapter Twenty-Three

Dave

The Northern Line at seven a.m is not the most relaxing place to be. I'm squashed between two workers in fast food restaurant uniforms who appear to have been taking maximum benefit of their staff discounts. Both are wearing giant headphones and nodding silently while tapping away on their mobiles. Thank goodness it's only two stops.

As we reach North Barnet I feel like a prop forward, as those leaving the carriage lock shoulders with those trying to get in. I used to do this every day but I seem to recall more genteel times of 'After you, sir. No after you, madam.' But, there again, there were far fewer passengers in those days.

Out of the station, the bitter cold of the early morning hits me. I check shop numbers to see which direction I need to head and set off at a brisk pace. I arrive at the police station slightly breathless and look for the intercom alongside the front door. Positioned beneath a newly graffitied bright blue arrow and the word 'PIGZ', it's not difficult to find. I despair for today's levels of literacy.

I press the button and tell the muffled, disembodied voice that I'm here to see DC Macintosh.

"Macca eh?" I hear a sharp intake of breath.

As I wait, the cold begins to take effect and the now familiar urge to pee has me hopping from foot to foot. I hope that Macca is not too long as my ability to hang on seems to be diminishing daily.

The intercom buzzes and I hear the door click. I pull it open and step into a sterile hallway. There's an empty desk ahead of me at the end of the corridor and I head slowly towards it scanning around for a door for a welcoming 'WC' or 'Gents' symbol. I'm getting toward the point of no return.

I hear footsteps skipping at speed down a stairwell. A door opens behind me. "Mr. Prendergast?"

I turn round. I was expecting a smartly suited, slight woman with stylishly coiffured auburn hair but when I meet the tall, slender, black haired bespectacled young lady wearing skinny jeans and a chunky sweater I realise that not all Scotswomen are Nicola Sturgeon.

"Yes. Pleased to meet you DC MacIntosh. Err sorry but could you point me in the direction of the conveniences before we start."

"Ah yes," she says looking down at a file that she's holding, "bladder problems."

I've flown under the police radar for over sixty years and when I finally come into their sights I'm there as an incontinent. I wonder if Reggie and Ronnie's files were littered with references to their urinary tracts.

She shows me to the toilets and waits outside. I am able to relieve myself without accident and, feeling refreshed, rejoin her.

She leads me to a door marked 'INTERVIEW ROOM 1'

I've seen these interview rooms on the telly a thousand times. Bare table, two chairs on each side. I look for the two-way mirror but there isn't one. The DC points to a chair. I take it.

She sits opposite me and puts a large, steaming mug with a Saltire on one side and a cartoon Nessie on the other down in front of her. She takes the file from under her arm and puts it on the table. I'm a bit taken aback by its thickness.

MacIntosh picks up her mug. "Can I get you one?" she asks.

I worry about a repeat performance and more notes on file about my weak bladder. I imagine a poster on their noticeboard 'WANTED' above my mug shot and below it 'WEE DAVE PRENDERGAST' or even worse 'DAVE THE PISSER'. I decline her offer.

"So, Mr. Prendergast. Thank you for coming in. You are not under arrest and are free to go at any time. I would just like you to help me with some enquiries."

"Should I have my lawyer with me?"

"Do you think you should have your lawyer with you?"

"No. It's just what they say on TV."

"We're not on TV now."

I nod in the direction of the recorder. " Are you recording this?"

"No. As I said, I just need some help with my enquiries. I'm a busy woman and I am sure that you are a very busy man so I won't hang about with pleasantries." She stands up, moves to a corner of the room and drags a large cardboard box towards her. She opens it and pulls a familiar object from it.

"What can you tell me about these handbags, Mr. Prendergast?"

"*These* handbags?"

She tips the box onto its side and about twenty identical bags each in a sealed plastic bag marked 'EVIDENCE' spill onto the floor.

"I don't know anything about them."

"You don't know anything? Eighteen fake Mulberry handbags each with a handwritten card inside initialed 'DP' and you know nothing about them?"

"I only know about one."

"So which one is that? The one that you sent to the widow in Chelsea before giving her the sob story about needing forty thousand pounds for urgent medical treatment in California? Or maybe the one given to the elderly spinster in Richmond who thought she was lending you a hundred thousand to put down as a deposit on the love nest on the river you were going to share together? Need I go on about the divorcee who lost fifty K? Eighteen handbags and eighteen tales of misery and loss. Same operation each time. Months of lovey dovey stuff by email on Match.com followed by the grand delivery of the," she does that thing making speech marks with her fingers "*expensive* handbag by motorcycle courier before the tales of woe begin."

"As I said. I only know about one and I think you'll find that that bag has nothing to do with widows, spinsters or divorcees."

"Aye. You're right. The..." fingers in the air again, " *Sugar Daddy* bag. Maybe there's another con artist using identical fake Mulberry bags to get himself laid by naive and gorgeous young women. Maybe, that is, Mr. Prendergast, if we hadn't managed to trace these bags back to a couple of African laddies who got kicked out of Venice for pedaling them there. They told us that they had thirty left and they sold all of them to one man. A man of about your age, Mr. Prendergast. A silver fox."

"Do I look like a silver fox?"

The DC looks over her glasses. "Well they did sell them almost a year ago now. You could have let yourself go a wee bit in twelve months."

"You've got the wrong man. Ask yourself DC MacIntosh would I use my real initials?"

"They all say that, Mr. Prendergast. It's only initials. There's been Don Pearson, Daniel Parsons, Denis Porter, Duncan Ponsenby and Derek Patmore to name just a few."

"No Dom Perignon?"

"This is no laughing matter Mr Predergast."

"Okay. Let me tell you everything I know."

Chapter Twenty-Four

Dave

As I get to the end of my story, DC MacIntosh leans back in her chair. She sucks on a pen before writing lengthily in her file.

"You're prepared to put all this in a statement?"

"Of course."

"So you know this penthouse flat then?"

"I don't know it," I look at my watch, "but I do know that around about now my wife will be heading there for," I now do the fingers in the air, "*coffee* and God knows what else he's got in mind. No doubt he'll be trying to pump her for information about my Yabu Meizan vases."

"Your *what* vases?"

"Nothing it's just something I collect. They're worth a few quid."

"Right. I'd like you to come with me."

"Where?"

"The penthouse. Where do you think? It'll save on formalities, warrants, that sort of thing. There are a few dodgy characters known to us in those flats. The reception and concierge people are well trained in, how shall I put it, the art of delay. We know he's going to be in. He'll let you in. We'll have him bang to rights."

"Bang to rights?"

She smiles for the first time since we met, "Isn't that what they say on TV?"

I try to enter into the spirit. I leap from my seat and point to the door. "To the Batmobile, Robin"

"I think it had better be 'To the Gents' Mr. Prendergast before we leave. We don't want any accidents do we?"

I'm clearly not Batman. My superhero alter ego will have to be The Urinator.

Fully relieved, I feel a rush of excitement as I follow the DC out of the rear of the police station into a packed car park. She's been joined by a partner - a young man in his thirties.

"This is DC Wood."

"Pleased to meet you," I say as we get into a black Mondeo.

I sit in the back with the two detectives in front of me. DC Wood opens the window and puts a blue flashing light into position on the roof.

"We'll get there in a quarter of the time with this," he says, "no need for the siren."

He's right and I am amazed by the way that the traffic parts for us like the Red Sea as we weave our way towards the river. The journey is shortened by at least half an hour and before long we are driving between rows of Victorian terraces.

"Right.. We'll park here," says DC Wood.

We're in a side street about a hundred yards from the impressive apartment blocks that line the river by the bridge. We get out of the car and walk towards them. As we approach, I see that there are electronic gates with an entry camera system.

DC Wood looks at me. "We need you to get him to open the gate and we'll follow you in."

I walk to the camera and scan the list of apartments. There are no names- just numbers. There isn't room for all those long Russian names that would no doubt fill most of the spaces. There it is 'Penthouse'.

I press hard on the button and smile into the camera like I'm taking a selfie.

"Is that *you,* Dave?" a disembodied voice floats through the speaker.

"No it's George Clooney. Of course it's bloody me."

"What do you want?" The tone is a little bit evasive and slightly disconcerting.

"You invited us for coffee."

"I invited Sheila for coffee."

I hear Sheila in the background. "What's he doing here? Tell him to go home."

I can't hear Martin's responses. He must be turning away from the speaker. A few muffled words follow and then it's clear again.

"Okay Dave. The gate will open. Make your way through and then to the revolving doors into reception. I'll buzz down and tell them to put you in the penthouse lift."

There's a buzz and the gate starts to move slowly open. I walk through and look behind me. No sign of my oppos. I head towards the entrance and take another look back. The gate has reached its fully open position and is now starting its leisurely journey back. The two officers step through. I wait for them at the revolving doorway.

"You took your time, DC MacIntosh," I say.

"We just wanted to make sure that he wasn't still watching on the entry phone."

We go through the doors into a plush, marble-floored atrium filled with exotic palms and flowers. It's like something you'd expect to find in Dubai. In the centre is a desk that looks like the reception at The Ritz (not that I've ever been to The Ritz so perhaps I should say that it looks like I imagine the reception at The Ritz might look). A very tall, extremely smartly dressed black guy looks down on us quite haughtily. He's wearing a name badge in his Armani lapel: 'Jeremiah'. We're perhaps not as well-heeled as the usual visitor and I half expect to be shown sniffily to the tradesmen's lift.

"Mr. Hetherington is expecting a Mr. Prendergast," he says when I announce my name, "He didn't mention other visitors. I need to check with him."

As if choreographed, Wood and MacIntosh, reach into pockets and flash their warrant cards.

"Just show us to the penthouse lift, please," Wood's voice is calm but authoritative.

"Certainly, officers."   Jeremiah leads us past two elevators near his desk to a glass lift at the far end of the atrium. The lift compartment is on the outside of the building. The concierge is wearing a ribbon around his neck. He pulls the ribbon out from inside his beautifully lined jacket and swipes the card hanging from it against a pad. The door opens. He gestures to us to enter the lift and turns to leave.

"You can come with us, Jeremiah," says MacIntosh.

"But I need to stay at my desk. We have some very important visitors due."

"Aren't we important enough for you then? No Jeremiah, I think you need to show us," MacIntosh pauses, "right to the door."

Jeremiah reluctantly joins us.

There are no buttons just another electronic pad. We wait.

DC Wood breaks the silence, "Come on then, Jeremiah. Let's get this thing going."

Jeremiah takes the card out again and waves it over the pad. The doors shut and in seconds we're whooshed skywards.

"I think I'll bring the kids here in the holidays," says Wood. "It's a bit cheaper than Thorpe Park."

Our journey is too short to fully appreciate the fabulous views over the river towards the city. As the lift comes silently and smoothly to a halt we can see the full extent of the enormous apartment that makes up the penthouse. All glass, there's very little privacy but I imagine that this level of luxury is there to be flaunted, not hidden away.

The lift door opens into the apartment's reception area. Martin is our one-man welcoming committee.

"You didn't say you were bringing your pals from the charity shop Dave," he says looking my companions up and down. "Who are these people, Jeremiah? Haven't I told you? Nobody comes here without my say so. *Nobody.* So hello and..." he waves a card like Jeremiah's, "*goodbye*".

The lift door glides shut but springs back as it catches MacIntosh's foot.

"You say goodbye. And I say hello," she says.

"Don't tell me...You're a bloody Beatles tribute band."

MacIntosh flashes her warrant card. "Of course we are,

Mr. Hetherington. I'm Sergeant Pepper (or Michelle to my friends). She pulls a pair of handcuffs from her bag. "Chains," she says, "I want you to come quietly down to the station where perhaps we can work it out."

Wood joins in, "Let it be, DC Macintosh. He wasn't born *yesterday*."

Martin turns away from the lift but Macintosh has her hand on his shoulder. "You're going nowhere, man."

As she slips the handcuffs on his wrists I'm sure I hear a muffled, "Help."

Chapter Twenty-Five

Dave

It's been a long day but we're home in time for *Deal Or No Deal.*

Sheila stands in front of the TV and juggles with the three remote controls necessary to switch on the TV, Sky box and sound system. It's a daily struggle watching her manipulating the controls time and again as one of the devices springs into life whilst another simultaneously clicks off. If I utter the magic words "Here, let me" I know that I'll find the largest of the remotes inserted where the sun don't shine. I hold my tongue.

Eventually all the components of the home cinema are functioning correctly and Noel Edmunds bursts onto the screen. Sheila eases herself down onto the sofa beside me "Police cars outside the house three times in a couple of days. What on earth are the neighbours going to think?"

"Does it matter? We've just helped solve a very nasty fraud. Hopefully he'll get ten years and I won't have to see the horrible oleaginous toad ever again."

"Not until after the court case that is. You'll be a lead witness."

"You think so?"

"Of course."

"Do you think he'll be remanded in custody?"

"Depends whether he can find anyone to stand bail for him. I imagine with his background he'll know a few well connected people who'll pull some strings for him in that department."

"So we haven't heard the last of the bastard just yet. He'll just go on living it up on top of his ivory tower until the courts have time to fit him in and you know how long it takes to put fraud cases together. I read about one that took years to come to trial and then, after six months of evidence, the jury said that they couldn't understand it and the case collapsed."

"You'll have to make sure that you're convincing then."

"I'll do that alright, but all his computer data should be enough to put him away."

"*If* the police find it. He's not an idiot. I wouldn't be surprised if any computers they find in the penthouse are clean as a whistle."

"You think so?"

"I'd lay my life on it."

"So where do you think he's been doing all his dirty work?"

"There'll be a laptop hidden away somewhere that he uses exclusively. It'll be in some bedsit miles away from here."

"But at least the African lads will be able to identify him."

"You think so? I bet Reggie and Bollie are back home in Ghana now."

"So. It's going to be down to me. Maybe I'll get witness protection."

"He's not a violent man. You don't need to worry on that score."

"You never know when there's a lot a stake," I pause "and anyway, how was the *coffee*?"

"I hadn't been there very long before you and Taggart arrived. It took Martin almost half an hour to show me around the apartment. It's crammed full of paintings and sculptures and he had to tell me the story behind every one of them."

"You mean he had to tell you how much they cost and how he was bidding for them against a Saudi Prince in Sotheby's New York or a princess in Monaco."

"I suppose so. Anyway, he suggested we skip the coffee as the enormous chrome espresso machine that took up half the kitchen needed time to heat up. He opened a bottle of Crystal and a jar of Beluga and said he wanted to show me the Picasso in the master suite."

"You sure that was real champagne and real caviar? Remember the handbags."

" I'll never know. He was just getting the ice bucket when your mug appeared on the entry system."

"It sounded like you weren't pleased to see me."

"To be honest Dave, I can't say that I was. I spend half my life inside these four walls watching stuff like this on TV and I find myself in a fabulous multi million pound penthouse with views across the whole of London being plied with champagne and caviar," she stops for a moment. The Banker has just offered the contestant a deal at thirty-five thousand pounds.

"Thirty-five thousand," I say, "Just watch the idiot say 'no deal' and go home with 50p." Sure enough the audience is baying for him to turn it down hysterically screeching "NO DEAL" even though it's statistically a fantastic offer. It's no deal and the show continues. "So you never got to taste the spoils of his crimes. Good job perhaps you'd be a receiver of stolen goods or maybe an accessory." I look at Sheila. She's still looking great. "A very glamorous accessory," I add, "I'll ply you with the best champagne and caviar one day. I promise."

"The story of my life. One day. One day I'll go to New York. One day I'll be in Mauritius. One day I'll be on death's doorstep and I'll still be waiting for one day. You'll probably have to prise open my coffin lid and pour the champagne through the crack – one day."

"So, what would have happened if I hadn't turned up with the cops and spoiled your tête-à-tête? Would you have gone inside and looked at his etching?"

"He's down to eight thousand now. Why do they do this every time?"

"Greed I suppose. Greed. That's what drives Martin. You didn't answer me. The etching?"

"You expect me to answer that? How long have we been together? If you don't know the answer you don't know me at all."

"Deal," I say.

Noel is commiserating with the poor sod whose thirty-five thousand has turned into two hundred and fifty pounds.

"Time for *Pointless*."

Chapter Twenty-Six

Dave

It's six o'clock in the evening and I'm sitting in the doctor's waiting room.

Half way through *Pointless* Sheila told me she's fed up with yellow stains in my underpants and she's fixed me up with an appointment. She got a late cancellation. It's good to know that she cares. She wanted to come with me but it's a cold evening and I told her to stay warm.

My name comes up on the screen and I make my way to the consulting room. They say that you know you're getting old when the police look younger. The same goes for doctors. I grew up with doctors in tweed jackets with patches on the elbows, heavy brown brogues and a whiff of Golden Virginia. Dr Thompson is sitting behind a desk and she looks like she's just left sixth form.

She taps on her keyboard and I see my name flash up on screen above a few coloured charts.

She offers her hand. "Pleased to meet you, Mr. Prendergast. I see that you haven't been to the surgery for a long time."

"I like to keep myself in shape," I say sucking my stomach in.

"So I see." She smiles.

She checks my details and goes through a number of questions on her screen. When she's recorded my smoking and drinking habits it's time for some measurements.

"Can you take off your coat and step onto the scales?" I do as she asks and wince as I see the read out.

"They need calibrating," I say.

"Afraid not. I think it's you who might need some calibration."

After my weight, she measures my height, my breathing and my blood pressure and inputs all the data into my record.

"Now. What did you want to discuss with me?"

"Well doctor. It's a little delicate but I seem to be developing a bit of a bladder problem."

"In what way?"

"When I've gotta go. I've really gotta go."

"Urgency?"

"Yes that's the word. Urgency. One minute I'm not even thinking I need to pee. Five minutes later and I'm almost wetting myself."

"And *do you* wet yourself?"

"So far I've managed to hold on but I've had too many near misses, a couple of dribbles but no full flows. I've been thinking of looking for trousers with Velcro flies."

"It's quite common in people your age. Particularly men. There are lots of causes but we need to get to the bottom of it and rule out any of the serious ones. When did you last have your prostate checked?"

"I've never had it checked. The only thing I know about it is watching Billy Connolly describing it in one of his routines but I imagine you're not old enough to have seen him."

She smiles. "Yes but all doctors have heard about his story. Don't worry it's not as bad as you think."

She asks me to lie on the examination bed on my side facing the wall and undo my trousers and pull them and my underpants down to my knees.

"Now raise your knees towards your chest," she says. I do as I am told. "This will be a bit cold." She smears some sort of jelly around my back passage.

I feel a latex coated finger being inserted and moving inside. My brain is screaming 'don't fart' at a hundred decibels and I find myself clenching my guts to make sure that I don't. To be quite honest it's not painful at all and, in different circumstances I might even describe it as a mildly pleasurable experience. I don't think I'll be suggesting that Sheila gives it a try, mind.

I feel the finger depart and enormous relief that it's removal is not accompanied by a following wind. "All done" she says handing me a tissue to wipe away the residual jelly. "You can put your clothes back on."

I adjust my pants and trousers and get down from the bed. She takes off her latex gloves and throws them into a clinical waste bin.

'Well?" I say.

"Feels good to me Mr. Prendergast. I'm going to get you to have a scan at the clinic for a second check and to have a look at your kidneys." She peers at her screen again. "You really are in luck. Another cancellation. They can see you tomorrow morning at ten. There's usually a two week wait."

She prints out an appointment sheet together with instructions. I have to eat nothing before the appointment and drink almost two litres of water in the morning before I go.

"So. If the prostate and kidneys are okay, what's causing the urgency?"

"Can be something simple. Perhaps too much tea and coffee. You may not be drinking enough water. There are plenty of possibilities but don't worry too much about it and let's wait until the results are here. Is there anything else you'd like to ask me? "

"No thank you doctor. And thanks for the speedy appointments."

Chapter Twenty-Seven

Dave

It's ten in the morning and I'm in another waiting room in the local health centre. It's been a couple of hours since I drank the requisite couple of litres of water My instruction sheet tells me to advise the receptionist if I start to feel uncomfortable but I don't want to push my way through a throng of patients to report that I'm desperate.

But I am desperate. And I'm getting more desperate by the second. I look around the waiting room. It's clear that I'm not alone. Several mature gentlemen are shuffling uneasily in their seats. Their feet look as if they're rehearsing for Riverdance. Their eyes are fixed on the screen that announces their turn to see the clinicians. The calls come through on both screen and a speaker. The receptionist makes the announcement like they do on *X Factor*. "Screening Room 1, Mr..." - pause. I swear she's going to smile, turn to us all and say 'we'll tell you after the commercial break.' Half a dozen of us put our hands onto the edges of our seats and lean forward like six Usain Bolts waiting for the starter's gun. "....Johnson."

Five start back on Riverdance while Johnson flies to the door as if the doctor has just threatened to put a finger back up his backside.

It's half past ten when I get the call and I make it to the screening room in seconds. I reckon *Guinness Book Of Records* should set up a branch in this place.

The sign on her desk tells me that the clinician is Angela Clemence. She's a smart woman in her early forties. She's wearing a white coat that reaches down to her knees. She has beautifully styled red hair set off by a pair of sapphire earrings. Her immaculately painted fingernails match her hair. I feel immediately at ease with her. This is a professional and I'm sure that she'll understand when I blurt out "Can we make it quick?"

She glances at her notes. "Bladder and kidneys. You're struggling to hold on?"

I nod.

"Okay. Unfasten your trousers and your shirt and lie on the bed. I'll be as quick as I can and then you can nip to the loo and when you come back I'll do the second set of scans."

She rubs, what feels like, the same jelly as yesterday on my back and I feel her scanner moving slowly around. I do whatever she asks. I follow her instructions turning this way and that, breathing when she tells me and concentrating on holding on.

She's good to her word and it's only a few minutes before she gives me my leave. I leap to my feet, leaving my shirt unbuttoned and holding my trousers up unfastened. I rush to the door.

"Which way?"

She points along the corridor. "Third on the right."

As I leave the room, the next door in the corridor opens and another of my Riverdance partners emerges in a similar state of undress. We look at each other briefly and both of us break into a trot. We start at a trot but the pace soon hots up and we speed along the corridor clutching our belts - shirts tails flapping behind us.

He's a bit older than me but it's a photo finish as we reach the door. I grab the handle and turn it. It's locked. We look at each other in mutual despair. He turns round and tries the handle on the next door. It opens.

"But you're not disabled," I shout.

"I will be if my bloody bladder bursts."

I turn back to the first door. It opens slowly and an ancient woman stumbles out. I reach out to catch her and, in doing so, lose my grip on my belt. As I bend down to grab the trousers from around my ankles she steadies herself on my shoulder. Glancing up I see that the door is right opposite the waiting room. They've had *X Factor*. Now they've got *Fawlty Towers*.

We both straighten ourselves up.

"Thank you young man. Are you practicing for *The Full Monty*?"

I haven't got time to chat. I rush into the cubicle and pull the door shut.

After a Niagara of a pee I take a few minutes to compose myself. I straighten my clothes, wash my hands and face and tidy my hair. I hope that Doctor Clemence didn't witness the floorshow. I open the toilet door and stare at the floor to avoid the sniggers of the waiting bunch of bobbers. I'm going to take as long as I like heading back to the screening room. That'll teach them.

When I return it's the same process as before but without the urgency.

"Okay Mr. Prendergast. You can button up your shirt and fasten your trousers. All finished."

"So how does it look Doctor Clemence?"

"It's *Mrs.* Clemence. Well I will be sending a full report to your doctor this afternoon but your kidneys look absolutely fine. Your bladder didn't empty completely but not to a worrying extent. Your prostate shows signs of very slight hardening but that would be expected in a man of your age. I think your doctor will be pleased with the results. Make an appointment with your surgery to go through them."

I thank her, shake her hand, say goodbye and turn to leave. As I open the door I notice a very familiar bag hanging on a coat-stand alongside a stylish black overcoat. I hesitate.

"Nice bag," I say.

"Thank you. It was a gift."

"Very nice. A very unusual colour. My wife would love it."

"Yes. I'm very pleased with it."

Mrs Clemence is a busy woman. I can sense that she's no time for idle chitchat. There may be another old bloke in extreme discomfort in the waiting room. Looking at the way she's dressed, it's probably a genuine bag and I should keep quiet. But...I find myself saying "I'm sorry. I don't want to interfere but the bag was not from a 'D.P' by any chance?"

"How *did* you guess that?"

"It's a very long story. I can see that you are very busy but you really need to know more. It's important. Let me give you my number." I gesture for a pen. She hands me a smart Mont Blanc fountain pen together with a Post It note. I write my mobile number down. I'm impressed by the beautiful calligraphy the pen delivers. "Please phone me when you finish work and, whatever you do, don't contact DP until we've spoken."

"I'm very curious," she pauses, "and more than a little worried."

I try to reassure her but I don't think I'm very convincing. As I take my leave she's busy tapping my number into her phone.

I decide to try and empty my bladder completely before I go home and I'm surprised that after Niagara ten minutes earlier there's still a Swallow Falls in there.

Chapter Twenty-Eight

Dave

When I get home I find Sheila pacing the floor in the dining room.

"Well?" she asks.

"All fine," I say.

"What do you mean 'all fine'?"

"What I said. All fine."

"But you usually have to wait for the results."

"I do but the screening woman indicated that I'll be happy with them."

"What did she say?"

"She said I'm fine. You're stuck with me for a bit longer I'm afraid."

"Is that all she said? You're fine. What did she mean? What is fine? Why do you keep rushing to the loo?"

"She didn't say."

"Well, did she do it properly?"

"Of course she did."

"She must have said more than *you're fine*. What *exactly* did she say? "

"Okay. Okay. She said my kidneys look good but my prostate is slightly hard."

Sheila immediately jumps onto this, "Your prostate? That could be serious."

"Don't worry. Very, very *slightly* hard. She said it's common in men of my age."

"What else did she say?"

"She said that my bladder didn't empty completely."

"What does that mean?"

"I don't know. I'll have to ask the doctor when I go for the results. Aren't you pleased?"

"Of course I'm pleased."

"So you'll be okay putting up with me then?"

She smiles. I put my arms around her shoulders and

draw her towards me. She holds me tightly around my waist and puts her face against my chest.

She looks up at me, "I don't know what I'd do without you after all these years."

"Me neither. Let's make sure we enjoy what we've got left as much as we can."

I'm toying with asking her if she fancies continuing our cuddle upstairs when my phone vibrates. I take it from my pocket. It's an unknown caller. I go to reject the call but Sheila tells me to answer and our amorous moment passes.

"Hello."

"Hello. Mr Prendergast?"

"Yes."

"Angela Clemence here from the clinic."

Sheila mouths 'Who is it?'

I put my hand over the phone. "The scanner woman."

"Oh no! Has there been a mistake? What does she want?"

I indicate to Sheila to be quiet for a moment while I listen. I take my hand away.

"Mrs Clemence. I hoped you would call."

"I've been worrying about what you said since you left. How did you know my bag was from a DP?"

"As I said Angela - May I call you Angela?)"

"Sure."

"It's a long story but there's been a conman giving out bags like yours to wealthy widows, divorcees and others he's befriended on Match.com."

"Match.com?"

"Yes."

"Well," I continue, "the bags, you see, they're not what they appear to be."

"Well. I did think it wasn't quite right – there was something about the stitching and the label but the man who sent it is an international banker."

"You've met him then?"

"Not yet but we've been exchanging emails and photos for a few months. The bag arrived last week."

"Not everyone on the Internet is what they seem to be you know. Your international banker could be a spotty youth in Southend, a guy working from a shanty town in Nigeria or even an old woman in Russia."

"But I've seen his photos."

"You've seen someone's photos and I'm sure that that someone looks remarkably handsome and sophisticated. Have you Googled him."

A long pause. "No. I didn't think I needed to. He seems so...nice. So genuine."

"Okay. Let me get straight to the point. Have you given him any money?"

This time the pause seems unending. I continue.

"Hello Angela. Are you still there? Have you given him any money?"

I hear a stifled sob. "I'm sorry, Mr Prendergast. I have to go."

"Wait. Angela. Wait. If you've given him any money you need to tell the police. D C MacIntosh at Barnet is dealing with it. Did you get that? D C MacIntosh."

I wait for her response but the phone is dead.

"Did you get all that?' I ask Sheila.

Sheila nods. "Another of Martin's victims?'

"Looks like it.

Chapter Twenty-Nine

Dave

It's early Thursday evening and we're snuggled together on the sofa watching *Pointless*. Simon will be home any minute with, no doubt, a caustic but very funny comment on our lovey-doveyness. Let him mock. It's strange how my minor health scare has strengthened a relationship that we were both, to say the least, somewhat *laissez-faire* about a few days ago.

We're trying to think of obscure Spielberg films that will be pointless.

"*ET*," I say.

"*ET*?" says Sheila. "No way will that be pointless."

"*Jaws*?"

"Duh. One of the biggest box office successes ever?"

"*Reservoir Dogs?*"

'Well, I'm sure nobody will have said that."

"There you go then. *Reservoir Dogs* it is."

"Because it was directed by Quentin Tarantino.

I'm rubbish at this but Sheila likes it and she usually comes up with some good answers.

The contestants answer with some titles neither of us has ever heard of and we're about to find out if they're pointless answers when my phone rings again.

Sheila tuts and pauses the programme.

I take the mobile out of my pocket and look at the screen. "It's Susie," I say.

"She doesn't usually phone you," says Sheila, sounding slightly peeved. She's right, mind you, Susie rarely phones me unless it's something extremely important or she needs something. I suppose I'm not that good at making small talk about toddlers. I slide the call answer button on the screen and say hello.

There's no response but there's a terrible racket in the background.

Crash. I hear something smash and a girlish scream. And then a man's voice, "Family. Your family grassed up my guvnor and you're gonna pay for it, you bitch." Another scream and a loud thud follows.

"Susie! Susie!" I shout but there's no response.

Sheila has seen the panic on my face. "What is it? What's going on?"

"Shhh," I say, "I need to listen."

The man's voice again, "No one ever gets one over on my guvnor. Ever! You listenin'? You can tell your family that we're watchin' them. We're watchin' them right now." I hear a slap and another thud. "**Right.** *Now.* And when my guvnor's in the dock they better remember this visit before they get into the witness box." I hear more struggling. "An' here's something for you to remember me by."

There's another scream. This one's long and sends a shiver down my spine. I hear a bump-bump-bump noise and the phone goes dead.

I'm shaking.

"What is it? What is it?" Sheila is shaking me. I'm looking blankly at the phone.

"It's Susie."

"I know it's Susie. What's going on?"

I'm frantically dialing Susie's number but the phone switches straight away *'Hi Susie here. Can't take your call. Probably dealing with a couple of naughty fairies at the moment. Leave your number and I'll get back to you.'*

I dial again and again. But she's still dealing with those naughty fairies.

I try to explain what I've just heard to Sheila.

"We've put our family at risk. Bloody Martin Hetherington. I never thought he'd resort to this. Poor Susie. We need to get there straight away. Get your coat."

Sheila switches off the TV. It springs back to life a couple of seconds later and Alexander Armstrong is sorry that one person knew the obscure Spielberg film. I grab the remotes, press the off button on each in turn and throw them down onto the settee.

Sheila snatches her coat from the coat hook in the hall and puts it on. I move to open the front door. "Wait" she says "shouldn't we call the police?"

"He said they're watching us. Who knows? They might even be bugging our phones. We can't put the family in any danger. You know what can happen to kidnap victims when their families tell the police."

"But they *aren't* kidnap victims."

"How do you know? We don't know what happened after the phone cut off."

"I'm still going to phone 999." Sheila takes her mobile out of her pocket.

I grab the phone.

"Don't," I turn back to the front door.

I am about to open the door when I hear the key being inserted. The door opens and Simon comes in.

"You two look in a state. What's up?"

"No time to explain now," I say, "Just get into the car. We need you."

"Calm down. Hang on. Wait a minute. What's going on?" Simon has his hands on my shoulders. He shakes me. "Dad. Listen to me. What's happened?

I explain Susie's call.

Simon takes his phone out of his pocket.

"What are you doing?"

"I'm calling the cops. What do you think I'm doing? You should have phoned them straight away."

His 999 call is answered immediately and the operator puts him through to the police. He hands the phone to me.

"Tell them exactly what happened," he says.

I tell the operator everything I heard. I give him Susie's address and he tells me that he will notify Suffolk Constabulary and get a squad car there as quickly as possible.

"I just hope that call hasn't put Susie in more danger" I say handing the phone back to Simon.

"Stop worrying Dad. The police will sort it. By the time we reach Southwold, Susie and the kids will be fine. I promise." He opens the front door. "Come on. *Now* we can get going."

We leave the house. Sheila jumps into the back, Simon's gets into the front and I settle into the driver's seat, start the engine, crunch the gears and reverse into the road.

I risk being fined what little life savings we have left for flying down bus lanes, jumping red lights and driving like Lewis Hamilton. Sadly it's more like the Lewis Hamilton who pranged his supercar after partying too hard in France than the one who won the world Formula 1 championship. I can feel the tension in the car as two right feet hit imaginary brake pedals and my passengers swing from side to side like a pair of metronomes as I take every bend as if I'm auditioning for The Stig. And, because this is London, we're only averaging fifteen miles an hour.

"Dad. I really don't get why you didn't call the police immediately."

"Like Dad said. We didn't want to put your sister at risk." His mum replies.

"But it's over two hours to Southwold. If we ever get there, the way Dad's driving. God knows what they'll have done to Susie and the kiddies by then. Where's Alec? No doubt at another sales conference in some hideous plastic hotel in the Gulf."

"He's in Dubai."

"Exactly."

Sheila takes my phone and rings Susie's number. It's still going straight to voicemail.

"Try the landline," I say.

"No chance," says Simon. "They never answer that. Susie reckons the only people who ever use it are cold callers and Grannie. And Grannie only ever calls on Sunday nights when *Antiques Road Show* finishes, so she's not going to answer."

Sheila gives it a try anyway. "This isn't a normal day. She might pick up" but sure enough there's no answer. There's not even an answering machine as Susie reckons there's no point in ignoring PPE callers if you're then going to listen to their patter on voicemail.

We weave our way slowly along the solidly packed suburban roads until we reach the North Circular. But it's going nowhere tonight. I've got the SATNAV on and every five minutes the estimated arrival time in Southwold is five minutes later.

Simon is messing with his phone. "I need to phone Maria and explain what's going on." There's a silence. "Shit."

'What's up?" I ask.

"Battery. Spent half an hour watching Netflix on the bus home."

"You can use your Dad's." Sheila passes my phone between the two front seats.

"Thanks Mum. Just one problem."

"What's that?"

"Her number is on my phone."

"Oh dear."

"I'm sure she'll understand, son," I say, "This is an emergency."

"I know. That's why I phoned the cops. Look Dad, it's a good job I did. We're not even up to the M25 yet. Susie could be bleeding to death for all we know."

"Simon's right, Dave. He did the right thing."

I know that Sheila and Simon are right. I've not taken rush hour traffic into account and by the time we hit Suffolk, if we ever hit Suffolk, we're bound to be stuck behind a combine harvester for half an hour. "Okay. Sorry son. You were right. I just didn't want to put them at risk."

We move slowly around the North Circular and then head up north towards where the M25 crosses the traffic nightmare that is the A12.

I'm trying to keep calm for Sheila's sake but my stomach is churning. If this is what happens to witnesses and their families it's little wonder that people are wary of helping the police. It's been an hour since we called 999 and I can imagine half a dozen police cars sealing off

Susie's quiet Southwold road. There'll be a helicopter hovering overhead with powerful searchlights illuminating half the town and hordes of coppers in riot gear crouching behind shields.

My phone rings.

"It's Susie," says Simon.

"Answer it!" Sheila and I scream as one.

We're about to pass a lay-by but with screeching brakes accompanied by the loud honking of a cut-up lorry driver I manage to pull into the farthest available space.

"Hello."

"Put it on speaker," I say.

He does as I ask and I am relieved to hear Susie's voice.

"Simon? Is that you?"

"Yes. Are you okay? We're still an hour away I'm afraid."

"Of course I'm okay. Okay apart from just having had the police interrupt a quiet evening in front of the telly with a bottle of Sauvignon Blanc and a Tesco ready meal that is."

"Blimey. When did the police start doing home deliveries?"

"Very funny Simon. Why are you answering Dad's phone and why are you on your way here?"

"I thought that would be obvious from your phone call."

"The police said something about a phone call and you reporting an assault. But I haven't made any phone calls. With Alec away I got the girls to bed early for once and decided to binge on catch up TV on the iPlayer."

"But I had a call from your mobile," I stammer, "Your name and photo came on screen. All hell was breaking loose. Crashes, bangs and a cockney thug making all sorts of threats against you and the family."

Susie goes quiet for a second. "Let me check the phone. I'll put you on hold." There's a pause. We look at each other in confusion.

"Butt-dial."

"Butt-dial? What are you talking about?"

"Butt-dial, Dad. The phone was in my jeans back pocket. When I sat down it somehow called you. It wasn't me who called. It was my bum. Sorry Dad."

"But that doesn't explain what I heard. Your bum doesn't talk like Henry Cooper. What about all the screams, the crashes and the bumps"

"It was just the TV, Dad. I was catching up on the soaps."

Simon smiles, he turns to face me. "Bump....bump.....bump bump tiddlebump."

Chapter Thirty

Maria

It is Friday morning. In a perfect world I might have been waking up to the smell of fresh coffee and pastries delivered on a tray decorated with a single red rose by the handsome gentleman who, after missing the last bus home, spent his night curled up on my couch.

But it is not a perfect world and I wake up to the usual scent of damp from the mouldy wallpaper and the sound of clanking central heating pipes that the landlord promised to fix last winter.

Simon said seven o'clock. I did not want to seem too keen so I was a little late but I mean very little, muy poco tiempo – maybe two minutes – not long enough for him to have given up and left me. No phone call. No text message. Just me standing outside Mr Ali's shop, dodging all the passers-by on the busy pavement. When I got myself dressed, as the English say, 'to kill', I had not thought that the killing would involve me freezing to death. I waited for thirty minutes in that ridiculous skirt and then I wondered if I had the right place, the right date, the right time.

I phoned. It went straight to his voicemail. I left a message.

Was it the empty shop doorway where we were supposed to meet? I walked back along the high street towards it. The sleeping bag was still there but no Simon.

"Ah Señorita Bamba," the old man crooned as he poked his head out of his nest, "We must stop meeting this way."

"Have you seen a tall man waiting around here?"

"Sorry, young lady. Been stood up?"

"Stood up? What is stood up?"

"It's when the geezer you're supposed to be meeting don't turn up."

"Yes. I have been stood up."

"He must be mad," he said. "how could anybody stand

up a gorgeous thing like you? If I were fifty years younger...
" he looked wistfully and a broad smile creased his face "I'd
have been waiting all day."

I shivered at the thought and rushed home as fast as my
stupid stillettoes would let me.

~

I get out of bed and wrap my dressing gown tightly around
me. I go to the bathroom and look at myself in the mirror.
Streaked masacara stains my cheeks. Estupida! I think.

I tidy my face up before I take a shower. I wash my hair
and bundle it up in a towel. I wrap a bath towel around me
and put my dressing gown on on top of the towel. This
bedsit is so cold. Another two dressing gowns would not
keep me warm.

I go to the kitchen area and fill the kettle. Whilst I wait
for it to boil, I go to check my phone. I was so unhappy
when I got home last night I just threw my bag and jacket on
the floor behind the door, got undressed and went to bed.

I check my handbag. No phone. I tip the bag out onto
the sofa. I shake the bag. I hold it in front of me and bend
to look deep inside like a donkey with his nosebag. I go
through all the stuff on the couch. The phone has not
turned into a make up compact or a purse. It is not there.

I shake my jacket. Just in case the phone has somehow
found its way inside the pockets that are still stitched up.

My world is in that phone. I had it when I was outside Mr
Ali's. I put it back into my handbag as I walked to the empty
shop. Did I put it down in the doorway? Could the old man
have taken it? Why would he take a phone and leave a purse?

I have never used it but I set up the 'find my iPhone'
app when I bought the phone. You pair it with your
computer. I do not have a laptop so Margarita set it up on
hers for me. I will phone her and check if she is in. But I
cannot phone her.

I dry and dress myself as fast as I can. I have not got the
time to dry my hair. It hangs around my face like stringy
rats' tails.

I rush out of the building and head to the bus stop.

It is half past ten when I arrive at Margarita's place She is working lunch shift today so she should still be at home. I ring the doorbell. No answer. Her parents both work, so they will be out. I try the bell again. Still no answer.

I give up and walk back down the drive. And there she is. She has her gym bag, so she must have been to a class at We Can Work It Out, although, looking at her perfect make-up and hair she looks instead as if she has been for a beauty treatment.

"Maria! Why are you here?" she asks me in Spanish, "Why did you not phone?"

"Because I have lost my phone."

She opens her front door and pauses to switch off the burglar alarm.

'Come in," she says.

We go upstairs to her bedroom. It is bigger than my bedsit. My landlord has fitted six bedsits into a house that is about the same size as Margarita's mum and dad's place.

"Remember you set up the 'find my phone' thing on your computer for me?" I ask.

"Of course."

She picks her laptop off the floor and opens it up. She finds her way to the 'find my iPhone' app.

"Okay," she says. "Let's see where it is."

And there it is, flashing away on the screen. The battery has survived and like ET my phone is sending me the signal to bring it home.

It is sending its signal from a derelict shop doorway on the High Street.

I tell Margarita about what happened last night and how Simon left me waiting in the cold.

Her fingers flash over the computer keyboard.

"What are you doing?"

"Look," she says turning the screen towards me.

A grinning, gap toothed, whiskery, wrinkled face beneath a mass of straggly white hair peers out from the screen.

"He's been practicing his selfies," she says. "If you can

wait while I get ready for work, I will come with you. You cannot go on your own."

I sit on her bed and wait. I pick up the open laptop.

"Can I use the laptop?" I shout through to her in her ensuite.

"Sure."

I log onto eBay. I scroll down to my unsold items. I click on the vases. I go to the 'relist this item' option. My finger hovers above the button. I click. My old listing comes up. I notice that I stupidly listed them under Pots And Pans. I change the category to Pottery and then, as they are Japanese, use the Oriental Pottery sub-category. It is unfortunate that I do not have better photos. I check all of the details in the listing.

Margarita comes out of her bathroom and starts to dress.

"What are you doing?" she asks.

"Selling Abuelo's floreros on eBay," I say.

"I thought that you sold them to that frog guy who was going to come to the restaurant.".

"He did not come. It was him I was meeting last night."

"Huh. He's got no chance. There's no way should you let him have them now."

She is dressed and ready for work. How can a short black skirt, white blouse and black shoes look so elegant? She sits beside me on the bed.

"Can I read it?" she asks.

I turn the computer towards her. She scrolls through my revised listing.

"Looks good," she says, "But don't the English call them vases not flower pots?"

"Flower pots came up when I checked the translator."

"Maybe but look at this," she opens a new screen on the laptop and Googles 'vases'. She clicks the image tab and I can see that she is right. I change the title.

"Do you really want to do this?" she asks.

"I have no room for them."

"No. Do you really want to do *this*?" she points to the shipping details. I have chosen 'will ship worldwide.' "That could be trouble. They are ceramics. They are fragile. Would you trust the post office in say Afghanistan? You should choose collection in person only."

I agree and change my selection as she suggests.

Maria scrolls down the screen. "Why not try this 'Buy It Now' too?"

I think that may be a good idea. "How much do you think I should put as the price?"

"Fifty pounds would be good."

"I started them at thirty last time and did not sell them."

"Maria, you need to think big."

I change the price to fifty pounds and complete the listing.

We leave the house and walk to the bus stop. On our way is a house that is being renovated. When they see us, three builders working on scaffolding begin to whistle and shout comments at us... I say 'us' but only one of us looks like she would be at home on the front of *Vogue*.

Does this happen every day?" I ask.

'Twenty times every day."

"How terrible. That is horrible. What do you do? How do you react?"

"You'll see."

As we pass the scaffolding Margarita looks up, gives the builders the finger and utters the foulest Spanish oath I have ever heard. It is one that would make my father blush.

I giggle a little. "We have plenty of Polish builders. We have plenty of Romanian builders. I hope we do not meet any Spanish ones."

We run to the bus stop. We catch the bus and it is not long before it arrives on the High Street. We get off at a stop very near to the shop doorway.

We link arms and walk together.

The sleeping bag is still in place and there are signs of movement inside. Margarita gives the bag a heavy kick.

The bag answers. "Oi. How many times have I told you. Ain't got no fags, no hash, no booze, no stash, no dope, no cash, so piss off home, yer poxy rash."

"Come out Kanye West," Margarita kicks the bag again.

The familiar white-haired head emerges from the bag.

"Oh it's little Miss Bamba again. Thought it was Freddie from down the big bins. Oh." He looks Margarita up and down and up and down again "and *big* Miss Bamba too." He shades his eyes from the winter sun that reflects off the shop window. "Blimey you really *are* a couple of stunners. It's the first time I've had a visit from a pair of beauty queens. My regular visitors aren't quite so fragrant." He starts to fumble in his sleeping bag.

Margarita's face distorts and she makes an oath that replaces the last one as the foulest Spanish phrase that I have ever heard.

"I don't know what you're sayin but it sounds a bit strong for a lovely señorita like you." He takes out a crumpled cigarette packet. "I was only gonna offer you a fag but I'll take that as a 'no gracias'. So ladies. Ow can I help you?"

Margarita takes her phone from her bag. She swipes the screen and brings up one of his selfies that she has transferred from her laptop. She holds it in front of his face. "Do you know this ugly face?"

"Rings a bell," he says, "'ansome geyser, inni?"

"The phone," I say, "Where is my phone?"

There's some more fumbling in the bag. "I was hopin you'd be back for it." He brings the phone out of the sleeping bag with a cackle. "I'm not a tea leaf. I might be 'omeless but I don't nick stuff. You ran off last night so fast yer phone flew out of yer bag and landed right here. Right in me lap. I wish it were someone like you who'd landed in me lap. But that's the story of me life."

He holds out the phone.

"You should put a stronger pass code on that," he says. "You've had some very interesting texts. Don't worry. I answered 'em all for you."

I snatch the phone from him and turn to leave.

Margarita gives the bag another kick accompanied by, what is now, the foulest Spanish sentence I have ever heard.

"Buenos knockers, Señoritas," is the last we hear.

Chapter Thirty-One

Maria

Margarita heads off towards Casa Nuestra.

"See you later," I say.

"What time do *you* start?'

"Five."

"Have a good afternoon."

"You too."

I cross the road to the bus stop. The bus arrives very quickly. I find a seat downstairs and check the phone. I realise I have been very lucky. The battery is down to 7% and just closing the photo album brings it down to 5%. If he had used it any more last night the battery could have run down before I got to Margarita's.

I look at the phone. There are five missed calls from Simon and dozens of dialed numbers that I do not recognise. There is a voice message but I do not think there is enough power to listen to it. I tap on messages. It opens on Simon Oxford and I see that the old man was not joking when he said that he had replied to my texts. I scroll up to the first message.

Yesterday 22:29

I'm so sorry Maria. I can explain. Please answer the phone.

Explain away then, you lousy pig.

There was an emergency. I had to go to Southwold. My battery was flat.

Your excuse is flat. Standing me up like that.

I can't tell you how sorry I am. Your number was on my phone. The battery was dead. There was no way to contact you. It really was an emergency.

Please forgive me.

Don't believe you.

It's true.

Sure it's true. You think I'm stupid?

Honestly

You DO think I'm stupid. Fucking bastard.

Maria!!!!!!! I said I was sorry.

Lying twat.

What are you up to? Where are you?

Givin a blowjob to that sexy George Clooney lookalike in the shop doorway.

Who is this?

Maria.

Sure. And I am the Pope.

Hail bloody Mary

Look. I don't know who you are and how you got hold of that phone, you bastard but if you've done anything to Maria you're asking for trouble.

Ooh. I'm shakin in me fucking boots. She's good isn't she. Best hand job I've had in years.

I am glad that Simon ended the conversation at that point. There are five or six more messages from the old guy trying to rile Simon with even cruder claims about what he has been doing with me but Simon did not respond. My battery is down to 3%. I attempt to listen to the voice mail.

'Maria. It's Simon. Call me. There's been an emergency. I can explain. I'm really, really, really sorry.'

The message ends and, as it does, the phone finally dies.

As soon as I get back to the bedsit I plug the phone in to

charge. When it springs back to life there is immediately a series of trumpet calls followed by a ker-ching. I check the screen. The messages are all from eBay.

Chapter Thirty-Two

Dave

I don't want another night like that. It was bad enough driving half way to Southwold at twenty miles an hour, but driving back with Sheila haranguing me about my idiocy at not being able to tell the difference between my daughter and a character from *Eastenders* and Simon pointing out that my stupidity had probably cost me any chance he had of getting the vases for me was a hundred times worse.

I'm cooking a late breakfast to try and get back into Sheila's good books. I've made her some freshly squeezed orange juice, a pot of green tea, some toasted artisan bread topped with perfectly poached eggs and a single rasher of bacon. I put it all on a tray and I'm preparing to take it upstairs when my phone signals a new email.

I put the tray down and take the phone out of my pocket. *'An eBay item you have been watching has been re-listed.'*

I click on the message. It can't be. It is. She's re-listed the vases. I anxiously follow the link to eBay. And there they are. It's a better listing this time and there's a Buy It Now Price.

I click the Buy It Now button and they're mine.

For just fifty pounds.

Chapter Thirty-Three

Maria

It is late afternoon and I need to get ready for work but I have time to check those eBay messages. The vases have sold and the payment has come from Paypal. I click on the details.

There is a message from the buyer.

'I am delighted to have won these vases. When and where can I arrange to collect them?'

I follow the link needed to send a message to the buyer.

'Thank you very much for your bid. I have to go to work soon but I will reply with arrangements later.'

I press send.

The phone rings. It is Simon.

"Maria? Is that you?"

"Yes. Hello Simon."

"What's been going on with your phone? Who was texting on it last night? I tried to ring you at least five times."

"I know, Simon. I lost my phone but, as you can see, I have got it back now."

"I'm glad it wasn't you sending those texts. I'm no prude but talk about Triple X! Look. I'm really, really sorry about last night. I hope you didn't wait too long for me. It was so cold. How can I make it up to you?"

"What happened? You said there was an emergency."

"My dad thought my sister was being attacked and we all rushed into the car and drove to Suffolk to rescue her."

"Like knights in - how do you say - shining armour. Is

she okay?"

"Oh, she's okay alright. I'm not sure that Dad's so good though; the stick me and Mum gave him on the way home. It turned out that she was being beaten up by Phil Mitchell."

"Who?"

"Someone from a soap. My sister accidentally called while the TV was on in the background and my Dad thought a fight was really happening. He's deaf. I don't know if he had his hearing aids in. It would have been quite funny really if you hadn't ended up shivering outside Mr Ali's. When can I meet you and try to redeem myself?"

"There is no point now."

"Why?"

"I sold the vases."

There is a short silence. "You sold them?"

"Yes."

Another, longer, pause. "Who to?"

"A user called Kinkozanfan."

"Can't you cancel it?"

"No. The buyer has already paid and asked me how to collect them."

"But you knew how much I wanted them, Maria. Why did you sell them?"

"I was not happy after last night."

"But -I've explained. You know it wasn't my fault. Look. I'll give you seventy pounds for them to make up for last night. You can refund the buyer. And it will save you the eBay fees."

"That is very kind but I do not go back on my promises. I have only excellent feedback. I know how much you wanted them Simon but you will find something else. I am sorry."

Simon's voice changes. "But you've still got them haven't you?" I know he says he is keen on frogs but he seems almost desperate.

I hesitate for a moment. "Yes. I have written to the buyer. I will let you know what happens."

"I'd still like to see you – vases or no vases."

"You would? Why?

"I thought that we got on well at the post office."

"Maybe."

"We did. Didn't we?"

"Yes but perhaps you were just being nice because of the frogs."

"It might seem that way but honestly the vases are not that important."

"Not *that* important but still important."

"As I said before. Vases or no vases. I'd still like to see you. Can I meet you sometime?"

"I am not sure."

"How about after you finish work tonight?"

"It is too late. It will be almost midnight. I suppose I could possibly meet you tomorrow morning if you are not working."

"You could?" He sounds genuinely pleased

"Possibly?"

"Make it definitely"

"Okay definitely."

"It's a date. There are no school activities this weekend. Where do you fancy?"

"How about coffee and croissants at Le Petit Pain. Ten o'clock?"

"Fine with me. I will see you there. Have a good night at work. Bye."

"Bye."

I put the phone down and start to change into my kitchen clothes.

A new eBay message arrives on the phone.

'Message from Kinkozanfan: What is your address? I will come to collect.'

Chapter Thirty-Four

Dave

I'm singing a Pharrell Wiliams song to myself when Simon comes home. He walks into the dining room where I'm sitting at the laptop.

"What are you so happy about then?" he asks.

"The vases," I say, " I've won the vases."

"But she's sold them to some Satsuma collector called Kinkozanfan."

"I know," I say.

"So why the smiles? Do you know this Kinkozanfan?"

"You're looking at him."

"You...you crafty bugger. I thought your eBay tag was DP and your birthday."

"It is usually but I've also got a secret undercover identity that I save for special buys."

"Congratulations Dad...You've just succeeded in robbing a poor Spanish cook of her one and only chance to get a leg up in life."

I put my hands over my ears. "Lah lah lah."

"True I'm afraid, Dad. If they are right that is." He goes to the cupboard and pulls out a particularly garishly painted and very ugly, cracked pot that I had opined was a Meissen piece when I clicked on the bid button and wasted seventy-five pounds.

"You've certainly got form when it comes to picking winners," he says.

Sheila comes into the room.

"What's going on?" she says, "Has your Dad told you about his buy?"

"Yes. Dad's just told me about his little windfall and I've just told him he's robbing a poor Spanish cook of her inheritance."

"But she sold them for fifty pounds. I assume she was happy with that."

"She will be happy, Mum. Until she finds out they're worth a hundred grand."

"Well. You know your Dad. He'll do the right thing." Sheila turns to me. "Won't you, Dave?"

My heart sinks. Conscience. Bloody, bloody conscience.

Chapter Thirty-Five

Maria

It is Saturday morning and I arrive at Le Petit Pain just as Simon is opening the door to go in. He turns to me, smiles and holds the door open. We step inside together and find a seat in a window table where we can watch the busy crowds enjoying their weekends.

"Good morning, Simon." I offer him my hand to shake but he kisses me softly on both cheeks.

"Good morning, Maria. How do you like your coffee?"

"Cappuccino," I say.

"That makes it two. Anything to eat? Those pains au chocolat look pretty good."

"Okay. That would be nice."

Simon gets up to go to the counter and order.

"Wait," I say fumbling in my purse for a ten pound note. " I will pay."

"Wouldn't dream of it. Least I can do after the other night."

He is back carrying a tray in a few minutes. He serves the coffee and pastries and goes back to the counter to return the tray.

"You could get a waiting job," I say.

He smiles. "I don't think I've got the looks."

I look up at him. He is not at all bad looking. "You do not have to be Brad Pitt to be a waiter."

"Oh. So I'm no Brad Pitt then. Benedict Cumberbatch perhaps? No. No, don't tell me, Marty Feldman."

"Who?"

"You don't know Marty Feldman?"

"Is he very handsome?"

"Was. No longer with us I'm afraid."

I smile. "Okay Marty," I say, "So how are you today?"

We pass a few minutes sipping our coffees, enjoying our pains au chocolat and chatting.

Simon asks me when I decided to leave 'sunny Spain' and head to England.

"It was four —no, five years ago now. I was cooking in a little place with rooms in our village in Catalonia. Mike and Stevie, a couple from Oxford stayed for two weeks and we chatted most evenings after dinner. They suggested that I should, as they said, *spread my wings* and *broaden my horizons* and they offered me work as an au pair. Our village was tiny and remote. I had been thinking about moving to Madrid but I thought England might be an adventure."

"And was it?"

"An adventure?" I raise my eyebrows and smile. "The place was beautiful. The house was fabulous but the *kids!*"

"Weren't quite as nice as when they were on holiday?"

"They were not on the holiday. Their grandparents looked after them while Mike and Stevie were in Catalonia. Stevie made them sound like angels."

"You should hear some of the mums and dads at Parents' Evenings. I have to keep checking that we're talking about the same kids. So you didn't last long as an au pair?"

I shake my head.

"But you liked England?"

"Yes. I liked England. I missed my parents and my little brother but I like the people. I like the crowds and, you may not believe this, but I like the weather."

"Oh I believe it alright. I love our climate." He smiles. "Hey. We've got something in common. I knew we would. Carry on. How did you get from Oxford to here? And don't say the X90 bus."

"The train actually."

He laughs.

"Casa Nuestra is run by some friends of friends of my family," I explain, "I phoned them and asked if they had any work for a cook."

"And the rest, as they say, is history.... You like Casa Nuestra?"

"I love it. We are like a big family."

"I can tell. That's why it's so popular. But how about your family? You said you miss your parents and little brother. How old is he?"

"He's not so little now. He's nineteen and almost as tall as you."

"What's his name?"

"Carlos."

"And what's he doing?"

"He's at university in Sevilla studying medicine."

"Great. And your mum and dad?"

"Oh they are fine. My dad is a fisherman and my mum works as a cleaner, where I used to work."

"They must *really* miss having you around."

"They do, but they have Skype."

"Ah Skype... what would we do without Skype? It's certainly been fantastic for people like you, living away from your family. I don't need Skype to talk to my mum and dad."

"They live nearby?"

"More than nearby. It's a bit embarrassing to admit it, but I live at home."

"You do not need to be embarrassed. I know how much rents cost."

He raises his eyebrows. "Tell me about it. That bottom rung of the housing ladder is getting higher and higher."

"Even for someone as tall as you."

He looks into my eyes and again he laughs at my weak joke. I am enjoying his company but, I have to talk to him about the frogs.

"Simon, I know you will be unhappy but I am sorry I cannot cancel the sale of the frog pots."

I am surprised by his response. I thought that he would be disappointed or even angry. "That's no problem. I'm sure they will be going to a good home."

"Why do you think that?"

"The buyer name. Kinkozanfan. Kinkozan was a Japanese potter. So the buyer is a fan of Japanese pottery so he should be pleased with his buy."

"And you are not disappointed?"

Simon shrugs. "Me? Why should I be disappointed? I'm sitting here drinking coffee and chatting with a *very* beautiful, young woman. Kinkozanfan will be looking at some very pretty vases. I know which one I'd choose every time."

I blush. "The frogs for sure," I say.

"Not in a thousand years. So have you arranged for him to collect them yet?"

"Not yet. I will send a message when I get home."

"Good. Be careful if you are arranging for the buyer to collect. I'm absolutely sure that he or she will be perfectly fine but, take care. You might be safer meeting somewhere public."

"I will take care."

We return to our chat and our coffees. Simon buys two more coffees for us and it is over an hour before we leave the café. It has been a very happy morning but, I have to go home and get ready for work.

"Thank you for the coffees, Simon. I have enjoyed our morning."

"Me too," he says, "Can we do it again?"

"Of course. That would be good."

We walk together to the bus stop. Two buses that he could catch come and go but Simon waits with me. As my bus finally approaches he looks down at me, he holds me in quite a tight embrace and kisses me gently on the lips. I close my eyes as I return the kiss. Opening them again I see that we have an audience.

"That was nice," he says with a smile. I'm not sure if he is talking to me or to the onlookers in the queue.

I turn back towards him as I get onto the bus.

"Yes," I say. "It was very nice."

Chapter Thirty-Six

Maria

Now that I have spoken to Simon I feel happy to arrange for Kinkozanfan to collect the vases. I am a little surprised that Simon was not more angry or sad about the sale but I will take his advice and be careful.

I send a message.

'Hi Kinkozanfan. I see from your location on eBay that you are in North London like me. I do not want to give my address so maybe we can meet in a public place. Could we meet at We Can Work It Out gym on Common Road in Finchley on Monday at 10.45?'

It is only a few minutes before a reply pings back to me.

'I know We Can Work It Out. Monday at 10.45 is great with me. See you there. My name is Dave. Who do I ask for?'

'Maria.'

Chapter Thirty-Seven

Dave

I'm in my usual spot at the dining table with the MacBook open in front of me when the message arrives in my inbox. Sheila is sitting opposite checking out Facebook on her iPad.

Yessss. I'm another step closer to getting the vases. I'm not sure about another trip to We Can Work It Out after my last performance but then again, perhaps I should be giving it another go and try and get myself in shape for Sheila. I log onto the gym's website and check out what classes are scheduled for Monday morning.

I pick HIIT – nothing like throwing myself in at the deep end. The class runs from nine forty-five until ten-thirty - pretty near perfect timing. I use the online booking system to make sure that there's a space in the class. There are four slots still available and I ask Sheila if she is interested in joining me for a taster.

"You think I need exercise do you? Don't I have enough exercise running around looking after you and Simon and this place? What are you saying?   I'm fat. That's it you think I'm fat – old and fat. Okay you put my name down if you think I'm fat, old, unfit and useless. Thank you *very* much."

"Sorry, love. I didn't mean that. Of course you're not fat or old."

"Okay, but I am unfit and useless then?"

"Of course not. You're neither fat nor old, unfit nor useless."

"So why did you think I'd want to go the fitness class then?"

"To be with me."

She shoots me a withering look. "Like I'm not with you enough?"

"Sorry. I shouldn't have mentioned it. I'll leave it."

"No, don't leave it now that you've asked me. You

obviously want me to go or you wouldn't have asked."

I tap on the keyboard. "Oh look. Sorry. Class is full. Panic over." I close the laptop.

"You're just saying that. Let me see."

I open the MacBook up again and take a gamble.

"Can't you just take my word for it. It's full. There were spaces but they've been taken."

I turn the screen towards her but she's more interested in Susie's new photograph of the girls eating ice cream on Southwold pier. She ignores the laptop screen and says "Alright but don't you go accusing me of being fat again." She keeps on looking at her iPad.

"You'll never believe what happens next?" I say.

"What?"

"This is amazing? You won't believe your eyes?"

"What are you taking about?"

"Facebook. All those click bait links trying to get you to watch a crappy video of some choreographed wedding dance or a baby laughing at its own farts."

"You've got your eBay what are you complaining about?"

She's right. What's it got to do with me what she chooses to watch? I decide to go down to the shops to pick up the papers.

The weekend passes slowly. I manage to read Saturday's *Times* and *The Sunday Times* cover to cover: magazines; travel; food; property - the lot. I even do the Sudoku puzzles and attempt the crosswords. The wait is agonising. It's as if I am trapped in a time warp.

I hardly sleep on Sunday. My head is filled images of a dusky señorita.

At first she is veiled and holding a fan in front of her face revealing only her eyes. "Dave Prendergast," she says, "Here are your frogs, Señor". She places two ghastly, pulsating, slimy creatures in my outstretched hands. A chef runs from behind her wielding a cleaver. "I need zehhr legs," he shouts in a Clouseau accent. He brings down his cleaver. The blade swishes past my head towards the amphibians. They leap from my grasp but the knife takes one leg from each. As the bloodied animals reach the ground, they transform into the most exquisite Satsuma pottery before smashing into a million pieces.

"Oh Señor," cries the woman, "I must refund your fifty pounds. Is it fifty pounds?" She pauses "Or is it a *million* pounds?" I see that she has now dropped her fan. Her face is shrunken, her body wasted, she looks like a model for a famine aid appeal. She holds out a desperate hand. "Fifty pounds for me Señor. A million pounds for you... and a copy of *The Big Issue*."

I jolt awake, shaking. Sheila turns on her bedside lamp and looks at me.

"What's going on? The bedclothes are all over the place. You're sweating like a pig but it's freezing in here."

"Bit of a nightmare. Sorry."

"Go back to sleep. It's three o'clock."

More dreams fill the hours before dawn. In each Maria is progressively less nourished until, at around sunrise, she appears as a skeleton wrapping the vases in her own shroud.

I'm up and about very early. I cook Sheila a bacon sandwich and take it to her in bed.

"I can't eat that. I'm too fat."

"You're not fat."

"That's not what you said yesterday when you were trying to book me into exercise classes."

I take the sandwich back. I go downstairs. I shout back up the stairs. "I'll bring you a cup of green tea."

Later, as I get myself kitted out in my gym stuff, I look in the bedroom mirror. Whatever comes of this episode I've go to do something about my fitness. If I don't I won't even get to see that State Pension. I pack the holdall that came in Djimi's gift pack with a towel, shampoo, shower gel, deodorant, comb and a change of clothes. I go downstairs to the cupboard where I keep the eBay failures and fish out some of the yards of bubble wrap that they arrived in and squash it into the gym bag.

I shout up to Sheila, "I'm off now, love."

"I thought that your class was at nine forty-five," she shouts.

"It is."

"Do you know what time it is now?"

I know precisely what time it is. "Nine-thirty ...ish?" I offer.

"Eight... ish! What are you going to do at the gym for nearly two hours? Check where they keep the stretchers? Or the defibrillator?"

"Okay, I'll hang on here."

Simon runs down the stairs.

"Morning, Dad. Do I smell bacon?"

"I made a bacon sarnie for your mum. You're welcome to it but it'll be cold now."

Simon takes the sandwich and its plate from the worktop and puts them into the microwave. He gives the food a short blitz and takes it back out.

"So what are you up to in that outfit?" he says, in between mouthfuls of sandwich.

"I'm going to meet Muchachabonita at the gym to collect the vases so I'm killing two birds with one stone and getting in a bit of exercise at the same time."

"You might be killing two birds with twenty stone if you fall on any of your classmates."

"Ha bloody ha. And I'm sixteen stone, if you don't mind."

"That's still four too many."

"You don't need to remind me. Why do you think I'm going?"

"To pick up the vases. Look, whatever you do please don't mention me to Maria when you meet her. I don't want her to know the connection."

"Why not? She'll find out sooner or later."

"Only if we start dating regularly."

"And how will you explain yourself then?"

"I'll cross that bridge if I ever come to it. But no mention. Please?"

"Okay."

"Any pangs of conscience?"

"I've been awake all night."

"Dreaming of your new found wealth?"

"No. Dreaming of Spanish women."

"You found porno-espanol.com then?"

"Isn't it time you got the bus to school?"

"Sure. Want to walk to the bus stop with me?"

We shout our farewells to Sheila. I'm still way too early but as I'm walking to the bus with Simon it's no longer a problem.

Chapter Thirty-Eight

Dave

I see Simon off at the bus stop and decide on an indirect route to We Can Work It Out. I don't want to be kicking my heels making small talk with Djimi, so I walk via the High St. I look in the charity shop windows and make a note to go back to a couple when they are open and tell them they've got a few bits of their bric-a-brac underpriced. It doesn't happen too often nowadays as most have got an expert who comes in and values donated goods for them but a few antiques still slip through the net and I'd rather the charities profit than someone who makes a living at car boot sales.

I reach the gym in plenty of time for my class and enter the building using my fingerprint. As the door slides open I see Djimi behind the reception desk. He looks at me with a somewhat startled expression.

"Morning Djimi. I imagine you weren't expecting me back after the last episode."

He's now searching frantically for something in his desk drawer. He pulls it out and waves it in front of me.

"So that's why it's called a *'waiver'*" I say.

Djimi groans as he hands me the form. The management seem to have added another three paragraphs since my last appearance – talk about covering their backsides!

"Can I have another signature please, Mr Prendergast?"

"It's Dave. And yes you can have another signature but it was only indigestion you know."

"Indigestion? Martin Hetherington told us how he performed CPR while his Merc was stopped at traffic lights. He said that he ran into A&E carrying you over his shoulder and rushed with you to an operating theatre they'd prepared for you through him phoning ahead to his friend, who is one of the World's leading cardiothoracic surgeons. He said that he waited outside the operating theatre while they carried out open-heart surgery to save your life."

"It was the NHS, you know, not an episode of *ER*. I suppose Martin wasn't expecting me back here then. Is he still coming regularly?"

"Yes, but he has been a bit quiet recently. Lost a bit of his swagger. He doesn't say much when we ask him if he's okay – just says he may have to go away for a while. It's all very mysterious the way he tells it. He taps the side of his nose a lot," Djimi demonstrates the nose tapping before adding, "as if he's on a secret mission."

I'm disappointed but, just as I expected, it looks like he's managed to find someone to stand bail. Damn.

"Oh well," I say, "As long as he hasn't booked into HIIT this morning our paths shouldn't cross."

After asking Djimi which studio I will be working out in, I go to the changing rooms to leave my holdall in a locker.

The urgency has diminished a little since my visit to the clinic. The doctor suggested that I cut back on tea and coffee and drink more water instead and her very simple solution seems to be doing the trick. I can't be complacent though and maybe my lack of emergencies has been down to careful planning rather than any medical change. It's good to have it under control and, after a quick, pre workout insurance visit, I look at myself in the changing room mirror. I'm a long way from my prime. I take a few deep breaths and walk to the studio.

The class passes without event. That is to say the class passes without a repeat performance of my dying swan – this time I leave with some modicum of decorum although shaking my sweaty head, like a dog coming out of the sea after a dip, didn't earn me too many friends.

I pass reception on my way back towards the changing rooms. I see the unmistakable long black hair and shapely legs of Margarita moving in the direction of the spinning studio. I think about shouting a greeting but have second thoughts. I could have explained everything but why bother? I'm unlikely ever to see her again so what's the need?

I look in the direction of the main glass door and see a young Mediterranean looking woman attempting to put her finger onto the scanner. She's struggling to keep the gym bag on her shoulder from swinging off as she leans towards the door. There's a flimsy box in her hands and she can't get her index finger free. The box wobbles precariously.

"Djimi," I say with mild panic. "Can't you just open the door for her?"

I look back to the door. The box is now crumpled on the floor and the young woman is on her knees looking anxiously inside it.

Djimi presses the necessary button and the door slides open allowing her to step inside.

She walks to the counter and puts the box down on it with far less care than I was hoping. As she does so the ominous rattling sound that I'm way too familiar with echoes around the reception area. So near and yet, so far.

"Shit," she says.

"Morning," Says Djimi, "What've you smashed, Miss Clumsy?"

"Mugs for the staff rest room. Picked them up at IKEA yesterday. The boss asked me to get them. Oh well. They'll be coming out of my pay now."

I'm aware of someone by my side.

"Are you Dave? Kinkozanfan?"

I turn to see another, clearly Mediterranean, face. Last time I saw this face I was at much closer quarters. I feel my cheeks flush so much they start to burn.

"Oh my God. What a small world. So you're *the* Maria. I remember you very well."

"Si Señor."

"Am I pleased to see you," I say with a smile. I offer my hand and she takes it and give me a firm handshake. "No need for kisses this time. How can I thank you for your efforts to revive me?"

"De nada. I believe that it was Martin who saved you."

"You should take everything Martin tells you with a pinch of salt. I'm fine. It was just a touch of indigestion after over eating at Casa Nuestra."

Now it's Maria's turn to blush. "Maybe I have to reduce the peppers." She smiles. "I am so pleased that you are well and I am sorry that I am late." As she speaks she unzips her gym holdall and takes out a carrier bag. "Here are the pots."

In taking them, I'm reminded of when I first visited Susie in the maternity ward and she offered me the tiny bundle that was Sally. I think I may even take the carrier bag with more care than I did my own granddaughter. I open the bag and peer inside. Two shapes wrapped in newspaper lie alongside each other.

"Thank you, Maria."

"It is a pleasure," she says. "They were my Grandfather's."

"And now they're another grandfather's," I say.

"I am sorry, I have to get to my class," she says. "If they are not okay, I finish before noon. See me here then."

"I am sure they'll be fine."

I find myself alone in the lobby cradling the bag. I resist the urge to unwrap the newspaper here and now and instead head back to the changing room like Gollum carrying his Precious.

Chapter Thirty-Nine

Dave

I return to the changing rooms and go to my locker. I unlock it and take out the holdall. I open the holdall and remove my clothes, wash stuff and the bubble wrap. I put the carrier bag down on a bench. I take out one of the newspaper wrapped packages and unwrap it as if I'm defusing a bomb. As the leaves of newsprint fall away, the package becomes smaller and smaller but in a few seconds I get my first glimpse.

That's all I need. One glimpse of one small section of one of the vases is enough to tell me that I have indeed made the find of a lifetime. The minute and immaculate brushwork is sheer perfection. My heart leaps. I hold back a gasp of delight as the changing room is filling with fellow exercisers returning from their routines in varying stages of exhaustion.

As I hastily rewrap the first vase in bubble wrap and do the same with the second without taking it out of the newspaper, I'm aware of a conversation going on in the communal shower. I glance in that direction. It's two oldish blokes. The first is showering conventionally facing the jets of hot water. His companion has his back to the water and, in even the briefest of glances, it's impossible not to notice that he's endowed with the most unfeasibly oversized meat-and-two-veg since the Great British Bake Off's squirrel. The shower stands, like a stage, a foot or so above the changing room floor and I half expect him to fling out his arms and regale us with a chorus of *I've got a lovely bunch of coconuts*. In true locker room tradition, I avert my eyes.

I put the bubble wrapped pieces into my holdall and lock the holdall back inside the locker. I can hear the old guys droning on about Council employees and local politics. I get out of my sweaty gym stuff and hear the shower stop running. The first man drapes himself in a towel and walks modestly to his locker; not so our Alpha male; he strides manfully across the floor and ends up at the locker next to mine.

I'm about to head into the shower when my phone beeps. I unlock the locker and reach into my gym bag and fish out the phone. It's Simon asking how I got on with Maria. I sit down to reply only to find Mr Big's tackle an inch away from my ear. I feel like I'm being eavesdropped on by an albino python.

I send my brief text - *Yabu Dabba Doo* - and head for the shower. As I shower the *blah-blah- blah* of council, golf club and office continues behind me. When I've finished my shower I see that the friend has had time to dry, dress, tidy his hair and put on his coat as well as run through the minutes of the Golf Club AGM. But our 'king of the swingers' has obviously decided to drip dry.

As the friend takes his leave he wishes everyone a Merry Christmas even though it's a month away. I, together with a few other members in various states of undress, attempt to ignore the elephant in the room. He moves to centre stage and starts doing some sort of stretching exercises. It could not be more obvious that he was staking his claim to the territory if he went and peed in every corner. The look on his face says it all: "I'm the cock of the walk. I'm the dog's bollocks". I'm surprised that he hasn't an arrow tattooed above his groin along with the message "LOOK WHAT I'VE GOT".

By now, I'm almost dressed and there's a palpable air of relief in the room as he returns to his locker and reaches for some clothes. He pulls out a shirt. I'm probably not alone in thinking "Bloody hell. He'll have his jacket and tie on before the crown jewels get put away."

As I finish dressing he reaches into his bag and takes out a huge pot of E45 cream. On taking a big dollop and starting to massage it into his buttocks he sparks a mass exodus of disheveled members stumbling to tie up laces and straighten hair. An instructor passes us in the corridor. "And they're off," he shouts.

"Too bloody right" says one of my fellow members "we're wondering if they'll ever be back on again."

As I reach reception the mobile rings. It's Sheila. I refrain from telling her that I've spent the last ten minutes as an unwilling spectator to a wanton display of exhibitionism. She says "Will you be very long?"

"Don't worry," I say. "I'll be with you shortly."

Chapter Forty

Maria

I go to my spinning class feeling both happy that the frog pots have gone to somebody who wants them and sad that one of my last remaining connections to my dear old Abuelo has gone. I know that he would have been more happy to see me with food to eat and my bills paid than having no money and two pieces of pottery. I tell myself that I have all my photographs and all my memories and they are so much more important than belongings.

I sit alongside Margarita in the spinning class. It is the first time that she has been to this Monday morning class. She has been away for the weekend. I tell her I have given the pots to Kinkozanfan and I talk to her about my Saturday morning in the café with Simon. She rolls her beautiful eyes and flashes her lovely eyelashes as she jokes about my new 'boyfriend'.

Martin, the guy I call Señor Libertino, comes to the class, late as usual. As always, he says something about my body and, as always, I pretend not to understand. I am glad that Margarita did not hear his comment or I am sure that she would give me another lesson in Spanish obscenity. He takes the bike next to mine and adjusts it to suit his size.

"How are you, gorgeous?" he asks.

I ignore him but after a moment I say. "Martin. What is the difference between a heart attack and indigestion?"

He looks at me oddly. "Why do you ask?"

"The man you saved and took to hospital."

"Dave?" he sucks making a hissing sound and shakes his head. "Nasty that. He just made it."

"How do you mean?"

"Touch and go, you know." He holds out his hand in front of him and makes small wobbly movements with it.

"He says to me it was indigestion."

"How do you know him?" Old Libertino is not as sure as he was.

"He was just here to collect something from me he bought on eBay."

His eyebrows raise almost to his hair. "Well one thing's for sure," he says.

"What is that?"

"You've been done."

I don't know this phrase and I turn to Margarita and ask her if she knows it. She, like me, does not understand. I say to him "No comprendo."

"Robbed. Stiffed. Ripped off. Swindled. Fleeced. Shafted. Screwed over. That man is mucho baddo."

"He was very nice."

"He looks on eBay for bargains that are going to make his fortune. His wife told me that he was looking at some Japanese vases worth a fortune that some poor sucker was selling for a few quid. What did you sell him?"

I do not answer but I think that my face may have answered for me. Our instructor arrives and starts the class warm up exercises.

Señor Libertino shakes his head. "It was you. Wasn't it? It was you." He shakes his head again and pedals furiously. He mutters "You bastard, Prendergast. You fucking bastard."

He tries to stop me as the class finishes but Margarita tells me that she does not like the way the 'viejo verde' has been watching her spinning and quickly leaves for the changing room. I follow her. As I leave the studio I hear him shout after me, "Don't let him get away with it."

As we change I tell Margarita what he has said.

"Do you believe him?" she asks.

"I am not sure," I say.

"I would never trust a man who looks at girls like he does. And did he not say that he had rescued your eBay man from a heart attack?"

"Yes he did. I do not think he would be exercising this morning a week after surgery."

"So he is a liar. Don't trust him. Forget him and remember who told you to put the price up to fifty pounds."

"Yes, but he did say *Japanese vases*. I did not tell him anything about what I had sold."

"Wasn't your boyfriend interested in those vases? You should ask him. He will tell you the truth if he really likes you."

"Simon did not appear to be upset when I said that I had sold them."

"So they were not important. Ask Simon when you see him again."

"*If* I see him again."

"What do you mean?"

"We have not set a date."

"Well, do it now."

"It is the man who should ask."

"It is 2017 not 1917."

Perhaps Margarita is right. I look for my phone in my bag. I take it out, unlock it and tap on messages. Before I can start my text, Margarita snatches the phone from me. She turns her back towards me and I see her fingers jabbing quickly at the screen. A few seconds later there's the whoosh sound of a message departing. "Okay," she says throwing my phone back into my bag.

I reach into the bag and take it out again. I look at the screen.

'Hey Simon. What U doin tonite. Want some Spanish fun?'

A message pings back *'Maria! Don't tell me you lost your phone again. Although, if by any remote chance that is you, Spanish fun sounds good to me. What do you have in mind? Bullfight? Flamenco? Fiesta?'*

I show Margarita the message. "*So* English," she says.

"How do you mean?"

"All that punctuation. But..." she pauses

"Yes?" I say.

"He does have a sense of humour."

"What should I say?"

"Give it to me." She snatches the phone back from me and immediately begins to tap tap tap onto the screen. "There," she says and hands it back. I check the screen.

'Hey Simon she like have v sexy time but she tell you take her to el cine Margarita ☺ ☺ ☺'

'Hey Margarita. Tell Maria el cine is good with me. I can meet her at 7.30 outside Cineworld. X-Men:Apocalypse looks good.'

I reply.

'Hi Simon. I rescued my phone from Margarita. Yes please See you at Cineworld tonite x ☺

We finish changing and leave the gym. I have a date for the first time in months. It feels good.

Chapter Forty-One

Dave

When I get home there's nobody about. Sheila has gone to Yoga with her friends and Simon is at work. I put the holdall down on the dining room table. Then I go into the kitchen area and find a pair of thin gloves that I picked up from next to the petrol pumps when I last filled up the car. I put the gloves on and go back to the table and open the gym bag. I carefully take out my two precious bundles. I've used so much bubble wrap it looks like I've got two footballs on the table. I roll them out one by one and, as the bubble wrap diminishes, I can see the newspaper-wrapped shapes, tantalisingly awaiting exposure.

I remove the paper and stand the vases alongside each other. I am blown away by the absolute perfection of the pieces. They are only about six inches tall but each is a perfect miniature work of art. Such is their beauty I feel a sense close to arousal.

I go to the sideboard and take my magnifying glass from its place on the rejects shelf. How many times have I used this to confirm my lousy judgement and rotten gambles? Today I only need it to get a better view of the intricate decoration painted with a single brush hair.

The design is so simple. Unlike some pieces of Japanese ceramics that are covered in garish gilt and crudely painted figures these have a few simple floral blossoms and tendrils around the top, and similar flowers around the bottom above a sensuous border of intricate gilding. In the wide cream-coloured gap between the floral bands there are a number of small, green and brown frogs in a variety of poses. Some stand; some crouch; some appear to be wrestling; others are in conversation; all are exquisite in their execution. The decoration is uncluttered; the frogs don't cram the space; just a couple here, one there and three or four beside them whichever way I look at each vase. Their faces are full of expression and must have been based on some of the old Kyoto characters known to the artist and his artisan potters a hundred years ago.

I open my laptop and bring up on screen the Lenhams vase that sold for sixty-five thousand pounds a couple of years ago. Although my vases are of a slender shape compared to the record-breaking example, the decoration is identical in layout but each frog, each leaf and each blossom is unique. I check the dimensions on the lot details. Their vase stood six and a half inches tall. I turn back to the sideboard and take out a tape measure. As I hoped, my vases are both exactly six and a half inches tall.

I am so excited by my good fortune that I haven't even studied the seal on the base. I don't really need to, but a rubbed seal can seriously affect the value of Satsuma pieces. I had no need to worry. The small seals, beautifully painted in gold, bear the unmistakable signature of Yabu Meizan. Each is perfect.

I sit down at the table and pick the vases up one by one and turn them over and over.

I click on eBay on the computer. I find the vases and click on the 'leave feedback' option. I input five stars for 'item as described', five stars again for 'communication' and five stars each for the dispatch and packing categories. I am lost for words on my written feedback. True feedback would contain words like 'absolutely fabulous', stunning' or 'unbelievable' and even those would not do justice to the pieces, but that would sound like gloating so I settle for *'Lovely vases, great seller. Thank you very much.'* As feedback goes that should win the world record for understatement.

Sheila and Simon won't be around for a while so I decide to photograph the pieces. Thank God for digital photography – as I take scores of photos I think back to the days of 36 shots on a roll and the trip to the chemist to get them developed. I upload the pictures to the laptop.

When I've finished I decide to get in touch with Lenhams. I'm on first name terms with the poor sod who has had to deal with dozens of my hopeful emails attaching photos of my latest finds. I imagine that he has a file somewhere on his computer called '*A hundred and one ways to let Dave Prendergast down gently*' as, every time I have written, I have received an immensely polite personal response telling me that the item doesn't quite fit their sales criteria and might be more suitable for a local auctioneer. Not once has he sneeringly suggested a jumble sale, car boot or the tip although I bet that he has been very sorely tempted. I just hope that he hasn't programmed his computer to auto-respond. His loss if he has.

I head up the email *A Pair Of Vases By Yabu Meizan*. I attach six photos although I know from experience that their expertise is such that they will only need one.

Dear Michael I write

I hope you are well.

I am attaching photos of a pair of vases that I am interested in selling. I believe that they are by Yabu Meizan.

Please let me know if you would be interested in handling these pieces for me.

I look forward to hearing from you.

I press send and close up the laptop.

I tidy away the pieces of newspaper from the unwrapping and put the vases on a display unit that sits beneath a spotlight in the corner of the room. They look superb and I feel a surge of disappointment that it will be impossible to keep them.

I sit back at the table and scroll through my photos. I zoom in to study the breathtaking intricacy. I tweak a couple of the pictures by re-adjusting the brightness. I crop a couple more hardly believing my luck to possess such fabulous works of art. I feel my phone vibrate in my pocket. I take the phone out and see a reply from Lenhams. They always respond within forty-eight hours but this can't have been more than forty-eight minutes.

Dear Mr Prendergast

Thank you for your email.

We would indeed be most interested in handling the sale of your beautiful vases for you.

I have forwarded your email to Matsuko Kimura in our Japanese Arts department and asked her to contact you.

I hear the front door opening.

"Hi, love," I shout.

I hear Sheila taking off her coat and shoes and I go into the hall to meet her.

"Hi," I say again. "Had a good time?"

"Not bad. What's up with you? You're grinning like a Cheshire Cat."

"Come and look," I say.

I step behind her and put my hands over her eyes. "I want this to be a surprise."

Sheila pushes my hands away. "You don't need to do that. I can keep my eyes closed."

I lead her through to the display unit, turn her to face it and say. "Okay. Look now."

Sheila opens her eyes. "So, these are what all the fuss has been about."

"What do you think?" I say.

"Well Dave, I have to say, they're very nice."

"Nice? They're not *nice* they're bloody incredible."

"That's what you say. How do I know?"

I go to the table and open the laptop and show her the Lenhams page. "Look," I say, "I showed you this before but have another look. They're identical."

"They aren't the same shape."

"I know. That's because I think they are part of a garniture of three."

"So what do you think they are worth?"

"I don't know, but that one was over ninety thousand

dollars so a pair has to be -what? A hundred and fifty thousand, at least."

"Pounds or dollars?"

"What does it matter? A hundred and fifty *thousand*"

Sheila smiles and looks at me. "So, you did it at last."

"Yeah," I say. "I knew I could do it one day. It was just a matter of time."

"And a matter of a hundred mistakes."

"These will make up for that, by a long, long way."

I hear the front door open again. Simon comes into the dining room still in his coat.

"Okay Dad. I got your message. Let's see them then."

I point them out glowing beneath the spotlight. Simon breathes in sharply and sucks whistling through his teeth. He shakes his head.

"Bloody hell Dad. These aren't just good. They're bloody fantastic." He pauses. "So how you going to square it with Maria then?"

Chapter Forty-Two

Maria

I get ready for my cinema date with Simon. I put on a black leather skirt. It shows my legs, but not too much of them – I can sit comfortably in it without it rising to my thighs. I try it with a smart white blouse with a frilled front. Although the blouse is modelled on a Ralph Lauren classic, I found it at Top Shop for less than thirty pounds. It looks good, but if Cineworld has the air conditioning on full I will have to sit in my coat all night.

I take off the blouse, put on a plain white camisole vest and a chunky white woolen jumper. The Internet described it as a *'chunky cable knit Nordic sweater - the essence of femininity and warmth'* and I think that it will be fine with anything Cineworld's air conditioning can blast at me.

I look in the mirror. Not bad, I think. I look on the Internet on my phone to see if I can find what to wear with the outfit. I Google 'chunky white sweater with black leather skirt' and click on the image results. Lots of photos come up and I scroll to one and click. It is a model called Karolina Kurkova and she is absolutely beautiful. She is wearing a skirt and jumper, like mine (but I guess with a hundred times the price tag) and she has worn them with a black coat and below-the-knee, black boots.

My choice is limited to just four pairs of shoes and one pair of boots but they *are* black boots and they *are* just under knee length. I have one coat. It is black. I put the coat and boots on and look in the mirror again. I am not Karolina Kurkova, but I feel happy as myself.

"Muchacha bonita?" I question the mirror. The mirror does not answer, but if it could it might say 'Muy guapa'

I take the coat and boots off and leave them on the bed while I go into the bathroom and finish my make up. I do not wear a lot of cosmetics but I want to get the lipstick right. Too deep red will make my lips stand out, but nude tones will have no impact at all. I choose coral and I am pleased with the look. I finish with a touch of mascara and a tiny dusting of blusher.

I take a free sample of Chanel perfume from the bathroom shelf. It was given to me at a high street store and I have been saving it for a special event like tonight. I put it in my handbag to use when I get to the bus stop.

I am early so I go back to the bedroom and sit on the bed. I take my phone out of my bag and look at the screen. I see that there is activity on the eBay app so I open the app and check what it is. There is a message from the buyer of the pans. *'Thank you for the super pans'* it says. *'It must have cost you a fortune to ship them. I will leave you great feedback.'*

I would have liked *'Thank you for the super pans. It must have cost you a fortune to ship them. Can I pay you some more?'* better, but good feedback is always good to have. I click on the feedback profile next to my user name. There are three extra feedbacks. They all give me five stars for everything. I read their comments.

'Fabulous pans. Great seller. Fantastic CHEAP shipping.'

'Super, sexy, silky. Thanks Muchachabonita – the dressing gown's nice too ☺*'*

'Lovely vases. Great seller. Thank you very much.'

I read that last one again and again. Martin's words come back to me. Have I been, as he put it, 'done'?

I click on Kinkozanfan's feedback. It tells me very little. He has not set up an 'About Me' page and I can see only that he joined in 2002. He has fifteen feedbacks and all are from sellers saying that he is a good eBayer and pays quickly. I try and find feedback that Kinkozanfan has left for sellers but only mine and one other show up as recent. I click on the other object that he bought. It is a Japanese vase. I look at the price. It was four hundred pounds. Maybe I have been 'done'. My vases were nicer and he paid just fifty pounds for two.

It's time to go, so I put my phone back into my bag, put my boots and coat back on and swing the handbag over my shoulder. I have a final check in the mirror and leave the flat. I get to the bus stop five minutes before my bus is due so I take the Chanel sample from my bag and dab the perfume on my neck and on my wrists.

I arrive at the cinema complex at seven-thirty and go into the foyer. I look for Simon but he has not arrived. The foyer is full of people queuing for tickets and each one takes forever to be served as the cashiers sell them popcorn, nachos, hot dogs and gigantic packets of sweets. I check the film times on the screens behind the cashiers. Our movie is on at 8.00 in 2D and there is a 3D screening in IMAX at 9.15. If Simon does not arrive soon we will be too late for the eight o'clock screening. I feel a tap on my back. I turn.

"Hope I've not kept you waiting, Maria."

"No. I have only been here for five minutes."

"Do you fancy eating first and catching the nine-fifteen screening?"

"Is it not too expensive?" I never go to the IMAX screenings as it costs about double the normal entry.

Simon smiles and holds his phone in front of me. "This will make up for it," he says. "I've been saving these for a special occasion."

I look at the screen. It's an email from Tesco with a list of fifty pounds worth of Clubcard codes to use at Pizza Express.

"Okay. I know. It's not exactly a candlelit supper but I love the American Hot and they do plenty of pastas and salads. What do you think? We'll only have to pay for the drinks."

I try to hide my opinion and show nothing in my face. He looks down into my eyes.

"Damn," he says. "I'm being a cheapskate aren't I?"

"I do not know a 'cheapskate'."

"Well you know one now," he smiles. "A bit stingy."

"Stingy?"

"Okay. I think you would say 'agarrado' or maybe 'tacaño'."

I smile. "No. You are not tacaño. You are 'sensato'."

"Sensible, but not very romantic, I suppose."

"Romance won't pay for the movie," I say. "Pizza Express will be good."

"Great," Simon starts to tap into his phone. "I'll book the nine-fifteen showing."

He chooses the seats on his phone, taps in the payment and a few seconds later he shows me the screen.

"There," he says, "Two seats. E-tickets. No need to queue for ages behind all those hot dog and coke-guzzling lard-arses"

"Lard-arses?"

"I think the exact translation would be 'manteca culo'. But let's just say large posteriors."

"Your Spanish is good Simon. You know 'manteca culo' 'agarrado' and 'tacaño'. It suprises me that you did not know the meaning of 'muchacha bonita'."

Simon holds up his hands. He smiles "It's a fair cop,Maria. You got me. Now what's the Spanish for—"

I interrupt "Tonteando?"

"Flirting?"

I nod.

He laughs. "Well at least my *frase para ligar* or chat up line did the trick."

He takes my arm, gently and leads me towards the exit doors. We leave the cinema and walk around the plaza of fast food restaurants and back onto the High St. We can see Pizza Express across the busy road. It starts to rain so we run the final few metres to the door, dodging between the slowly moving traffic. It is a buzzing restaurant but the waiter is with us quickly. At Casa Nuestra we like to seat our most attractive clients where they are seen so that people think it is a restaurant for cool people so I feel very good when he shows us to a table in the window.

I feel my face colouring.

"Are you okay?" Simon says.

"Sure," I say. Simon helps me take off my coat and holds my chair while I sit. He takes off his leather jacket. He takes both to a coat stand by the door and hangs the up before returning and taking his seat

"They usually hide me in the back by the kitchen," he laughs as he sits.

I am a little surprised by this as Simon certainly does not have 'by the kitchen' looks. I decide not to talk about how we do things at Casa Nuestra. It is possible that Pizza Express do things differently but I look at Simon and I look around the tables and I think that maybe we are the hottest couple in the place.

"I love your jumper" he says, "and your skirt. You look great. You smell fabulous too."

I feel my face reddening again. I brush back my hair from my cheek and stare at the menu.

"Sorry. Am I being a bit forward? It can be confusing for men nowadays."

"Not at all. You look good too."

We both look at our menus. We decide to share a starter and Simon picks his American Hot Romana pizza and I go for the low-calorie Leggera option.

"I don't want to be too forward again but you really don't need to count the calories, Maria."

"I do not need to count the calories because I do count the calories. If you understand what I mean."

He smiles again. "I certainly understand. I understand everything you say. Your English is really good. When I first read your eBay listing for your flower pots I thought you might not be very fluent."

"There are plenty of words I do not know, so I use Google. I am pleased that you mention the frog pots. I gave them to the buyer today."

"What was he like?"

"An old guy called Dave. I actually knew him. I have seen him at my gym before. He seems to be a nice guy."

"Did he like the vases?"

"He didn't look at them when I was there but he left good feedback. Are you still unhappy that you did not buy them?"

"No. Water under the bridge now."

"No comprendo."

"Sorry. It's in the past. I am sure that the buyer will be pleased with them. Anyway, I've decided to give up on my frog collecting now. It's all going to the charity shop next week. That period of my life is over. It's a bit of an odd obsession for a bloke of my age isn't it?"

"If you say so, but..." I pause, "a man at the gym he tells me that Kinkozanfan has robbed me."

"What man? How has he robbed you?"

"The guy is called Martin. He is about sixty but likes to think that he is a young man. He makes sexy comments to the women and looks at their bodies when he thinks we do not see him."

"A bit of lech then."

"In Spanish we say viejo verde. He is quite handsome and slim and fit and some of the older women seem to like him and answer him with more sexy comments."

"Like I said before, I don't approve but it *can* be a bit confusing for us blokes sometimes. Mixed messages and all that. So how has this Dave robbed you? He paid what you asked didn't he?"

"Martin said that the frog vases are worth thousands and thousands of pounds. I am sure that he is wrong but he said that he knows Kinkozanfam's wife and she told him that her husband had spotted some very rare Japanese pots on eBay."

Simon pushes his lips to one side and screws up his face. He lets out a breath slowly and shakes his head.

"I'd just forget it if I were you, Maria. You sold them for a price you were happy with. Even if they were worth a fortune, he's not done anything illegal."

"Not illegal. But sneaky, maybe."

"He doesn't know you, Maria. If he is an expert on Satsuma then he's been lucky and okay it would have been lovely if he had said 'Hey, Maria. Those vases are very, very valuable and I'm going to sell them and give you half of what I get' but, let's face it, how many people would? Would you? Would your friends?"

I think for a moment. "I know that Margarita would say 'no way Jose' but me? I am not sure."

Our food arrives and we start to eat.

We do not speak again about the vases. We talk about work; we talk about girlfriends; we talk about boyfriends; we talk about Spain; we talk about cooking; we talk about everything. We are still talking when Simon checks his watch and says "Christ. We're going to miss the film."

He jumps up and goes to the coat stand and collects our coats. The waiter hurries across with our bill and Simon pays with his phone codes and cash for the drinks. I notice that he gives the waiter a very generous tip.

Simon helps me into my coat before putting on his jacket and opening the door for me.

"Hope you're okay with me opening the door," he says with a smile.

It is dark and wet as we again weave between the slow traffic and cross the road to the plaza. Simon holds my hand as we run around the plaza and back to the cinema. His steps are longer than mine but he slows so that I can run by his side. We reach Cineworld and rush to the IMAX screen queue. Simon holds up his phone and the attendant scans his e-tickets and hands us our special glasses. We go into the screen. The dark is lit up with a hundred mobile phones glowing into their users' faces. Simon holds his glowing screen downwards and uses it to inspect the row numbers. We find our seats and settle into them.

"Just in time," Simon says. "Only twenty minutes of adverts and we can enjoy the film."

Chapter Forty-Three

Dave

I am struggling to sleep. I've had variations of the skeletal señora and the frog dream constantly. Only, now that I have the vases, the frogs have taken on the characters of wizened, Japanese men who wink and leer at me as I hold them.

Simon's question 'How you going to square it with Maria?' is constantly echoing in my thoughts. I was in bed when he came home from his night out with her. I heard him climbing the stairs and clunking around in the bathroom very late. I wanted to get up and talk to him, but I didn't know if she was with him. I'm pretty sure he was alone but some of his girlfriends have had the stealth of cats, and I've given three of them quite a fright when I've walked unawares down the landing in only my Y-fronts while they were on their way to the bathroom. Simon accused me of doing that on purpose but why on earth would I want to subject my potbelly and sagging buttocks to the ridicule of nubile, young women whose reactions were more likely to be 'yuck' than 'buck'? Any chance Simon had of another rhyme on those nights disappeared as quickly as their dashes to the night bus.

As dawn breaks, I shuffle bleary-eyed into the en-suite and perform my daily ritual of pee, shave and shower. I put on my dressing gown and walk along the landing. I hear Simon showering in the bathroom. His bedroom door is open so I peek inside. It's obvious that he's spent the night alone.

I go downstairs and start to make some tea and toast. I don't make anything for Sheila. She's still fast asleep and oblivious to my night of tossing and turning. I sit at the dining table and open up the MacBook. I check my emails. The inbox fills with the usual daily pile of sales promotions that I must somehow have unwittingly signed up for.

Simon comes downstairs. I didn't think it was his fortnightly shave day but he looks smarter than usual and seems to have more of a bounce in his step.

"Morning Dad."

"Morning, son. How did last night go? You didn't bring Maria back here."

"How could I bring her back here? She might have seen you."

"I told you there'd be no more night time Y-front trips to the fridge."

"I'm not talking about that - I don't ever want to talk about that. I don't ever want to *think* about that." He grimaces. "Remember she's seen you. She doesn't know we're related. And it's a good job too. Martin Hetherington told her you'd robbed her."

"Martin Hetherington? How could he have the temerity to call *me* a robber? Cheeky bastard. When I went to collect the vases, Djimi at the gym told me he's still going to classes. You should have heard what he told them all about my hospital trip. Talk about Hans Christian Andersen! "

"He's definitely still going. Maria saw him at her class yesterday. He's out on bail."

"Phew. That was lucky for me then. I must have only missed him by a few minutes. Well, I won't be seeing him again. I think my gym days are numbered... Why didn't you stay at her place?"

"If you must have all the details, Dad, we went to Pizza Express and then we went to Cineworld to see the new X-Men movie and then I took her home on the bus."

"The age of chivalry is not dead then. Hardly likely to sweep her off her feet though. Pizza and X-Men is not quite a sunset cruise down the Thames with a candlelit dinner and string quartet. I hope you didn't pay with Tesco vouchers."

"I'm a teacher, not Lord bloody Rothschild. I paid for everything mind."

"You did, didn't you?"

"What?"

"Tesco vouchers."

"Leave it Dad."

"Did she ask you in for coffee?"

"Yes."

"And?"

"I went in and she made coffee."

"And?"

"I drank my coffee, washed up my mug, kissed her on the cheek and came home."

"You're losing your touch then."

"I'm not losing any touch. Maria's not a one-night stand. She's not that sort of woman. And I'm not sure that I'm that sort of guy."

"I beg to differ. That's not what nights of clanging bedposts tell me."

"That's in the past. There'll be no more clanging bedposts in this house."

"Tell me about it," I say.

"Seriously, Dad. You need to think about things with Maria and those vases."

"Do you think I haven't been thinking about it? I've not slept a wink worrying about doing the right thing. What if I go and speak to her and you never see her again."

"To be honest, Dad, my relationship with her doesn't affect the morality of the situation. She might be an extremely gorgeous, young Spanish cook but she could equally be a foul hag. Whoever she is, you've knowingly paid an ignorant and innocent party a fraction of what those vases are worth. I've always respected you and I always will, because you're the one person I know who always takes the honest option."

I sigh. "Honest Dave. I've always been 'Honest Dave'. Why couldn't I be 'quite honest, but not honest enough to throw away a fortune Dave?'"

Simon smiles. "Because that's not who you are, Dad."

I continue, "By the way. She might know my name. I said I was Dave but she might have heard Djimi at the gym call me Mr Prendergast. Does she know yours? There aren't that many Prendergasts around here. What are the odds on two being the only ones interested in her vases?"

"I'm not going to lie to her, but funnily enough we haven't got around to surnames yet."

"Okay, son. I won't let you down. I've got to talk to your mum about it. Don't say anything to Maria. You haven't said anything have you?" Simon shakes his head.

"Good. I'll speak to you when you get home from work."

Simon takes a couple of slices of toast and holds them between his teeth as he goes into the hall and puts his shoes and coat on. "Okay Dad," he mumbles through the toast, "I knew I could rely on you."

Chapter Forty-Four

Dave

I've got a quiet day ahead. After the excitement of the last week there's nothing pressing; just a bit of shopping to do later at Waitrose. After Simon leaves I go upstairs to check on Sheila's plans for the day and to talk to her about my conversation with Simon.

She's still in bed.

"Morning," I say. "Want anything for breakfast?"

She stretches and yawns. "I'll get something when I'm out."

"Where are you going?"

"You know where I am going.

"Do I?"

"Well, I've told you half a dozen times."

"Have you? I'm sorry. My memory's like a sieve at the moment."

"Either that or you haven't been wearing your hearing aids or, more likely, you haven't been listening to a word I've been saying...as always."

I mumble, "Sorry, love. Promise I'll wear them all the time."

Maybe they *are* invisible. I *have* been wearing them all the time.

"Okay. Just one last time. Where are you going?" I ask.

She sighs. It's a long sigh and it's accompanied by a shake of the head.

"The hairdressers. I should be able to afford the full works this time now that we're going to have a bit of money. I might ask them to do a manicure too."

"That would be nice. As you mentioned it, can we talk about the money?"

"You've been telling me we'll be coming into a hundred grand all week. Don't tell me we're not."

"It's not that. It's just—"

"It's just what?"

"It's just that I've been talking to Simon, and he's been questioning my ethics in taking the vases."

"You didn't *take* them. You bought them at a price someone asked for them. She wouldn't have a leg to stand on if it came to court. But Simon's right, in a way. I told him that you'd always do the right thing."

"So, what is the right thing in this?"

"Well...there are a number of options."

'Such as?"

"You find this Maria; take the vases back to her; ask for your fifty quid back and tell her what they really are."

"That's a bit steep. There's honest and there's bloody stupid."

"Okay. Option two. You get in touch with Maria. You tell her what the vases are, and you offer to keep one and give her the other back."

"You must be joking. They're a pair. I'm not splitting them up."

"Fair enough. Option three. You get in touch with her; you tell her what the vases are; you tell her you're selling them at Lenhams and you'll give her half the proceeds after fees."

A wave of relief washes over me, "Are you sure?"

'I'm sure. If Simon says it's the right thing to do, it's the right thing to do."

"What about Simon though? I think he's quite smitten with her. If she thinks anything sneaky has been going on it could ruin his chances."

"Well, there's nothing more certain than the saying *truth will out*. So the sooner the truth is out there the better the chances of him keeping his girlfriend."

"Okay. I'll try and get in touch with her later. I don't want to go to the gym in case Martin turns up and I don't know if she's working at Casa Nuestra today. I'll probably send her a message via eBay."

I leave Sheila to get up and ready to go for her hair appointment. I go downstairs, make her a cup of tea and take it up to her. I go back down and pass the time getting on top of an ironing backlog. As I get to the final sheet, - I hate the sheets so they are always the last - Sheila comes into the dining room. She's got her coat on and she's ready to go.

"Want a lift?" I ask.

"No. I've got plenty of time. I'll walk."

"Okay. Enjoy it. Make sure you get that manicure and, if they've got someone available, get a pedicure done too."

"I will," she says. She comes over to me at the ironing board and gives me a peck on the cheek. "Have a good day."

I think how good she's looking as she leaves. She'll look even better when she gets home. I'm lucky that she puts up with me. I've got to get my act together or I'll be spending my retirement on my own.

I put away the ironing board and drain the water from the iron. I leave it to cool on the drainer and take all the ironing upstairs and distribute it to the right wardrobes and cupboards. As I'm hanging the last shirt I hear the doorbell ring.

I go into the front bedroom and pull the net - voile Sheila would say - curtain to one side. I see a familiar face looking up at me and wonder what on earth they might want.

"DC MacIntosh. I wasn't expecting you," I say as I open the door. "Come in."

"I was in the area and thought I'd come and have a quick word with you. Let you know how we're getting on with the case. Or *not* getting on with the case, as it turns out."

I show her into the lounge and ask her if she would like a cup of tea. She nods, takes off her coat and sits down on one of the sofas. I go into the kitchen to make us both tea.

"Nice place," she shouts through to me. "Been here long?"

"Longer than I care to think about," I shout back. "We've been married nearly forty years and we've been here most of the time."

It's not been long since the kettle last boiled so the tea

is ready quickly. I ask her how she takes it, add the necessary and bring it through to her. She's standing now and inspecting our photos and accumulated knick-knacks.

"Your kids?" she asks.

"Yes. Simon and Susie. Susie's got two of her own now. Simon's still with us, as I think you already know." I gesture to her to take her tea. She takes it and sits back down on the sofa. I sit on the other sofa and put my tea down on the coffee table. She leans forward and puts her cup and saucer alongside mine.

"So," I say. "Things aren't going too well."

"Nah. We're struggling a bit. No way of finding those African laddies to testify about the bags so we've just got eighteen distraught women and very little else to go on."

"Surely eighteen women is plenty?"

"Aye. It would be if any of them had ever met him. If any of them had ever spoken to him even."

"What about his computers?"

"Clean as a whistle. Not a thing on any of them. A bit of a porn habit but show me a computer that hasn't got a trace of porn on it."

"So. What *have* you got on him then?"

"Well there's your evidence about the bag that ended up with you and, at the moment, that's about it."

"What about his identities on Match.com?"

"He's wiped all those. We can go to the website and ask for the historic information but our IT guys think it's not going to get us anywhere. They reckon he'll have been using software that hides every keystroke, he'll have been using it from an insecure wireless hot spot and whatever laptop he's been using will be as hard to find as Lord Lucan."

"What about Angela? Did you get anywhere with her?"

"Angela? Who's she?"

I hesitate. It's not up to me to report a crime on Angela Clemence's behalf. She may not want the hassle of court. She may not want the embarrassment. She may not have lost any money.

"No-one," I say. "Just someone I know. Thought she might have been in touch with you."

"If you know something. You need to tell me. This guy needs to be punished. He's a menace. Tell me about Angela. Who is she?"

"I can't tell you, but look, I will speak to her and try and find out more."

"I don't want you withholding any information. We need everything we can get."

"Give me twenty-four hours. If don't get anywhere I will phone you and tell you more but I don't want to get someone involved in a police investigation unless I'm sure of my facts."

"Twenty-four hours. Nae more than that."

"I promise. Nae more than that."

My attempt at bringing in a bit of humour merely brings me a withering look.

MacIntosh drains her cup. She stands and puts on her coat. I show her back to the door. I open it and she steps outside. She turns to me on the step. She's still buttoning her coat. "Twenty-four hours."

"I'm on to it right away, officer."

And I am onto it straight away. As soon as I shut the front door I look for the telephone book in the drawer beneath the hall table where the landline telephone sits. You need a degree in logic to find your way around the thing and I wonder how we managed in the days of hefty Yellow Pages, Local Directories and enormous phone books. I put the directory back where I got it from and go to the laptop. I can power it up and find the clinic's number in half the time it takes to find it in a book.

I dial the clinic.

"Is Angela Clemence available?"

"Mrs Clemence has a patient with her right now. Can I leave her a message?"

I leave my number and it's not long before I get a call back. I tell Angela I need to talk to her and we arrange to meet when she finishes at 3 p.m.

Chapter Forty-Five

Dave

We arranged to meet at a Costa that's a few miles from home so I decide to walk and get a bit of exercise. Mrs Clemence is already there when I arrive. She's got a seat in the window and she waves to me as she sees me peer in.

I go inside and walk across to her table.

"What can I get you?" I ask.

"Just a cup of Earl Grey for me."

"Nothing to eat?"

She shakes her head.

I go to the counter. I order and pay for our drinks and bring them back to the window table.

I give Angela her tea and put mine down on the table. I take off my coat, put it over the back of my chair and sit down.

"I'm sorry to drag you here on a cold afternoon," I say "but you'll remember our last conversation."

"Remember it? I'm not likely to forget that conversation in a hurry."

I smile thinly. "No. I suppose you're not. I was really sorry to be a bearer of bad news."

"You did me a huge favour. Saved me a lot of money."

"Ahh..." I lean back in my seat. I tilt my head back and then nod. "So you *didn't* give him any money."

"I didn't say that. I gave him *some* money but it was only peanuts compared to the cheque I'd just written him."

"You gave him a cheque? You don't see many cheques nowadays. It's all bank transfers and anonymous stuff like Western Union."

"I know. I sent seven hundred and fifty at first."

I splutter into my tea. "Seven hundred and fifty! You said peanuts."

"Let me finish. I sent seven hundred and fifty at first by Western Union. That was his choice. But then Brian's words about tracing payments by cheque came into my mind for some reason—"

"Brian?"

"Sorry. Brian was my husband. I lost him five years ago. Brain tumour. Nothing they could do for him. This guy, whoever he is, was my first foray into the world of dating since Brian died."

Tears start to well up in her eyes and trickle slowly down her cheeks. I put my hand on top of hers by way of comfort.

"I'm so sorry, Angela. Men aren't all bastards you know."

She takes her hands from beneath mine and clasps mine firmly. We've got our elbows on the table. Any onlooker might think we're holding a prayer session as she stares into my eyes. Her gaze is strong and I find myself returning it.

"I know," she says. "But this guy sure is."

"So why didn't you report him to the police?"

"How do you know I didn't?"

I take my hands away from hers now and sip my drink. I explain how I have been helping the police with their enquiries and how they haven't got a great deal to go on.

"I don't want to get involved," she says. "What will my kids think of their stupid mother getting ripped off by a romantic conman? What if all my emails are read out in court? I see patients at the clinic every day. They'll be sniggering behind their hands at some of the things I wrote. And the nurses will be worse. I dread to think of the jokes they will come up with."

"You said you didn't lose much. Seven hundred and fifty pounds sounds like a lot of money to me and anyway victims in these cases can sometimes be granted anonymity." I'm not sure of my grounds on that but I really want to see Martin put away. "How much was the cheque you stopped for?" I pause. "If you don't mind me asking."

"Twenty thousand."

I splutter into my tea again. I put my mug down on the table with such force that drops of tea speckle my glasses. I take off the glasses and wipe them with one of the paper napkins that came with the drinks.

"Twenty *thousand* pounds." I find myself whistling and shaking my head. "How did he almost take that from you?"

"We'd been chatting by email via the website for months. I really felt that we were building up a relationship. He was a real gentleman. He seemed interested in everything I said."

"He laughed at all of your jokes. Your love he didn't need to coax!"

She smiles at my *Maggie May* reference.

"That's the way it was. After five years on my own there was suddenly this presence in my life. Loving. Caring. Interested in me. Interested in my career. Interested in Brian. Especially interested in Brian. Oh yes. He wrote email after email about Brian. He must have researched him. It was almost as if he knew him. And then he hit me with the seven hundred and fifty."

"So what was the excuse?"

"He'd been diagnosed with a brain tumour. There was only one hospital with the expertise to operate on this particular tumour. It was in LA and he needed the money towards the cost of flying there. He said he could cover his hotel for a few weeks while they carried out tests to see if they would be able to operate but he was short of the airfare."

"I get it. So two weeks later you got the good news email that he had had all the tests and he could be saved but the medical bills would be twenty thousand. You don't get much treatment for twenty thousand in America."

"I know. He said that the bills would actually be close to a quarter of a million but the twenty thousand would cover him until some investments matured and he would then pay me back and pay for the rest himself. I'd lost the love of my life through a brain tumour. How could I lose another? I couldn't live with myself. Brian had enormous life insurance policies and those, plus our shares in his company, left me set up for life. I could afford it. I could easily have given him the full quarter of a million and, you never know, I might have done so if you hadn't spotted that bag. I just couldn't let Damian Proudfoot be another victim."

"Damian Proudfoot? So that's what he called himself this time. So that's when I came into it. My dodgy waterworks saved you a fortune." I smile.

"Yes. And, do you know, that was the only time I ever took that handbag to work with me?"

"Blimey. You deserved a bit of luck though. I realise that you say that you don't want police involved but if it helped to put Martin Hetherington behind bars and perhaps even got some money back for some vulnerable women who maybe couldn't afford to lose the money he took from them, would you at least think about it?"

"Martin Hetherington? Is that who he is? How do you know? How are you involved?"

"It's a long story and I'm not going into it now but at the moment the police need every scrap of information they can get and a cheque might just be the start of a paper trail that leads them to catch him. How did you get the cheque to him?"

"He sent a motorcycle courier. Told me that time was short. He couldn't wait for the post."

"Did you get the details of the courier?"

"I certainly did. I got a receipt from his company *and* I took details of his bike."

"Brilliant. It's a pity that the stopped cheque will have gone back to him. There might have been some fingerprints."

"But it didn't go back to him."

"How come? I used to work in a bank. That's the way it works. You stop a cheque and they send it back to the bank it was paid in at, and they return it to the customer."

"Not this time. I'm on good terms with my manager Henry. I've known him for years. Brian owned a very big and very successful business. Henry used to invite us to hospitality events; Wimbledon, Ascot, you know the sort of thing. I told him there might possibly be some investigation so I asked him to help me with it."

"Did *you* never work for the business?"

"No. Brian always wanted me to but I liked the independence of having my own career. I never needed to work. I still don't but I enjoy it."

'So what did Henry do to help?"

"Firstly, he arranged for the payment to be stopped. He notified his fraud department and they contacted Damien's bank's fraud department. *They* cancelled the credit on Damien's account and wrote to him asking him to contact the bank immediately and telling him they would hold the stopped cheque at his branch for him to collect. He didn't collect it and I believe that it's now somewhere safe in a sealed plastic bag in case the police become involved and it's needed as evidence."

I'm amazed at her foresight. "Fantastic. You may well have enough to get MacIntosh back on course."

"MacIntosh? That's the DC you told me to contact isn't it? I wrote the details down after we spoke but I just couldn't bring myself round to getting in touch."

"Would you mind if I tell MacIntosh what happened to you? It really could help a lot of women."

"How many?"

"I don't know, but at least eighteen at the last count."

"Okay. Give MacIntosh my card." She hands me a calling card. It reads simply

'Angela Clemence' together with email and home addresses a landline number and a mobile.

"I will," I say.

Angela delves into her handbag and takes out a small compact mirror. She looks at herself in it.

"Look at the state of me" she says inspecting the thin black streaks that stain her cheeks. She takes a small packet of wipes from her bag, opens it and uses one to clean her face. She looks out of the window.

"Luckily the sun's shining," she says. She puts the mirror and packet of wipes back into her handbag and takes out a thick, black glasses case. She opens it and takes out an elegant pair of sunglasses. Sitting with someone so glamorous and chic gives podgy, out-of-condition, me, something of an ego boost.

"Thanks for seeing me, Angela. And thanks for letting me give DC MacIntosh your details."

"Tell him that Thursdays are best for me."

"It's her," I say.

"That's good. Why do we always jump to those conclusions? Exactly the same happens at the clinic."

She stands up. I stand up and help her with her coat. She leans across towards me and kisses me on each cheek.

"Thank you, Dave. It was good to talk. You know. You're the only person I've told about this. Don't speak to anyone else will you?"

I put my finger to my lips. "My lips are sealed."

Angela puts on her sunglasses. We leave the coffee shop and I give her a small wave as she heads off along the crowded pavement.

The tea is beginning to take its effect on me. I don't want to take a chance on making it all the way home so I step back inside Costa. I look for the toilets. I can't see any so I ask at the counter. I'm directed downstairs.

"You need the code. It's on your bill," the cashier tells me. I root in my coat pocket and find the bill. I see the code on the bottom.

The tea only started to take effect on my bladder a minute earlier but I'm experiencing urgency again as I reach the foot of the stairs. The loo is straight ahead and there's a pin code keypad alongside the door. I key in the code with one hand whilst unbuttoning my coat with the other. The door springs open and I make it but it's a close shave. The doctor told me to cut back on tea, so *what* do I pick off the menu? Duh. As I sit, I notice an advert on the back of the door. It's a photo of a male torso and thighs wearing a smart pair of white underpants. The picture is emblazoned with the words 'Perfectly Engineered'. His body certainly appears perfectly engineered. I wonder if the old guy from the changing room has branched out into modeling. He looks like he's wearing one of Henry VIII's codpieces. Beneath the photo is a blurb exhorting me to be drier and more confident with Tena Men.

Jasper Carrot used to say that you knew you were getting old when you found yourself looking in the window of Dunn & Co and thinking 'Hmm. Nice cardie.' I'm sitting on the loo looking at an ad for Tena Men thinking. 'Hmm. That might not be such a bad idea.'

Chapter Forty-Six

Dave

As I leave the toilet, my mobile rings. It's an unknown number. I answer "Hello."

A very quiet female voice replies, "Is this Mr Prendergast?"

"Yes."

"Good afternoon, Mr Prendergast. This is Matsuko Kimura from the Japanese Arts department at Lenhams."

"Good afternoon, Ms Kimura. Thank you for calling."

"I wanted to speak about your vases. They are very exciting. I would very much like to handle their sale for you. I think that I can offer you a very competitive commission and an excellent catalogue entry. We are having a very fine Japanese sale in four months. The vases would look perfect on the catalogue cover and, if you can get them to me here in London in the next week or so, we should be able to make the deadline."

The cover of a sale like this is something that an antiques collector can only dream about. It's like a model getting the front cover of *Vogue,* a fisherman and his fish landing the front of *Angling Times* or an author getting a mention in *The London Review Of Books*.

"That would be wonderful," I say. "I'm out at the moment but when I get home I'll check the calendar and see when I can get to you."

"Fine. Thank you, Mr Prendergast. I look forward to meeting you soon."

On my walk home I phone DC MacIntosh and outline my conversation with Angela. She is delighted that I've given her a fresh lead and tells me that she will be following it up straight away. I give her all the details on Angela's card. "Go easy on her," I add, "She's been through the mill."

MacIntosh reassures me that Mrs Clemence will be treated with the utmost sympathy. I phone Angela and tell her to expect a call from MacIntosh to set up a meeting on Thursday.

It's getting late when I finally get home.

"Hello," I shout as I open the front door. "Are you back?"

There's no reply. I step inside the hall, take off my coat and hang it on a coat hook. I take off my shoes and leave them on the mat. I walk into the dining room. Sheila's handbag is on the table.

"Hello," I shout and again, there's no reply.

I walk upstairs. I open the bedroom door and walk in. It's dark but I can sense Sheila's presence. "Sheila? You alright?"

Something flies past my ear. I put my hands over my head and crouch down as another missile misses me narrowly and hits the wall behind me with a muffled thud. I switch on the light.

Sheila's sitting on the bed. I see from the indentations that she has been lying down. She grabs another cushion and flings it at me. I look at her and see her cheeks streaked with mascara. Two mascara streaked faces in one day. It's too much for a bloke to handle.

"Your hair looks nice," I say ducking a pillow, "and your nails....Lovely colour."

"Bastard!" Sheila screeches between sobs. "Don't you try buttering me up. Where have you been? No. Don't tell me. I'll tell you. You've been to Costa Coffee staring into the eyes of a glamorous woman. Is she what you'd call a MILF? No. A bit classier than that. High class escort? I get to spend the money on my hair and you - *you* -you're spending it on - on - on. I don't even want to *say* what you're spending it on. Is *she* why you've suddenly found an interest in the gym? Is *she* why you've started looking at yourself in the mirror? Where did you meet her? *Who is she?* I saw the way you were staring into her eyes and holding her hands. Your case is packed." She points to a suitcase at the foot of the bed. "Take it and get out".

"But. Sheila. There's—"

"No buts. There's the case. I said take it and get out."

There's little point in arguing with Sheila when she's like this. I take the case and go downstairs with it. I put on my coat and open and close the front door. Then I take my coat back off and go into the lounge and sit down. I need to sit this storm out. And I *really* need to think about that eye contact with Angela.

Chapter Forty-Seven

Dave

I'm still sitting in the lounge when Simon gets home.

"What you doing sitting in the dark? What's happened to *Pointless?* Don't tell me the TV broke. There's a match on tonight. Where's Mum? And why's there a suitcase in the hall?"

I point upstairs and then put my finger to my lips.

"There's been a bit of a misunderstanding with your mum. A bit of a falling out."

"Not again. This is becoming a bit of a regular thing. At least your glasses are in one piece this time. So what's happened now"

I explain the events in full to Simon. I don't tell him about the feelings I had when I gazed into Angela's eyes. I know it was *that* gaze and our entwined hands that Sheila saw and I know that, whilst my meeting was entirely innocent, at that moment there was something - some sort of frisson - on my side at least. I feel guilty and, as it says somewhere in the bible, 'anyone who even *looks* at a woman with lust has already committed adultery.' Maybe Sheila's got me bang to rights.

"Don't worry, Dad. I'll sort it with Mum. I'll explain everything and she'll have you back. But tell me one thing."

"What?"

"How are things between you - you know - in the bedroom department? Don't think I missed your line about the clanging headboard."

"It was bedposts. Headboards don't clang."

"You know what I mean. Is everything okay?"

"We've been married forty years. It can't be sexy every minute."

"No, but it can't be miserable every minute either."

"It's not. Anyway, that side of things is private. We have some good times together."

"Like when."

I hesitate. I think. I hesitate a bit more. "Like watching *Pointless* together."

"That's hardly Romeo and Juliet. Do you think 'The number of times Dave and Sheila Prendergast have made love this year' would be a pointless answer?"

"Like I said. There are some things that are private between your mum and me. I'm not going there. Maybe the conditions in this household are not always conducive to nights of passion."

Simon's face falls.

"Are you blaming me? Am I in the way? Is it me who's a cuckoo in the love nest? Look, Dad I'll try and get my own place as soon as I can afford it. The job's going well and I could be offered department head next term. I don't want to be a marriage wrecker."

I look at Simon. Poor kid. I know he's a man but he'll always be a kid to me. He'll always be the bouncy individual who'd find the only puddle in a desert to fall in, let out the noisiest ever fart at an ancient relative's funeral or quiver with excitement when the latest Transformers toy hit the shops.

"We love you very much, son. Your mum loves having you here."

"But you don't?"

"No. Of course you're welcome here. It's just different from when you were away at uni. You can stay as long as you want. Anyway, when we sell the vases, perhaps we can give you a leg up to find your own place."

"That would be good. So? Did you talk to Mum about the vases?"

I nod. "Yes. I spoke to your mum and she's fine. She's fine with me doing the right thing. She told me to contact Maria but I wanted to wait until I'd spoken to you."

"Don't do anything just yet. I'm going to go upstairs and talk to Mum. We'll talk about what's best to do later."

Simon goes upstairs and I can hear a muffled conversation being held in the bedroom. I switch the TV on. I don't want to hear what's being said. Simon's gone for at least half an hour. When he comes back downstairs he's changed from his school clothes into a pair of jeans and a polo shirt. He sits beside me on the sofa.

We're half-watching some guys in a vintage car driving around to antiques centres and buying antiques to sell later at an auction. It's a bit like me going down to News & Booze, buying some beans and trying to sell them back to Heinz at a profit.

"She'll be down in a few minutes," he says. "I can make myself scarce if you want to try and patch things up."

"No. You stay. We've got to sort out this business with Maria. Are you seeing her tonight?"

Simon shakes his head. "Nah. She's working and she won't be finishing until after midnight. I may get the chance to see her later in the week. Gives us time to sort out this money business."

Sheila comes into the room. She looks at me witheringly.

"So you didn't go then. You never do what I ask, do you?"

"I tried to tell you. It was all entirely innocent."

"Not the way I saw things. How long have I known you Dave? I know you and your expressions inside out. I know when you're not listening, I know when you're bored, I know when you're sad, I know when you're tired and I certainly know when you are mesmerized. Don't come over all the *I was just helping the police with their enquiries* with me. Talk about *take me to bed* eyes. Those where *take me here on the bloody table* eyes."

I try to change the subject. I can't think of what to say. I feel myself blushing.

"See, Simon your dad's gone all *no comment*. There's nothing that condemns a man more in those police interviews than *no comment*. Every *no comment* means guilty as charged."

"I didn't say *no comment*."

"Tell me you don't fancy her then."

"I don't fancy her." I'm looking at the floor.

"Look at me when I'm talking to you. Tell me you don't fancy her."

I look straight into Sheila's eyes. "I...do...not...fancy... her. There. I've said it."

"You've said it but I don't know if you've meant it."

Simon stands up.

"Look you two," he says, "It's beginning to feel like a RELATE session in here. What are we having for tea? I'll go and make it."

Chapter Forty-Eight

Maria

I am at home in the bedsit. I think about the past few days and how life has suddenly changed and become more exciting – more interesting.

I had such a good night with Simon. The movie was great and the IMAX effects were fantastic. My head was still throbbing with explosions as we left the cinema and while we were on the bus home.

I invited him in and we had coffee but that was all that happened. Even though my bed is in my sitting room he made no attempt to guide me towards it. He treated the bed as if it was invisible and sat down on the sofa while we chatted about the movie. I would not normally go to see a superhero film, but with my own tall superhero with me, I was happy. Maybe next time I will choose what we see...if there is a next time.

We did not set a time or place to meet again and he did not contact me at all yesterday. He knew that I was working late and I was at work when he left school but I had hoped for a text or even a quick call. Maybe he does not find me attractive - although the kiss he gave me at the bus stop after our coffee morning did not leave that impression. He did not kiss me like that here in the bedsit. Perhaps he worried about being in my bedroom. He does not know me well yet. Could he be like the old fashioned English gentleman I heard so much about when I was a kid? If he is, he will be the first I have met.

I wonder if Margarita would have done things differently. Would she have said "Oh. It is so hot in here." and taken off her sweater? Or would she have clumsily spilt water in his lap and offered to pat it dry with a towel? No. Margarita would not do anything like that but I do think that if she had invited him here for coffee Simon would have enjoyed much more than coffee. I gave him a Hobnob.

I think it is time to forget the vases. If Simon and I do keep dating and if one day we even fall in love, the vases will have brought us together and more than paid me back.

It is almost time to get ready for work when my cell phone rings.

"Hola Bonita."

"Hi Simon. I was thinking about you."

"Good thoughts I hope."

"Sure."

"Not *too* good though?"

I laugh, "No. They were a little bit bad."

"Sounds good. Tell me more."

"Not now. I have to get ready for work."

"What time do you finish tonight?"

"Midnight. Why?"

"I've got something I need to talk to you about."

"That sounds very mysterious. What do you need to talk to me about?"

"I'd rather tell you face to face. It's something quite important."

"I am worried now. What is so important that you cannot tell me on the phone?"

"It's something good. I promise. It's something that will make you happy. At least I hope it will."

I feel agitated. Is he going to take out a ring, go down on one knee and propose?

"I do not like surprises," I say.

"Okay. I'll give you a clue. *Ribbit ribbit.*"

"*Ribbit ribbit*? I have no idea what you are saying."

"Well, you'll have to keep guessing. When and where can we meet?"

"I think that coffee on Saturday again will be best."

"Same time? Same place?"

"Sure. I will be asking everyone at work about *ribbit ribbit*."

Simon laughs.

"Adios Bonita," he says, "te veo el sábado.'

"Adios Tonto. Goodbye silly."

Chapter Forty-Nine

Maria

On Saturday morning, I arrive at Le Petit Pain and find that Simon is already there. He has chosen a sofa at the far end of the café away from the street and the bar. He waves when he sees me and leaps from his seat when I approach. "Hi Bonita," he says, and kisses me softly on each cheek. He helps me to take off my coat and I sit down on the sofa beside him.

"Have you been waiting for very long?" I ask.

"No. I only beat you by a few minutes but at least I beat you this time." He smiles warmly. "You look fabulous, if you don't mind me saying?"

"I do not mind you saying and you do not have to keep saying *if you don't mind me saying*. Say what you think. I will tell you if I mind."

He laughs. "Well I hope you won't mind what I've got to tell you. But before I get round to that, what can I get you?"

I choose a large mocha and a pain au chocolat. Simon gets a pain au raisin and a large cappuccino. He brings the tray back and puts it down in front of us.

"Excuse me." I hear a voice behind me.

I turn and see a very very old man and woman.

"Yes?" I say.

"Is this sofa taken?" The old man points to a sofa opposite the one that Simon and I are using.

I can see disappointment in Simon's face. "No mate. Help yourself," he answers. Simon moves our plates and drinks to our side of the low coffee table. He stands up and helps the old couple into their seats.

"Lovely day," says the woman settling into the sofa.

"Yes," I say. I turn back to Simon. I shrug and smile. "So what were you going to tell me?"

"Thought it was going to be cats and dogs when I drew the curtains back this morning but it's turned out really nice. Hasn't it Alf?"

The gentleman, I now know is,'Alf' puts his hand to his ear and says "Eh?"

The woman's voice rises several decibels, "I said 'cats and dogs' we expected this morning, didn't we? But it's turned out nice hasn't it, Alf?"

Alf nods. "But that Shaffeenakke feller on the radio says it might snow later."

"Ooh. Love a bit of snow, I do. Mind, dear, you don't look as if you get much snow from where you come from. Let me guess. Italy?"

I smile and nod.

"I knew it Alf. I said didn't I? I said 'let's sit down there where that Italian girl and her feller are sitting'.

"You did," Alf nods. "You did, Elsie. She's good, my Elsie, you know." Alf says to both me and Simon, "Very perceptive. Knows her onions. So where in Italy are you from? I was there at the end of the war."

"Leave them be, Alf." She looks at me and Simon. "Don't encourage him. He'll be telling you all about his exploits at Monte Cassino."

Simon is sitting back in the seat. I see that he has eaten all of his pain au raisin. His coffee is disappearing quickly too. I eat my pain au chocolat and sip my coffee. The conversation has died.

"I'll have what she's just had, Alf" the old woman says, "She wolfed that down. Must be delicious. What do you call it love?"

"Just ask for a chocolate croissant," says Simon, "They'll know what you mean."

Simon slaps his hands onto his thighs and leans forwards. He checks his watch. "Well," he says, "Right Maria, it's time for us to go. Have you finished?"

I drain the rest of the mocha. I dab my lips with the paper napkin that came with the croissant and stand up. Simon stands and helps me with my coat. He picks up his coat and puts it across his arm.

"Lovely to meet you both," he says.

"And you," says the old woman, "You make a lovely couple." She nudges her partner, "They do, don't they, Alf?"

"What?" says Alf, with his hand to his ear again.

"A lovely couple," she shouts.

Simon and I spill out of the coffee shop onto the pavement and burst into laughter.

"What a laverly couple we are," says Simon, in a poor imitation of Elsie. He puts his arm around my shoulder and looks into my eyes. He says it again "a laverly couple." We both laugh.

"Come on, Miss Italy. We'll have to find somewhere else now for my revelation."

The pavement is too crowded for us to walk together so Simon takes his arm from around my shoulder and keeps a step behind me as we weave through the crowds. I hold my hand behind me and he takes it. "You'd think there was a match on," he says. "Never seen it so crowded."

We pass the tube station and see that it is closed due to engineering works. "Keep going," Simon says. "We'll head into the park. If you're warm enough."

We walk through the wide stone gate of the park and in an instant we are in another world – a world of peace. We walk along a tree-lined avenue. Simon is inspecting the benches that line the path. He is like Goldilocks. "This one's too dirty," he says of one. "Bird shit," he says at the next. The next is filled by a sleeping bag. A crop of dirty grey hair is poking out of the bag. Simon shakes his head "We'll find one. I promise."

After passing ten or more benches Simon is finally happy. "There we go," he says. He sits down and I sit alongside him. He is leaning against the arm of the bench. I snuggle alongside him and rest my head on his chest. He puts his arm around me and draws me closer.

"Are you going to be able to hear what I've got to tell you down there?" he says.

"Sure. Go ahead."

"Before I start there's something else I want to do." He bends his head down and kisses me on my lips. It is a long and passionate kiss and I am happy to return it. After a minute he pulls away.

"I wanted to do that at the bedsit the other day," he says.

"Why did you not do it?"

"Not sure. I didn't want to give you the wrong messages. Or maybe I just thought you might not enjoy my American Hot breath."

"Well, your cappuccino breath is fine," I laugh. "It will soon be time to go to work again and I have not heard the big news you want to tell me."

"Okay. Here goes." There is a very long pause and he takes a long breath. "Forgive me Maria for I have sinned."

"Oh. That sounds serious. When was your last confession?"

Simon draws another deep breath. "Right. I have lied to you. I don't really collect frogs. I know nothing at all about frogs. I bloody hate frogs."

"Is that it? Your big confession? You do not like frogs."

"Well that is just the start of it. Here's confession number two. My full name is Simon Prendergast, well Simon Stephen Prendergast to be precise."

"I know."

"How do you know?"

"You showed me your ticket email at Cineworld. It said *to Simon Prendergast*."

"And didn't that ring any alarm bells?"

"No. Why?"

"Kinkozanfan on eBay. What was his name?"

I struggle to remember. "Dave...er....Dave... He just said Dave. I cannot remember another name. Oh, wait. Yes I can. Martin called him Dave Prendergast."

"Dave Prendergast. Correct."

"Oh." I stop and pull away from the warmth of Simon's coat and sit up.

"So, you are related to Kinkozanfan. Is he your father?" What Simon is telling me is beginning to become clear. "And you pretended you collected frog things and you contacted me to try and get my eBay vases?" I feel tears beginning to form. I try to hold them back. "You took me out for that coffee to try and get them. You were not interested in me. You were only interested in what I had." I stand up.

Simon grabs my hand and pulls me back down. I do not resist. I sit back alongside him. He puts his arm back around me. I pull away and move along the bench leaving a space between us. I fold my arms and stare down at my feet.

"Look," he says, "Think about it. If I *were* just interested in those vases I would have disappeared by now. You wouldn't have seen me for dust. But I'm here sitting on a bloody freezing park bench making a confession."

"So they *are* important? Martin at the gym was right when he said that I have been *done*."

"Yes, Maria. Please look at me....Yes they are important but you honestly have not been done."

My eyes are fixed firmly on a cigarette butt on the ground in front of my feet. "Why? What are the vases worth?"

"A lot."

"How much is a lot? Fifty pounds was a lot for me. Two hundred pounds?"

"A lot more than that. I don't want to raise your hopes but they are worth thousands."

"Thousands!"

"I'm not going to exaggerate so let's just say more than ten thousand."

I tighten my folded arms.

"So, why have I not been *done*. They belong to your dad now."

"Not quite."

"What do you mean?"

Simon reaches inside the front of his coat. He pulls out an envelope."

He slides it along the bench towards me. "Here," he says. "Read it."

I pick it up from the bench. The envelope is not sealed. I lift the flap and take out a single sheet of handwritten paper and read silently.

Dear Maria

Please take this letter as my agreement to pay to you one half of the sale proceeds (after deduction of the auctioneer's fees) of the pair of vases I bought from you and identified by eBay number 0231825389553

Yours truly

David John Prendergast

I read the letter again. I shiver a little. I put the letter back into the envelope and put the envelope in my handbag.

"Well?" says Simon. "Have you been done?"

I am not sure what to say. Am I happy to have the chance to have more than five thousand pounds or am I angry with myself for having lost something worth ten thousand pounds? I shrug. Simon moves towards me and tries to put his arm back around me but I brush it off.

"It's okay," he says. "I know it must be a bit of a shock and I know that you must be upset at me lying to you—"

I turn to look at him. I cannot hold back the tears and they flow down my face. I sob. I shake my head.

"I am sorry Simon. It is a lot for me to—" I am interrupted by a harsh voice.

"You alright, Bamba? Where's yer sexy-legs mate? What you done to upset 'er, lanky?"

Outside his sleeping bag the old man is scarily thin. His arms are covered in goose pimples and he is unsteady on his feet. He has a thin scrap of cigarette between his lips and holds a can of strong lager in his hand.

Simon stands up to face him.

"Nothing to do with you mate."

"Spare me a quid for a cup of tea?"

I fumble in my handbag. Simon unbuttons his coat "Leave it Maria," Simon says. He takes off his coat. The old man takes a step back.

"Whoa. No offence, mate. If it was you sendin' the text

messages, I was only havin' a bit of a laff."

"Here," Simon says to the old man. "Take it."

He holds out the coat. A shaking hand takes it from him. Simon takes the beer can while the old man struggles to put the coat on. It swamps him. He fastens the buttons and holds out his hand to Simon. Simon shakes his hand.

I know that he was reaching for the can. The three of us stand in silence for a second. The silence is broken.

"Now what's this? What's going on here? Excuse me sir," Sergeant Marley looks at Simon. "You know it is an offence - drinking alcohol here, in a public space."

I see the humour in her eyes. She continues "Has old stinky here been giving you any bother?"

"That's *Mr* Stinky to you Sergeant," says the old man. I feel as if I am watching a well-rehearsed double act.

"No, Sergeant. Everything is absolutely fine." Simon looks into my eyes and takes my hand. "At least I hope it is."

I shake my head. I pull my hand away from Simon's.

"I am sorry Simon. Everything was fine," I say, "but it is not fine any more." I cannot hold back my tears. I start to walk quickly towards the park exit. I do not look back.

Simon shouts, "Maria." I hear his steps behind me. I feel his hand on my shoulder. I shake it off.

"Leave me. I am late."

"But I've just given you a letter worth at least five thousand pounds."

I turn and face him. "It is not money Simon. I have *never* had any money. You lied and you cheated me. I would prefer to have a frog collector and no money than a liar and five thousand pounds. I do not want to see you again."

Simon looks at me. I can see that he is confused. I think that there are tears in his eyes.

"Please don't do this, Maria."

"I am sorry, Simon. Goodbye."

I walk away without looking back.

Chapter Fifty

Dave

It's Monday morning when I hear from MacIntosh again. She contacts me to tell me that Angela has been in touch with her and arranged to visit the station to help with enquiries.

"When's she coming in?" I ask.

"This afternoon. Four o'clock. Do you think you could join us?"

"Me? How can I help?"

"Seems that you've got her confidence. She spoke very highly of you." I feel my heart miss a beat.

"And you think that she'll be more at ease if I am around? Wouldn't she be better with just another woman?"

"That's what I'd like to think but seems that you've persuaded her to talk to me. I don't want her going back on that."

"Okay. I'll just check if it's okay with Sheila." I put my hand over the phone.

I shout up to Sheila who is in the bedroom.

"Is it okay with you if I go down to the police station later this afternoon. DC MacIntosh wants to run through my statement with me?"

"Again? How many times do you need to go through a three page statement?"

"She says it won't take long," I say.

"Okay. I'll come with you and we can go out later and have something to eat."

"No," I shout back. "I'll bring something home."

"So you don't want me with you?"

"I didn't say that. Just didn't want you to have the hassle of going out on a day like this."

"Fair enough. Don't be long though."

"I won't." I take my hand away from the phone. "That's fine DC MacIntosh," I say. "I'll see you at four."

I find myself outside the police station at a quarter to four. It's a bitterly cold day but instead of ringing the bell and sitting inside I find myself scouring the passing faces for Angela. It's almost four when she arrives. She looks surprised to see me.

"Dave!" she says. "What brings you here?"

"DC MacIntosh said that she was seeing you and she thought it might be good if I joined you."

Angela smiles. "Well it's good to see a friendly face. This might be an ordeal for me." She kisses me on the cheek. "So, where do we go?"

I press the door entry button. Before there's an answer the door opens and DC MacIntosh welcomes us in.

"I've been watching for you on the CCTV," she says. She leads us along the corridor and then upstairs to an interview room.

She tells us that this is an informal interview and there will not be any recording. She offers us hot drinks and phones through to someone to give them our order. I am quite surprised when it's DC Wood who comes into the room with a tray of drinks. He nods in my direction.

I return the nod. "I'm on tea duties today," he says. "Let me introduce myself," he offers a hand to Angela, "DC MacIntosh's oppo, DC Wood."

"Pleased to meet you." I see Angela shift nervously on her seat.

"I'll be off now," he says.

MacIntosh says, "Okay. Can you carry on with the bank paperwork and check with fingerprints if there's any news on that cheque?"

"Will do." Wood leaves us and Angela relaxes.

MacIntosh looks kindly at Angela. "He doesn't bite you know."

"I know. It's just—"

MacIntosh interrupts, "I know. We coppers are better in wee doses aren't we?"

Pleasantries over, Macintosh begins the proceedings.

"We've been in touch with the banks, Angela and, as

you'll gather from what I just said to DC Wood, I'm pleased to say that they've released the cheque to us and it's with fingerprints at the moment. If anything positive turns up it could give us the break that we've been waiting for."

Angela sits back in her seat visibly relaxed. "I really hope that it helps you, Detective. When Henry, my manager, first told me what the banks had done, I expected Damian to collect it and destroy the evidence. He was so plausible in everything he wrote to me I thought that he would waltz into the bank, spin them another of his lines and walk away."

"It's easy to be plausible in cyberspace, Angela. These scammers hide behind and inside the Internet like ghosts. The last thing they ever want is a physical presence. There *are* instances of physical contact with their victims but they're rare and usually come from desperation when the scam is faltering. He knew that you'd rumbled him. He wasn't going to take a chance of walking into a trap. So.... Let's start at the beginning. How did you first contact him, the man you know as Damian Proudfoot.?"

"It's so embarrassing to admit it Detective but, as you already know, it was online dating. Match.com. His profile seemed to be a pretty perfect match. He had so much in common with Brian - my dead husband - he was good-looking, liked art, opera, fine wines, rugby and he appeared to like what he saw on my profile."

"You say he was good looking. He sent you photos?"

Angela nods. She looks into her handbag and takes out an iPad. She taps in her passcode and swipes to the photos. She selects one and holds the screen towards MacIntosh. "Here's one," she says.

"He's certainly good looking, Angela. I've seen this photo quite a few times during our investigations. His name is Aaron Goulding. He's a fashion model working in New York. Handsome enough to have a portfolio of shots on the web but not a household name, at least not over here."

"And totally oblivious to any of this I suppose?" I ask.

"That's right," says MacIntosh. "Our Cybercrime people contacted his agent and told her how her client's photos were being used to seduce women. She said that her client would be flattered but she wouldn't be adding it to his CV. She asked us to apologise to the victims on behalf of Aaron but there wasn't a great deal that he, or she, could do about it."

Angela shakes her head. "No. Of course not. So, he set more than just *my* heart racing before he came up with his sob stories." Angela starts to tell MacIntosh how the relationship developed over months.

"And he never suggested meeting up?"

"Well, he did. He told me he had tickets for Covent Garden. It was a sell out – five stars in *The Times* – tickets were like gold dust and he had centre stalls seats *and* an exclusive dining package."

"And then he told you he was sick?"

Angela smiles. She looks into the distance. "I was in Mayfair looking for an outfit for the opera when I got the first email about the tumour. I went straight home and we exchanged scores of emails. It became extremely emotional."

"And he asked you for seven hundred and fifty pounds?"

"Yes."

"Were you not surprised or suspicious that someone who loved such fine things and had scored top seats at Covent Garden couldn't find seven hundred and fifty?"

"With hindsight, I suppose I should have been suspicious but the emails were so passionate and he was going to be spending so much money on medical fees it seemed understandable at the time. And there was such urgency."

"You sent the money there and then?"

"Yes."

"And there was never a suggestion that you speak to each other, or used Skype or FaceTime instead of corresponding by email?"

Angela blushes. She looks down at the table in front of her. "It sounds so stupid, doesn't it?"

"Of course not. You're not the only one."

"I'm not?"

MacIntosh shakes her head. She scribbles something on a piece of paper. "I know what you're going to tell me but I'd like to hear it from you."

"Skype or FaceTime would spoil the magic when we finally met."

MacIntosh nods. "And the phone?"

Angela looks at me.

"Do you want me to leave?" I ask.

"No but you're going to think I'm an absolute nincompoop. He said that he wanted the first time I heard his voice to be the day we met – when the first words I would hear would be *I love you* whispered into my ear," Angela groans. "I couldn't make this up, could I?"

"You're not making it up, Angela." MacIntosh holds up the paper she had scribbled on. *Spoil the magic. Whisper I love you.*

The interview goes on. Angela continues with the full story up to the point when I arrived at the clinic. MacIntosh prepares a lengthy statement and, as the interview starts to wind down, she hands it to Angela for her to read and sign if she's happy with it.

The phone on the interview room wall buzzes. MacIntosh gets up and answers it. She talks for a short while and comes back to the table "I've got some good news" she says. "That was DC Wood. He's been following up the cheque and there *are* fingerprints."

"And?" I say. Both Angela and I lean forward in our seats.

Two are unknown. One is probably yours Angela, we'll need to take yours to eliminate them, and another will be someone at the bank but the third is a definite match."

"Martin?" I say.

MacIntosh nods.

"Yesssssssss. We've got the bastard," I leap from my seat and punch the air.

The interview ends and, after taking Angela's fingerprints, MacIntosh escorts us from the station.

"Take care," She shouts after us.

I take Angela's hand and squeeze it.

"Well done, you," I say.

"Thanks, Dave. Have you got time for a drink?"

I check my watch. I shake my head.

"Sorry," I say. "Sheila will be wondering where I am. I promised to bring some food home. Maybe next time."

"Will there be a next time?"

I feel my face colouring. I look at Angela and squeeze her hand again.

"I certainly hope so," I find myself saying.

We head off in opposite directions. I catch a bus towards home. I sit and muse on my final words to Angela. 'Stupid old fool' I think. What on earth are you playing at behaving like a love struck schoolboy when you've got a life-partner at home; a life-partner who is probably at this moment checking her watch and waiting behind the front door.

Chapter Fifty-One

Dave

I get off the bus and go into Mr Chips. I decide on cod and chips for me and then spend an eternity reading through the menu looking for something that Sheila will be happy with. I don't see anything and I wonder what the hell brought me to a chippy. I leave without placing my order and walk along the street to the Marks and Spencer food store.

Marks have an offer on 'Dine In For Two for ten pounds'. That's better. I choose very carefully - a lasagne main, green salad side, and two lemon possets for dessert. The offer includes a bottle of wine too, so I opt for Sheila's favourite - a dry white. I pay at the till, pack them carefully and walk home.

The door opens as I reach it.

"You said that you wouldn't be long."

"I wasn't but it's a long way to Barnet, you know. And I had to get us some food on the way back." I hold up the carrier bag like a peace offering.

"How did you get on with MacIntosh?"

"Fine. She's okay when you get to know her."

"And it looks like you've really got to know her."

"What do you mean?"

"She's left her mark."

I've no idea what she means. My face must be a perfect blank. Sheila opens the cloakroom door, grabs my shoulders and turns me to face the mirror.

"Chanel, 'L'Amoureuse - if I'm not mistaken. They must be paying the police well at twenty-six pounds a tube."

I see my reflection with Angela's lip print on my cheek and put my hand towards it to rub it away. Why on earth did neither she nor MacIntosh point it out?

"We just did one of those French kisses on each cheek when we met that's all."

"French kisses? I'll give you French kisses if you think I'm falling for that one. Who is she? I don't really need to ask do I? She took one look at your naked body when you were in that clinic and that was it. Couldn't wait to get her hands on you."

"It's not like that, Sheila, honestly."

"Are you telling me that's not her lipstick?"

"No, I'm not. Look. MacIntosh invited Angela to the station and she asked me to join them. Angela simply pecked me on the cheek when we met. Do you think that if anything had gone on we wouldn't have wiped away the evidence? I might be thick but I'm not *that* thick." I get out my phone and bring up MacIntosh's number. I hold the phone in front of Sheila. "There. Call MacIntosh and ask her. She'll confirm everything I've told you. Come on. Let's not fall out. Look. I've got us a special dine in for two meal." I hold up the M & S carrier bag.

"Special? Marks and Spencer? You *really* know how to win a woman over don't you Dave? I would have been happy with fish and chips."

There's sometimes no way that I will win. Well, to be honest, there is no winning as far as Sheila's concerned.

I sigh as I take the Marks and Spencer dinner into the kitchen and put it into the fridge. Sheila follows me to check that I'm putting everything on the right shelf.

"Why are you sighing?" she asks.

"I just can't seem to get things right. I went into the chippy and was about to order us some fish and chips when I thought 'No. That's not good enough for Sheila. I'll go to Marks' and get something a bit better.' Not my best decision was it?" I shut the fridge door and turn towards her.

She looks puzzled.

"What's happening to us Dave?" she asks.

"What do you mean?"

"This relationship. It seems to be going downhill fast."

"I know, love, I know," I shake my head. "But let's get it back up again. I'm not giving up on forty years. We've had some pretty good times together haven't we?"

Sheila comes closer and looks me firmly in the eye.

"Yes but I'm not sure that I can remember the last one."

I put my hands on her shoulders and draw her towards me. She puts her arms around my waist and her face against my chest. I fold my arms around her and hold her tightly. I can feel faint sobs. I look down at her and she looks back up at me. I wipe away the tears with a finger. She starts to speak.

"Shhhhh," I say., "Let's just make the most of this."

Our embrace continues. I don't know which of us starts it but our faces move together and our lips touch. I hold Sheila's face gently between my palms and our kiss lingers and becomes slightly charged.

"Remember when we'd do this and you'd drag me upstairs to the bedroom like some Neanderthal and rip all my clothes off?"

"Those were the days," I say. "Hasn't happened since Simon moved back in."

"Well he just phoned and said he won't be home till late. He's staying behind to help with the play rehearsals and then his pals are going out for a drink. So, come on Barney Rubble, now's your big chance."

I don't need any encouragement.

I attempt to put Sheila over my shoulder but she's almost in a fireman's lift when I stumble. I panic but manage to ease her down gently and decide to give up. She's no heavier than she's ever been.

"So that gym's not working yet," she says. "Don't worry I'll do the dragging."

She takes my hand and leads me from the kitchen. She starts upstairs at a jog pulling me in her wake.

I stumble onto the landing. Sheila turns back to me.

"Come on," she says, "Strike while the iron's hot."

She moves into the bedroom and starts to undress. She still looks great in her matching bra and pants. She pulls back the bedcovers and climbs into bed.

"Aren't you taking them off?" I ask.

"I thought I'd leave *some* of the work to you." She's

watching me as I struggle with my shirt cuff buttons. It feels like an eternity as I fight to get them undone. One button pings off but at least it leaves me a free hand for the other. My shirt's on the floor and I start on my chinos. The belt's undone in a trice. I unbutton the flies and, as the chinos slip to my ankles I kick off the legs one at a time. I bend and, hopping on one leg, one by one, I remove my socks.

I look at Sheila. She has her hand over her mouth. I can see that she's suppressing a giggle.

"What *on earth* is that?" she says.

"What?"

"In your pants?"

"What do you think is in my pants? It's been there for the last forty years."

"Not like that it hasn't. It might have been a long time, Dave, but my memory's not that bad. Come on spill the beans. You look like a Shakespearean nobleman – or should I say 'knob'leman. Marry, here's grace and a cod-piece; that's a wise man and a fool."

I put my hands up. "It's a fair cop."

"Not a fair cock then?"

"Ha. Ha,Tena Men," I mumble.

"What? Like in the Chinese square? So is that one of the tanks or are you just pleased to see me?"

Sheila starts to laugh. She laughs. And she laughs more. Tears start to stream down her face. I jump into bed beside her.

"This is the first time we've done this in ages," I say.

"Done what?" she says stifling another giggle. "We haven't done anything yet."

"Laugh," I say.

Chapter Fifty-Two

Dave

It's Tuesday and I'm in my white towelling bathrobe in the kitchen making breakfast when Simon joins me.

"What's up with you this morning?" he says.

"Nothing's up with me. Why?"

"Haven't heard you whistling in ages. What's happened? Another eBay find?"

"Nothing's up. Can't a man whistle in his own kitchen? And never mind what's up with me. What's up with you?"

"What do you mean?"

"We've hardly seen you since you came home on Saturday. You've eaten virtually nothing and you look as if you're carrying the weight of the world on your shoulders."

"There's nothing the matter. I've been busy catching up with some work and I've just not been very hungry."

"Well, at least have a bit of toast before you go to work or your mum will start worrying about you."

I put a couple of slices of bread in the toaster.

"Alright. If it'll make you happy....When are you going to Lenhams?"

"Don't change the subject. Trouble with Maria?"

"Listen, Dad, I said it's nothing. Leave it."

I hear Sheila come downstairs. I turn towards her.

"Morning, love," I call.

Sheila walks into the kitchen. She's still in her bathrobe too. She walks straight to me, puts her arms around me, gives me a kiss on the cheek and says "Morning, Barney." She winks as she removes her arms from around me and glances across to Simon whose jaw is hovering a few inches above the floor.

"Morning, sweetie," she says to him.

"Bloody hell. I don't believe it. Should I be making myself scarce? I don't want to be a gooseberry. What's up with you two?" Simon's look could best be described as mystified.

"Nothing's up with us two," I say. "Let's just say that your mum and me are trying to sort things out."

"Thank God for that. It's been like living in Siberia here for the past few months. Good luck with it." He picks up the toast I've buttered for him, walks across to Sheila, bends and kisses her gently on the cheek. "I'm off now Mum. See you later." He comes to me and kisses me in the same way. He puts his lips to my ear and whispers "Great stuff Dad. Keep it up." He pats me on the shoulder and turns towards the door. "Have a good day you two." He puts the slice of toast between his teeth.

As he puts on his shoes in the hall he shouts to us in a toast-muffled voice "I'll be home at the usual time tonight."

Sheila looks in his direction, "Where's your coat? You can't go out without a coat. You'll be frozen."

"He's a grown man, love," I say. "It's up to him."

We hear the front door open and then slam shut.

"He's not been himself since the weekend," I say.

"No. He's not. Do you think something's gone wrong between him and Maria?"

"I just asked him that and he nearly bit my head off."

"Sounds like you touched a raw nerve."

"I think so."

"I'll try and have a word with him when he gets home." Sheila puts her arms back around me and gives me a kiss. "And if he's coming home early we might as well make the most of the time now," she says. She takes her arms away and pulls her robe back from her shoulder, "If you're up to it."

We head back upstairs. I'm a little nervous as I'm not sure that my body can cope with sex twice in under twenty hours – it's not something I've attempted for a very long time.

I needn't have worried; things work as they should.

We lie together in a warm fug. We talk more than we've talked in years. We try and open up with each other and explain our frustrations. I promise to get myself into shape and to spend less time on eBay. Sheila promises to be a bit more tolerant - although we laugh and agree that I will never have the last word. We don't want to kick Simon out but we know that, however much we love him, his presence has been something of a dampener on our relationship since he came back. We know that we've spoilt him but we both feel sorry for his situation and that of thousands of others who can't afford to live in London on their own. We decide that when we sell the vases we'll try and give him a leg up onto the housing ladder.

"But what about Susie? We can't give Simon money and nothing to Susie." Sheila says.

"We've given her plenty. She won't mind," I say. "She's not like that."

"I know a lot of people who have thought that and been surprised."

"How do you mean?"

"Ann and Peter's kids didn't speak to each other for years after they gave Charlie a car."

"Yeah, but Charlie needed that car. Steve had a company car and was earning megabucks."

"Made no difference. Steve thought they were favouring Charlie. I think it was their nan's funeral about five years later before they spoke again."

"That won't happen with Susie."

"Maybe, but you'd be surprised. It only takes Alec to make a comment and get her to start thinking she's being treated unfairly and, before you know it, our kids aren't friends anymore."

"Well, after giving half to Maria, there's not going to be an enormous amount left. If we're going to help Simon *and* Susie we might end up with that long weekend at Butlins instead of cruising the Caribbean."

"I know. But I'd rather see the kids happy than waste the money on ourselves. We can manage."

"Okay, love. Whatever you say. But don't ever say that I didn't offer you that Caribbean cruise."

The bedside phone interrupts us. I pick it up to hear a familiar very soft-spoken female voice.

"Mr Prendergast?"

"Yes. Hang on a moment please," I put the phone down and take my hearing aids from the bedside table and put them in. Sheila is mouthing 'Who is it?' to me. 'Not sure. Lenhams I think,' I mouth back.

I turn back to the phone. "Sorry about that. Yes. This is Dave Prendergast."

"Good. I hope I haven't disturbed you. This is Matsuko Kimura from Lenhams again."

I turn to Sheila and nod 'Yes, Lenhams' I mouth.

"Ah yes. Hi again Ms Kimura."

"Please call me Matsuko," she pauses briefly and then continues, " I was wondering if you had thought any more about bringing the vases in. I have been looking at your photographs and they are indeed a beautiful and very rare example of Yabu Meizan's work. You are probably aware of the vase with similar decoration that sold in New York. "

"I certainly am. Do you think they are part of a garniture?"

"It is very possible."

"What sort of value would you give them?"

"I don't want you to be over influenced by the New York sale price Mr Prendergast. It is possible that sale was exceptional. Two very keen collectors bidding against each other can sometimes result in extraordinary prices."

"I know. But the high bidder will be very keen to get hold of a full garniture."

"That is true, but he or she might not be in the market. Conditions in their life might have changed. I am not trying to say that your vases are not important, I simply don't want the New York sale to raise your expectations to an unrealistic level. I would suggest, providing that the vases are in perfect condition without restoration, we should offer them with a reserve of thirty thousand pounds."

"I'll have to think about that."

Sheila mouths to me 'How much?' I shake my head and put my finger to my lips.

"I think you will find that we have consistently gained the best prices for Yabu Meizan pieces for the last ten years, Mr Prendergast. I am sure that no auction house will provide you a better service or get you a better price."

"Do you think they might sell for more in New York?"

"Not at all. I feel certain that our Bond Street saleroom will produce the best results."

"Okay. So what's the next step, Matsuko?"

"Of course, as I said, I will need to see them first. When would you be able to bring them in?"

"Hang on a moment please. I need to check with my wife."

I put my hand over the phone and turn to Sheila.

"I need to get the vases into town for them to see them. How are we fixed this week?"

Sheila shrugs. "Nothing much planned. Just fit in with them."

I take my hand away from the phone. "Name the best time for you Matsuko. I'm pretty free this week."

We agree that I will take the vases into the Bond Street office on Thursday. I put the handset back on the charger.

"So?" Sheila says, "How much?"

"Not a lot. But I didn't expect them to go overboard with a valuation. She suggests a reserve of thirty thousand."

"Thirty thousand! After Lenhams' fees and Maria's share we won't have enough to help Simon to find a shoebox never mind a flat."

"They've got to be conservative. They don't want to scare bidders off. They want to get as much interest in them as they can. Put an estimate of eighty thousand on them and there will only be a handful of bidders. The market might have changed since the New York vase sold. I'm pretty sure they'll go way over eighty thousand. Let's face it, a hundred pounds would be a hundred percent profit. We can't be greedy and they really do get the best prices."

"Well, make sure that you negotiate a good commission. Those vases will bring collectors from all around the world to the sale. Lenhams should be paying you for the privilege of selling them."

"Don't worry, love. I'll make sure they give me a good commission rate."

I lean across to Sheila and kiss her. "And thank you," I say.

"What for?"

"For everything," I say.

Chapter Fifty-Three

Dave

It seems to take forever for Thursday to arrive, but at last I'm on my way. I've packed the vases in so much bubble wrap that each bundle is the size of a large watermelon. I put the vases carefully into my gym holdall and leave the house.

I've decided to go by bus and I trudge through slush that has accumulated on the pavements. After a couple of days of snow a slight upturn in the temperature has brought on a thaw. My shoes are soon wet and soaked through. I carry the holdall across my shoulder and head towards the High Street.

I reach the bus stop and check the timetable. The journey is about half an hour. I wonder if my bladder will cope. There's no sign of any activity down there but despite my improved control, I never know when the dreaded 'urgency' will strike. I decide that, after a large mug of tea at breakfast, I should find a loo as a matter of insurance. Matsuko was very flexible with my appointment and only gave a vague time slot so I've got plenty of time.

I'm quite near the Costa where Angela and I met. I feel in my pocket and I've still got the bill with the code for the loo on it. I won't even have to buy anything. I walk into Costa and head straight downstairs. The place is busy but the toilet is unoccupied. I take the code out of my pocket and key it in. The door fails to open. I try it again. No luck.

I walk back upstairs and go to the counter. I wave the receipt in front of the barista. "Sorry but the code's not working."

She takes my receipt from me.

"This isn't today's code sir."

"Sorry. What is today's code?"

"You'll have to buy something sir. The toilets are for customers."

I fumble in my pocket for some change and look for the cheapest thing on the menu. "No minimum spend is there to spend a penny?"

"No sir."

I order a small espresso coffee. I take my receipt and change and put them in my pocket. I look for a table. I might as well drink the coffee and use the loo afterwards so I can catch the bus with no worries about the efficacy of the Tena Men. The place is almost full. Every table is taken. I recognise a woman sitting near to the counter. There is an empty seat opposite her at her table for two. I walk across.

"Hi. You might not remember me but we shared a spinning class. Do you mind if I share your table?"

"Not at all" she says. She smiles and adds "Of course I remember you."

I look at her as I put my coffee down on the table. I shake my head and roll my eyes "My performance was *that* memorable?" I slip the holdall off my shoulder and put it under the table. I sit down.

"The most exciting class ever."

"I'm glad I livened it up for you. My moment of humiliation wasn't exactly my finest hour."

"Well it's good to see you back up and about. After hearing the stories going around the classes I thought we might not see you again. You look like you've made a full recovery."

"It doesn't take long to get over indigestion. Don't believe everything Martin Hetherington tells you."

"Don't mention that dirty old lech."

"I thought you were pals. You were bantering with him."

"I just keep him talking to try and keep his eyes off my boobs. He wants locking up."

"Tell me about it," I say. I try to think of something to change the subject. "So, what brings you to the High Street today?"

"Just bringing a few bits to the charity shop," she says. "My partner and I have been having a bit of a declutter this week."

I nod. "Which one are you donating it to?"

"Not sure yet. There are about fifteen to choose from. I had been thinking about the British Heart Foundation after your episode at the gym."

"Like I said, whatever Martin Hetherington told you, that was *not* a heart attack."

"That's such good news. So maybe I'll donate to the RSPCA, or Cancer Research... so many to choose from."

I sip my coffee. It only takes a few seconds to drain the tiny cup. I look at my watch.

"Well," I say. "Lovely meeting you again." I stand up and take the holdall. I put it over my shoulder. "Bye," I say as I turn and head downstairs to the toilet.

I arrive at Lenhams about an hour later. I walk to the magnificent glass front with my holdall over my shoulder. There's an apparently endless stream of limos stopping outside and disgorging Chinese men and women onto the pavement. Security men in expensive uniforms welcome the visitors and guide them through the revolving doors. I join the queue and soon find myself standing in a bright and airy reception area.

There's a reception desk in front of me and I introduce myself and tell the fashionable young woman that I have an appointment with Ms Kimura. I am told to take a seat and wait. I wait in a comfortable armchair near the desk and watch as more Chinese people head into the room opposite me. The room is all glass and it looks like a museum gallery filled with plinths on which the most exquisite examples of Oriental porcelain stand. Each piece is beautifully lit. Some pieces are under glass. Others are accessible and some of the visitors are picking these up and examining them closely. 'You couldn't do that in a museum' I think. I pick up an illustrated catalogue from the table alongside my armchair. *Chinese Works Of Art*. The sale is tomorrow and today is the final viewing.

I am fascinated by the quality of the setting. In my local saleroom there's no illustrated catalogue – just a couple of sheets of paper with lists of numbers on them and a couple of words alongside each. We fight elbow to elbow to get a look at tables piled high with dusty junk and to rummage through lots described as 'box of bric-a-brac'. This is so much more civilized. I think their minimum lot price is a thousand pounds.

A young Japanese woman approaches me. She's about five feet five tall, model-slim, bespectacled and dressed immaculately in a pale-blue, silk blouse and something below it that appears to be a cross between a grey skirt and a pair of grey trousers.

"Mr Prendergast?"

"Yes. Matsuko?" I stand up.

We shake hands. She indicates for me to follow her and we go through the Chinese gallery to a door behind. She swipes a security card and we head into a corridor. I follow her down the corridor. We make the usual pleasantries about the weather and my journey and soon arrive at another glass-paneled room. Matsuko swipes her card again and the door opens. There's only a table with two chairs on either side of it in the room. I feel as if I am back in Barnet Police Station waiting for the questions to begin.

Matsuko indicates for me to take a chair. I sit down and put the holdall on the table.

"My colleagues and I are all very excited about your pieces, Mr Prendergast" she says. "Would you mind if they join us?"

"Not at all," I say.

She picks up the phone on the table and dials through to her office. She asks me if I would like coffee while I wait but I decline the offer. I don't really want to be asking to use the facilities in a posh pace like this.

There's the sound of footsteps in the corridor and a knock on the door. Four people enter. One is a young Japanese woman, two others are young floppy haired men – they could be twins in their cream chinos, brown brogues, cravats and tweed waistcoats. The other is an older man. I've seen him on *Antiques Roadshow*.

"So Mr Prendergast," the older man says "Let's see these fascinating vases."

They all move to the table and stand opposite me, leaning forward in anticipation.

I stand up and unzip the holdall. They lean further forwards. I look inside. I zip it back up again. I unzip it again and look back inside. I put my hand in the bag and pull out a carrier bag. It's got a piece of notepaper taped to it. Written on it in felt-tip pen is.

Charity Shop Stuff

Chapter Fifty-Four

Dave

I'm running down Oxford Street with the holdall flapping against my back as I run. I glimpse at my watch. Two hours before the charity shops close.

I keep repeating to myself, "Oh my God. Oh my God." I've no idea why I am doing this. I don't even believe in God.

I change it to, "How did this happen? How the fucking hell did his happen?" Of all the tables in all the coffee shops, in all the towns, in all the world, why did I have to find one with another We Can Work It Out holdall parked beneath it?

It's busy on Oxford Street and I'm dodging between the burka-clad women carrying armfuls of yellow Selfridges bags; the Hen Party in their white boots and pink cowboy hats; I'm skipping past someone busking by playing a 'tune' - I use the term loosely - on a row of tin cans, a plastic bucket and a battered tray; I almost collide with a man wearing a sandwich board that proclaims THE END IS NIGH. "Even closer than you might bloody think," I say as I try to work out how I am going to get out of this one.

I leap onto a bus and sit down. It grinds to a halt and I see my imaginary self run past and far into the distance.

It's four-thirty when I get off the bus. Most of the shops close at five-thirty. Which way? I choose to go right. I run to the first – Barnardo's. The girl in Costa seemed like a caring sort. Barnardo's is a possibility but - hey - they're *all* a possibility.

The woman behind the Barnardo's counter shakes her head. No vases and no donations in a black holdall today.

"Sorry," she adds. ,As too do the British Heart Foundation, The Red Cross, Marie Curie and Cancer Research.

I arrive at Oxfam at five-thirty.

"A black holdall?"

"Yes" I say.

"Yes. I do think we had a black holdall handed in around lunchtime. Now. Let me see. I don't think we've got round to checking its contents out yet. Give me a minute."

The boy in beanie hat, polo shirt and ripped baggy jeans goes to the end of the shop, pushes aside the multi-coloured strip blind and goes into the store room.

I rest back on my heels. I tap my fingers in anticipation. "Please God," I say, "Please God. Even if I don't believe in you."

'Here we go," says a muffled voice from the storeroom.

The strip blind moves aside again and the beanie hat emerges. He's got a black strap over his shoulder. He walks through the shop to where I'm standing at the counter. He swings it around onto the counter top.

The holdall is black alright. It's also got the word ADIDAS on it in huge white letters.

"This not it then?" He doesn't really need to ask as I'm already heading to the door. The lights are going off in the shop windows. A bus passes just as I walk alongside a puddle formed by the last of the thawing slush. It's a sort of final straw – that Hamlet moment.

I walk slowly past the closed shops. I peer into the windows in desperation. I can't go home.

I walk past the new Diabetes shop. I look in the window. I carry on to the Donkey Sanctuary shop and I stop. I walk back to the Diabetes shop. I peer into the window again. What are those shapes at the back of the window behind the soup tureen and next to the golf club? Could they be? I put my hand flat above my eyebrows and peer harder. It's a possibility. My spirits rise. Yes. Definitely. The harder I look the better my eyes adjust to the low light. I can even make out a price ticket. Forty-five pounds.

Even though I know it's locked, I try the door. There's a doorbell alongside it. I push the doorbell and wait. There's no answer. I turn away and trudge back in the direction of home.

~

I open the front door.

"Had a good day?" It's a warm welcome from Sheila. She notices my soaking clothes. " Look at the state of your coat."

"I know," I say. "Bloody bus driver. I should be reporting him."

"Never mind, love. If you want to go and get out of all that wet stuff, I'll run you a nice, hot bath and you can tell me how you got on. You're much later than I expected."

I undress slowly and go into the bathroom. The bath is filling with lavender scented bubbles.

"I'll go and get us both a glass of wine," Sheila says.

As she goes downstairs I test the water temperature, add a touch of cold water and mix it around a bit before climbing in and relaxing back beneath the bubbles.

Sheila comes back and hands me a large glass of chilled Chablis. She puts the toilet lid down and sits on it cradling her own glass in her hands.

"You can join me if you like," I say.

Sheila shakes her head. "No. Don't want to mess up my hair. So? Lenhams? How was it?"

"Fabulous place. Quite amazing. Must cost an absolute fortune to run. They've got a big Chinese sale on tomorrow and the place was packed."

"So, what was Miss Kimura like?"

'Lovely," I say. "Beautifully dressed." I know Sheila's interest in clothes. "She was wearing something that looked like a cross between trousers and a skirt."

"I've seen those. Georgio Armani . I think they call them Skousers."

"I thought that look was tracksuits, curly perms and 'Calm down, calm down,'" I say moving my arms in my best Harry Enfield impression.

Sheila laughs. It's good to be laughing together like this.

"So. Was she on her own?"

"No I saw her entire team. That bloke you like on *Antiques Roadshow* was with her."

"Which one?"

"You know. Tall. Moustache. About our age."

"Great. Did he like the vases?"

"Loved them," I say, "They all did."

"So, what have you done with them then?"

"Left them with them. They need a few months to prepare for the sale."

"That's a pity. I liked having them on display here."

"Yeah, but can you imagine if Susie and the kids came to visit? They wouldn't last five minutes."

"You're right. Did they do you a good rate of commission?"

"Yes."

"How much?"

"I can't remember exactly. About two percent, I think."

"Where are the forms? I'll check the small print."

I pause. "Don't check them now. Simon's still out. When I'm dry we could carry on from where we left off the other morning."

Sheila smiles and takes a sip of her wine. She leans forward and puts her hands into the bubbles. She takes a handful of bubbles and smears them across my face. "Not now, you old goat. I need to check those terms and conditions. Where are they?"

"In my coat pocket."

As Sheila leaves the bathroom and goes downstairs to rummage through my coat pockets for a non-existent receipt and contract from Lenhams I gulp my wine in the vain hope that it will inspire a lie of the utmost brilliance.

It doesn't.

Chapter Fifty-Five

Dave

Talk about the ups and downs of a relationship. It's turned extremely frosty in bed. I lie awake thinking about the vases. Sheila, meanwhile, doesn't stop telling me how stupid I am.

"How could you possibly lose a signed contract and receipt for the most valuable things we've ever had? How? I just don't understand."

"I don't know. I'm really sorry. I can't say it again. I've already said it a hundred times. It's not a problem, I promise. I'll email Matsuko in the morning and ask her to send me a PDF copy. Don't worry."

"Do it now."

"What's the point it's almost midnight? She won't be in her office now."

"No, but if you do it now she'll have it as soon as she arrives in the morning."

"I'll do it in the morning."

"***Do it now.***"

I throw back the covers, turn on the bedroom light and go to the dressing table where my iPhone is sitting on charge. I tap in a few characters and write an email to myself. I walk back towards the bed and press 'send' holding the phone near enough to Sheila for her to hear its departing whoosh.

"There," I say, "Done." I walk back to the dressing table and plug the phone charger lead back into it. I switch the light off again.

"Let me read it," Sheila calls from the bed.

"Not now, love. I need to get to sleep."

I climb back into bed. I feel the bedclothes tighten as Sheila lies rigidly on the edge of her side of the bed. She feigns sleep but I know that she isn't sleeping. I don't attempt any contact. I simply whisper "Good night. It'll be sorted tomorrow I promise...Sorry."

Eventually Sheila succumbs to the exhaustion of having told me what an idiot I am a thousand times and she's lying besides me, still and breathing gently.

Hours pass, but I just can't nod off.

There's little point in lying wide-awake and worrying. I've been thinking hard about getting to the Diabetes shop before it opens. I pull the covers back gently and slide out of bed. I tiptoe out of the bedroom and creep along the landing. I go to the airing cupboard and open the door. I take out the spinning woman's holdall from where I hid it behind some sheets. I put it down quietly on the carpet. I leave the holdall on the landing.

I tiptoe back into the bedroom. I can hear Sheila's regular breathing. I fumble around with my hands in front of me trying to find my wardrobe. I find the door and pull the handle gently. I put a hand inside the wardrobe and reach up to where my jumpers hang. I lift one out and drape it over my arm. I reach back inside and find a pair of trousers and some shoes.

I shuffle further round the room to the dressing table. I unplug my iPhone from the charger and stuff it into my pyjama bottoms' pocket. I daren't get my glasses from the noisy bedside drawers.

I creep back out of the bedroom and shut the door silently behind me. I stand on the landing and pull on the jumper and trousers over my pyjamas. "Shit," I whisper. I've forgotten my socks. No point risking waking Sheila for the sake of a pair of socks. I put the holdall strap over my shoulder, pick up the shoes and feel my way along the wall to the stairs. I find the bannister and edge my way gingerly downstairs to the hall. I put the gym bag down. I still can't risk the lights so I fumble around the coat hooks and find my coat. I pat the pockets. Yes. My wallet is in there. I pat my trousers and realise that my iPhone is still in my pyjamas. I unbutton my trousers and lower them to retrieve the phone from my pyjama pocket. I refasten my trousers and straighten my jumper.

I put on my coat and tuck the iPhone into a pocket. I sit down on the stairs while I put on my shoes and tie the laces.

I stand up. I smooth my hair with my hand, pick the holdall back up and feel my way to the front door. I open the door and pull it gently behind me. Sheila's been asking me to oil that door for months and I cringe at the haunted-house creak followed by a loud bump as it shuts behind me.

There's no turning back now. I scurry down the path and walk briskly towards the High Street.

I check my iPhone. It's six o'clock. I've got hours before the Diabetes shop opens. But at least I will be there. I will be like one of those people you see interviewed on the telly waiting in shop doorways for the January sales on Oxford Street.

I reach the shop. There's somebody covered in blankets sleeping in the doorway. There's a notice on the window. I use my iPhone to light the notice up and I read that the shop has been set up by two mothers of children with diabetes to raise funds for research and to supply insulin pumps to those who can't get them on the NHS. I walk to the Donkey Sanctuary next door and put the holdall down in the doorway. I shuffle my feet and blow into my hands to stave off the cold.

I would have been better off lying awake in bed. I try sitting down but the floor is ice cold. I stand and shuffle again. I walk a few paces in an attempt to generate some warmth but I soon hurry back to make sure that nobody jumps the queue. It's too cold to stay still so again I walk a few paces and hurry back. I'm like a caged lion in an old zoo – ten paces right, turn, ten paces left.

Each time I pace, I try to see the vases in the window. Every time a car passes, the headlights illuminate the display briefly and I can see that they are still there – so tantalisingly near. I feel a drop of rain and take shelter beneath the Donkey Shelter's canopy. I hear a voice behind me.

"Spare some change for a cup of tea?"

I turn round to find a scrawny figure in an oversized coat holding out a hand.

As I turn he looks me up and down.

"Sorry mate."

"Sorry?"

He shakes his head. "Not seen you before on this patch." He looks down at my holdall. "That yer bundle?"

I don't reply. I put my hand in my pocket to see if I've got any change.

"Where you dossin? You'll struggle round here. This is Jimmy's gaff." He points to the Donkey Sanctuary doorway. "That's Maggie next door." He nods in the direction of the Diabetes shop. "An that's my place." He points to an empty shop across the road where I can make out a pile of blankets and cardboard. "But you might be okay tonight at Marie Curie. Razor's gone on holiday."

"Anywhere nice?"

"Belmarsh. Three stars on Trip Advisor. A lot warmer than it is 'ere, mate. I can tell you." He shivers exaggeratedly. "If you're lookin for fags or booze come and see me later." He nods in the direction of the derelict shop. "Jimmy should be back soon with supplies."

He crosses the road and settles down into his makeshift nest.

I need to check my iPhone. It's been vibrating like a sex toy with a faulty battery since I left the house. I fumble in my coat pocket for it. I check the time. I've been pacing for what seems like hours but it's only seven forty-five. There are fifteen missed calls from Sheila and Simon. I swipe across to messages and find a similar number of texts. I can't usually read texts without my specs but Sheila's has used the iPhone equivalent of shouting and they are all a variation of '**WHERE ON EARTH ARE YOU**?' Simon's are a series of WTFs and other acronyms that mean absolutely nothing to me but, judging from the number of Fs in them, I get the gist.

I tap into the phone. '*Don't worry. Everything okay. Home before ten. Explain then. xxx PS. Sorry.*' I send it to them both. I imagine that Simon will be messing about on my computer trying to get into the 'find my iPhone' app. I don't think he'll manage to crack my password. I got the

Mac to suggest it and it's about thirty characters of mumbo jumbo. He'll be typing DaveSheila1976 or something like that.

As the road gets busier and cafes and shops start to light up I catch a view of myself in the window. I flatten my hair and rub my fingers across my teeth. I rub the stubble on my chin. It's still freezing so I turn up the collar on my coat and shuffle some more. I pick up the gym bag and slide the strap across my shoulder. I smooth down the front of my coat. The vibrations are still coming at regular intervals. I don't look at the latest messages. I take the phone from my pocket and turn it off.

I walk back to the Diabetes shop and the lumpy bundle in the doorway. 'Wake up Maggie.' I think of the words to the song. I look at her shabby bedding. I take all the loose change I have from my pocket and drop it into the plastic cup beside her. There's more than enough for a very decent cooked breakfast.

The coffee shops are open on the High Street. The Diabetes charity opens at nine so there's still plenty of time for a coffee, the loo and a quick tidy up so I reach back down to the plastic cup to take back enough change for a drink.

"Oi. You! What the fuck are you doin?" I feel a shove in the back.

I turn round and find my friend with the voluminous coat. The coat has a strangely familiar look to it.

"It's not what it looks like," I say.

"It's exactly what it looks like. I know it's hard out 'ere mate and you look like you're new to it but there's rules on the street. You don't rob yer mates."

I stand up, throw the change back down into the cup and go to walk away. He gives me a helping kick on the backside

"And you don't piss in the doorways," echoes behind me.

Chapter Fifty-Six

Dave

I move ten yards away from the shop, stop and turn. Big Coat is still watching and waves his hands to indicate I've not gone far enough. I walk a bit further and look back again. Again, not far enough. Twenty yards more and it seems that he's happy now.

He disappears after a while and, a few yards at a time, constantly vigilant, I gradually ease myself back to my goal.

I linger in front of the window. It's getting lighter and I can see inside the shop more clearly. As I peer in, a light comes on inside. There's no sign of anyone in the place so I assume the light's on a timer. The vases are still there and, yes, they are definitely my vases. My holdall is in the window too. It's got a five pounds price ticket. I look back at the vases and cringe as I realise that some ignoramus has stuck price labels onto the body of each. It's going to be a painstaking job to soak those labels off without taking away some of the gilding and delicate decoration. A couple of thousand pounds could be wiped off their value with every spoiled frog. I shudder as I imagine the perfect signatures spoilt by stickers.

I start to sense my bladder trying to grab my attention. I do my 'urgency' dance to try and stave off an accident but I see from the clock inside the shop that it's going to be another half an hour before the staff open up.

I look away from the window and see Big Coat's back. He's glaring at me. He makes a shooing gesture. "Go on. How many times do I have to tell you? On yer bike."

I cross the road to a coffee shop. Now changeless, paying for an espresso with a twenty-pound note does not win me any new friends and the direction to the toilets is indicated with a grudging nod. I leave my espresso on a table and go to relieve the urgency and smarten myself up – not an easy job when you discover that you're wearing one black shoe and one brown.

I drink my coffee and try to cross back over the road. The traffic is constant but I can see between the cars that there's some activity in the Diabetes shop doorway. A heavily tattooed woman sporting a purple Mohican, a denim jacket and leather trousers is shaking out her bundle and collecting the coins from her cup. Her skin is corpse white. There's another figure in the doorway alongside her– an old guy - in his seventies I guess. He's got white hair and a white, clipped moustache. He's wearing a navy blue blazer, white shirt, red striped tie, grey flannels and brown shoes. I risk life and limb rushing across the road while holding my hands up in apology to angry motorists.

To say that my heart sinks when I reach the shop would be an understatement. I've waited, freezing, shuffling and pacing for hours and now I'm standing outside the shop *behind* someone I assume to be another customer.

"Good morning," I say.

He looks at me.

"Hello, old chap," he puts a hand in his pocket and brings out a coin. He holds it out to me. "Can I get you a cuppa?"

I shake my head. "No. No," I say, "I'm here to buy something from the shop."

He looks surprised.

A pure white arm decorated with skulls and snakes pokes in front of me.

"You can buy me a cuppa pal."   The old man puts the coin in her palm and closes her fingers around it.

"Of course," he says, "You're welcome."

"*Twenty pee*. You takin the piss?" she throws the coin down and walks away.

"The youth of today eh?" says the old man picking the coin back up. "No gratitude."

He looks back at me.

"So what are you hoping to buy?"

"Oh," I say, "Nothing much. How about you?"

"Well, old chap, between you and me, there's something *rather* special in the window."

My heart sinks further.

"Special?"

"Yes. Spotted them last night but the shop closed early. Got up at the crack of dawn to be here before they open."

My stomach is churning. I've hung around in a freezing doorway; I've alienated and worried my wife; I've risked a mugging; I'm not even the first in the bloody queue; in front of me there's an old codger who appears to have recognized the value of some obscure Japanese pottery by merely looking in an unlit charity shop window.

"So what is the *something* in the window?" I say, with what, I hope, sounds like an air of nonchalance.

"You'll see soon. Look, they're opening up."

A woman is standing inside the shop. She's got a ring full of keys and she tries one after another until the door opens and we spill inside.

"A rush," she says. "I've not had that before." She walks back into the shop and stands behind the counter.

The old man walks briskly to the window. He leans inside. I hang back. My stomach is in a million knots. He reaches down and almost in slow motion he emerges with his prizes. He holds one in each hand inspecting them closely, shaking his head as he does.

He covers his mouth with his hand and whispers to me "A blacksmith made cut-off nose track iron and a gutta-percha ball *and* a twenty pounds price ticket for the two. Looks like it's my lucky day, old chap. "

He takes a golfing stance and holds the iron above his shoulder. He swings the club through and into the window space. I see the contents of the window quiver in the rush of air as if a small earth tremor is passing beneath the London suburbs. My vases wobble on the inadequate tiny plinth that someone has unwisely displayed them on. I watch the wobble exaggerate as the pressure waves from the old buffer's swing take their full effect. I can't look. I put my hands in front of my eyes and take a deep breath. I hear an unmistakable smashing sound as something crashes into the window display. I make a chink in my fingers and peer through.

"So terribly sorry madam. I must pay you for that mug."
I exhale sharply.

As he moves away from the window I sidle to within touching distance of the vases. He hands the club and ball to the woman behind the till. "Would you take ten pounds, madam? The ball *is* rather cracked."

"Well, now that you point it out, I suppose it *is* a bit cracked. It's probably not much use as a golf ball anymore. Could we say fifteen pounds for the club and I'll throw the ball in for free?"

The buyer shrugs. He wrinkles his nose. He hesitates and makes to move away from the counter. But then he turns back. "Make it fourteen, madam, and it's a deal."

"It *is* for charity, sir."

"Oh well," he sighs. "You drive a very hard bargain, madam." He takes out a wallet from his blazer pocket, removes two notes and hands them to her. "After all" he says, winking at me, "it *is* for charity."

"Oh, and..." he says reaching into his trouser pocket. "I forgot the breakage. Is twenty sufficient for the mug?"

"That would be very generous, sir."

He hands the woman the coin that Maggie rejected.

The woman looks at the coin.

"*Very* generous," she says. She coughs and looks over the man's shoulder in my direction. "Can I help you over there? You might want to check our shoe shelves. Some lovely matching pairs down there." She nods toward the opposite end of the shop. "Another thing," she adds, "There's a branch of Shelter down the road you know. They'll offer you a cup of coffee."

I catch sight of my reflection in a mirror. Unshaven; my hair a greasy mess; pyjama material sticking out from the bottom of my trousers; odd shoes without socks. I'm surprised she's not suggesting Tramps R' Us.

"I'll wait until you've finished serving."

She finds some bubble wrap beneath the counter and with one eye on the golf club and the other eyeing me with suspicion she wraps the ball and the driver carefully before handing them to the old man.

"Thank you, madam." He turns away from the counter with a jaunty air and a swaggering walk.

"Are those what you're looking at?" he says nodding in the direction of the vases in the window.

I nod.

"Can I take a look?" He bends and peers at the vases. "Hmmm. Jolly nice. I didn't spot those."

I snatch the vases quickly from their plinth - one in each hand.

"Oh. They're nothing really."

"Well, if you say they're nothing and you're not interested," he says. "I might make an offer myself."

I hold the vases tight to my chest.

"No. It's okay. I think my wife will like them."

The shop assistant looks across to us.

"Is everything alright? Can I help you?"

Her interruption is welcome. I move towards the counter.

"Very well then old chap. Make sure you drive a hard bargain."

The man leaves the shop. I shake my head. If he's right, he's just robbed young children with diabetes of a small fortune.

'Oh my God,' I think. There's a voice in my head '*You're robbing them of a fortune*'.

"Course I'm not," I say it out loud. "They're mine." Now I'm talking to myself.

I take the vases and put them down on the counter. I go back to the window and take the holdall.

"I'll take this too. It's a bit newer than mine." I take the existing holdall off my shoulder and put it down alongside the one I'm buying.

The woman looks at the vases.

"These are nice," she says. "They weren't here on my last shift."

I nod.

"Yes," I say, "They're lovely aren't they."

I take my wallet out of my coat and find three twenty-pound notes. I take them out of the wallet and hand them across the counter.

"Thank you. I'll find you some change."

"Don't worry about the change. It's for a good cause."

The woman wraps the vases in plenty of bubble wrap and hands them to me. I unzip the holdall. I realise it's the wrong one. It makes me think of how those West End conmen are so successful with three cups and a ball. I zip it back up again. I unzip the right one and put the vases carefully in place.

I hold up the spinning woman's gym bag

"And this is for you," I say, pushing it in the charity worker's direction. "I've been having a bit of a clear out."

She accepts it with a wrinkled nose as if I were a toddler offering a soiled nappy that I've proudly managed to remove all by myself.

She reaches beneath the counter and takes out a pair of gloves. She puts them on.

"Sorry" she says "Health and Safety." She unzips the holdall and takes out the carrier bag. Its handles are tied together. After much fiddling she unties the handles and reaches inside. She takes out the first item like a magician bringing a rabbit from his hat and holds it up. She shakes her head.

"Sorry. We can't take underwear."

She hands an enormous bra back to me. I take it off her.

"You could have signed it 'Erica Roe' and put it with the sports memorabilia," I say before stuffing it in my coat pocket.

She delves back into the carrier bag as if she's at the bran tub at the local fete. After a good rummage she produces the next item with a flourish.

"Ah yes. Yet another addition to our fifty shelves of E L James."

She's back in the bag again. I pick up the holdall and begin to back away towards the door. As she takes out the next items I take one look and quickly beat a hasty retreat.

She follows me out of the door brandishing a Gift Aid form in one hand and a black leather whip and a pair of pink fluffy handcuffs in the other.

"Wait," she shouts, "We haven't finished yet."

I stumble into a scruffy figure on the pavement.

"Blimey," he says, "We only get *coffee* at Shelter."

Chapter Fifty-Seven

Dave

"But I sent a text. I told you not to worry."

"Of course you did." Sheila holds her phone briefly in front of my face.

"I can't read it. I left my glasses at home."

"Let me," she says. She turns the phone towards herself and reads, " *'Front worru Evetuthing bjist hone GeForce ten xxx ps dontru.'* That's very reassuring to a woman whose elderly husband has disappeared in the middle of the night and gone out in the freezing cold without his glasses...or his hearing aids."

"Hey," I say, sitting back in the sofa. "Go easy with the *elderly.*"

"Why? That's what people with Alzheimer's do – wander off in the dark. Go to the shops at midnight. What do you expect me to think when you disappear and all I get is a message written by a bloody chimpanzee three hours later. Three hours!" Sheila continues to pace the lounge floor in front of me.

"I tried not to wake you."

"Well you didn't try hard enough. How many times have I asked you to sort that front door?"

"Lots."

"And why didn't you answer any of our calls? We were going frantic."

"I told you everything was okay in my text."

"But I don't speak ape. What were you doing?"

"Sorting out the vases."

"Those bloody vases. They've taken over our lives. I haven't heard of anything else all week."

"You were worried about me losing the receipt. I wanted to sort it."

"You told me it was no problem. You told me your Japanese woman would send a duplicate, no problem. You told me to stop worrying a hundred times. No problem."

"But you told me I was stupid a hundred times. It was preying on my mind all night after we'd had such a nice week."

"So how was going out in the dark going to sort it?"

I take a breath.

"Sit down," I say patting the seat beside me on the sofa, "and I'll explain". After pacing a little more, Sheila sits down next to me.

"So?"

"I was being a bit economical with the truth. I didn't lose the paperwork."

"So why all the lies?" I can almost see Sheila's thought process. She's silent for a few seconds. "I get it now. You didn't want to tell me they were worthless."

"Of course not. You saw them didn't you? Look. I didn't lose the paperwork and that's the honest truth...I lost the vases."

"You *what*?"

"I lost them. But don't worry. I got them back."

The holdall is between my feet. I unzip it. I take out the bubble wrapped bundles and put them down gently on the coffee table.

"They're here."

"How could you possibly lose them? All you had to do was take them into town and deliver them to Lenhams. It's not exactly rocket science. Where did you lose them? Don't tell me. A toilet break was involved wasn't it?"

I nod. "Sort of."

"When are you going to sort it out? You've had all your tests and you've seen the doctors and you're no better."

"I am a lot better. I'm watching my drinks and I'm making sure I go before I need to. I told you, the doctor says it's just my age."

"So you left them in the loo somewhere?"

"Not quite. But look. It doesn't matter now. I don't need to give you a blow by blow account. I made an almighty cockup, but I've been lucky and I'm really, really sorry.

They're back now, safe and sound. I'll get them to Lenhams later but I need to go and get a shower and a shave first and tidy myself up."

I get up off the sofa. I bend and pick up the vases carefully and gently put them back into the holdall.

As I'm bending I feel a tug at my coat pocket."

"Hang on a minute," says Sheila.

"What?" I say.

Sheila's dangling a pair of 38DD cups in front of me.

"I think you do need to give me a blow," - she thumps me hard on my arm - "by blow" - another thump - "account."

Chapter Fifty-Eight

Dave

My arm's still smarting from Sheila's pummeling when I arrive back at the tube station with the vases in the holdall. She forgave me after my honest and full account of what happened and was full of remorse when she saw my black and blue biceps. I don't hold grudges – that's Sheila – it's part and parcel of living with a passionate woman. At least she cares.

She cares enough to join me on the journey back into the West End to make sure that the vases suffer no further mishaps. Matsuko is waiting for us in the reception area this time. She looks anxiously at her watch as we arrive. She holds a form.

"So sorry we're a bit late, Matsuko. Tube delays. Let me introduce you to my wife, Sheila."

"Very pleased to meet you, Mrs Prendergast." The women shake hands and Sheila compliments Matsuko on her stylish outfit. It's different from the one she wore when we last met. The very skinny black jacket, matching tight black trousers and tiny black shoes with impossibly thin heels emphasise her slightness.

She tells us that she has to leave in a few minutes to visit a client so we will need to do business in the vast reception area. She guides us to a table and chairs well away from the activity of the room and, half expecting another catastrophe of some sort, I put down and nervously open the holdall to reveal my treasures.

"No nasty surprises this time," I say, as I take the vases from their bubble-wrap swaddling. I put them on the table and sit down. Sheila sits next to me.

Matsuko sits down at the table. She picks the vases up one at a time and examines each in turn with a small magnifying glass that she took from her tiny handbag. We're silent for several minutes as she checks them over. She smiles as she completes her examination.

"Perfect," she says, "and you are happy for us to handle the sale on the terms agreed?"

We discussed charges and commission on the phone before we left home and Matsuko puts the paperwork she was holding down in front of us.

"I think I have filled in all the details correctly," she says, "but please check carefully before signing where I have indicated." She hands me a gold and enamel pen that wouldn't look out of place in one of their sales.

Sheila takes the triplicate form from me. She is brilliant when it comes to small print and she goes through the page meticulously. She doesn't find anything wrong; the commission rates and the charges are as agreed. She slides the form back to me.

"All looks fine to me."

I sign and hand the paperwork back to Matsuko. She tears off a copy and returns it to me and puts her copies with the vases.

"I want to ask just one thing before you go," she says.

"Yes?"

"Would you be willing to wait for a later sale?"

"I thought that you had an auction coming up in a couple of months."

"We do, but I think that the sale after that in May will be even better. Some of the lots in the February auction are unsold pieces from the November sale and are not fresh to market. In addition there is a major Japanese Art exhibition scheduled for the V&A in the spring and its opening, which coincides with the first viewing day for our sale, will create a huge amount of publicity for Japanese Art. It is your choice."

Sheila looks at me and says "Maria might be disappointed, but when you tell her the reasoning, she'll understand."

"You're the expert, Matsuko," I say, "we'll take your advice." I hand her pen back to her.

"Good." She stands up and we follow suit. She shakes Sheila's hand and then she shakes mine.

I offer the holdall to her.

"I won't be needing this."

She thanks me and puts the vases carefully into the bag. She walks across to the main reception desk and hands the holdall to the young woman in charge.

"So that's that," I say, "Mission accomplished."

"Thank God. It was nearly Mission Impossible a few hours ago," says Sheila.

Chapter Fifty-Nine

Maria

There is an important football match on and the restaurant is unusually quiet. Margarita joins me in the kitchen and asks if there is anything she can do to help me. I hand her a pair of thin plastic gloves and ask her to cut some bread while she waits for customers. Once the football is over, Casa Nuestra will be full and we both hope that the result is the one that the customers want as that will mean a top night for tips.

Margarita teases me about my 'boyfriend'.

"He is not my boyfriend."

"Two dates in Le Petit Pain and one at the cinema says he is. Tell me all about him."

"He is not my boyfriend – not anymore."

"Oh no. What happened? You seemed to be so happy. I have never heard so much laughing in this kitchen."

"There is not a lot to tell you. We spent a lot of time talking about Abuelo's vases."

"I get it. He invited you to see his frog collection. *Very* exciting." Margarita feigns a yawn.

"No. That is not it. You see, he is not interested in frogs. That was a lie."

"A lie? Why would he invent a lie like that? I can imagine him lying about a car or a job to try and impress you, but claiming to collect frogs was not exactly going to get you to rip his trousers off."

"He lied because of the vases."

Another fake yawn.

"Very sexy," she says. "He's a thirty year old man. He should be interested in your boobs and your legs not your grandfather's old pottery. Does he collect stamps too?"

"No, he does not collect stamps and he does not stand at the end of railway platforms with a notebook either. But there is something that I want to ask you about. "

I explain how he acted for his father in contacting me about the vases. I say that the vases are valuable but I do not say how valuable.

"That stinks. A man who cheats like a snake? A man who not only cheats like a snake but then *tells* you he has cheated you like a snake and *gloats* about how valuable the vases are? He is a creep. He takes your inheritance and repays you with a pizza and a trip to Cineworld? You were so right to get rid of him. Adios, Simon. Adios, you bastard."

I take out Simon's father's letter from my pocket.

"There is one thing though," I say.

"What?"

"This."

"What is it?"

"It is from his father."

"Dear Maria. Please take back my pathetic son. I have your vases but he loves you and he promises not to take your grandmother's inheritance too?"

"Just read it".

She snatches the letter from me in rage. She scans it quickly. "What's this number? His Tesco code for Harvester?"

"It is not a joke. Please read it properly."

She reads slowly.

She reads the letter again. She shakes her head. Her mood changes "This is good. This is very honest. I do not know very many people who would do this. I do not know any person, especially a man, who would do this. He must be in love." She hands the letter back to me.

I blush.

"He is not in love. I think that he would have done the same thing if you had sold them to him or Miguel or even Abuelo. I can feel that he is a good person."

"Or his father is a good person."

"Both perhaps."

"So, why did you finish with him?"

"I was not thinking straight. It was a shock when he

told me the truth. I was angry; sad; I felt cheated. Now, I am not sure."

"He *was* sly and yes, he did cheat you, in a way. But he gave you this letter. He could have disappeared and you would never have known any different. Perhaps you were wrong telling him you don't want to see him again. He may be one to keep." She pauses, "If he is good in bed too... Is he?"

I blush.

"One to keep?"

"No. You know what I mean. Is he good in bed?"

I say nothing.

"You do not know do you?" she says. "Life is short Maria. You must get back together and find out soon and if he is no good take the money and say goodbye."

"Simon said that I will not get the money until February."

"February?"

"Yes."

Margarita shakes her head.

"You might be having a lot of bad sex this winter."

"But I might be having a lot of *good* sex."

"You're going to take him back?"

"Maybe."

"I hope you do."

"Take him back?"

"Yes. A*nd* have lots of good sex."

There is a lot of noise in the restaurant. We look through the kitchen door window. The place is filling with men in red shirts with foreign names across their backs. They all look happy.

"Tonight is going to be a good night," I say.

Margarita pulls up her skirt about ten centimetres.

"Tonight is going to be a very good night," she says, smiling.

Chapter Sixty

Maria

It *is* a good night. Monreal scored the winning goal and the fans' love Spain more than ever. Even though the restaurant was quiet before the match, we share our best ever night's tips for just a few hours' service.

After we close, Margarita and some of the waiters leave with a group of fans who are Casa Nuestra regulars. They head into the West End to join in the partying but I sit and drink a coffee in the restaurant before I go home. Miguel joins me and sits opposite.

"You didn't want to party with Margarita and the boys?"

I shake my head and look into my coffee.

"What's the matter? You look very sad."

"It is nothing, Miguel."

"Would you perhaps like to go somewhere for a drink with me? It is a bit gloomy here now that everyone has gone."

I shake my head again.

"I am sorry Miguel."

"I know. I keep trying."

"I like you very much Miguel."

"As a friend."

I nod again.

"So, phone him."

"Phone who?"

"Whoever it is that is making you look so sad."

I look at my watch.

"It is too late."

"Maria. It is only one. He is probably lying awake thinking of you."

"You think so?"

"I *know* so. Go on."

Miguel stands up and starts to tidy the restaurant.

I take my phone from my bag. I dial Simon's number. He answers immediately.

"Maria?"

"Yes."

"It's really you."

"Yes."

There is a long silence. We both say the same thing at the same time.

"I'm sorry."

We laugh.

"Why are you sorry?" he asks. "It's me who should be sorry."

"I am sorry for being angry with you."

"I deserved it."

"No. You were being fair to me. It was just a shock."

"I understand. Please don't say any more. You'll let me see you again?"

I nod silently.

"Maria. Are you still there?"

"Yes."

"Yes - you're still there or yes - you'll let me see you again."

"Both."

Chapter Sixty-One

Dave

"How are you fixed to meet up for that drink?" I ask.

"I'm busy today but I could meet you tomorrow evening when I finish work. Do you know The Golden Lion? It's a nice place. We often pop in there for a glass of wine after work."

"What time?'

"I should be away by six and it's only five minutes. If you find yourself a seat I'll join you as soon as I can."

"Thanks Angela. Looking forward to it."

I tell Sheila what I'm up to. We've had a long talk to clear the air and I think she trusts me to nip things in the bud.

"Just one drink mind. From what you've told me she's a vulnerable woman. I don't want you giving her any encouragement. I still don't see why a very wealthy and glamorous forty-year-old widow might be interested in you."

"Perhaps it's my charm and my sparkling personality she's interested in."

Sheila looks me up and down. "Well it's certainly not your body."

When I arrive at The Golden Lion the small bar is empty. There are two comfortable armchairs in front of a glowing log fire. I walk to the armchairs, take off my coat and drape it over one of them. With my territory claimed I walk back to the bar and order a half of best bitter and a glass of dry white. I take the drinks back to the armchairs and put them down on a small table between them.

I'm glad that I arrived early as, before long, the pub fills up with regulars winding down before beginning their commute home.

I smell Angela before I see her. I sense her expensive scent and turn to see her approaching the fireplace. I stand up and kiss her quickly on each cheek.

"I got you a Chenin Blanc. Hope that's okay."

"Perfect," she says with a smile.

"How's your day been?" I ask.

'Busy as usual. How about you?"

"All the days blend into one when you're retired. I've not done much. Had a look on eBay while Sheila went to yoga with some of her friends."

"eBay? What were you buying?"

I tell her about my bargain hunting hobby.

"I promised Sheila I'd cut down on it though. It was starting to take over my life."

"I can imagine it can be addictive if you are finding exciting stuff but you could be addicted to a lot worse. What's the best thing you've found?"

I tell her about the vases.

"Well done," she says, "that is remarkable. And you're selling them at Lenhams in Bond Street?" I nod. She sips her wine. "I'll have to look out for them. I'm on their mailing list."

I take a long pull on my beer. After all that she's been through I need to let her down gently.

"Angela," I say. I look deeply into her eyes. She really is a beautiful woman and I need to shake off this schoolboy infatuation before I say something that I regret.

"Yes?"

"Angela. I'm sorry, but I've been married to Sheila for forty years."

"Why are you sorry? That's quite an achievement in this day and age." She looks at a point somewhere beyond my right ear. "If only Brian..." her voice trails off.

I reach to take her hand.

"What I'm trying to say Angela. What I'm trying to say is... I'm not available."

She snatches her hand away. She puts her hand over her mouth. What starts with a small puff of breath from one nostril is soon followed by another and another and before long it appears that she's doing a steam train impression. Tears start to flow down her cheeks as the steam train turns into an express. She lets out a hoot. And then there's a bellow and then she doubles up. Her body convulses.

"Oh, Dave," she says, "that's the funniest thing I've ever heard." She snorts. She reaches into her handbag for a tissue. She takes one out, unfolds it carefully and dabs at her cheeks and her eyes. She pats my hand. "Sorry." She's still laughing. "Did I give you the wrong signal when I suggested we meet up for a drink?"

"Well."

"I did, didn't I?" She opens her eyes wide. "I can see it now. Yes. When you were being sympathetic. You took my reaction for something else. You thought I was on the rebound from my Internet letdown. You thought I was looking for solace in an avuncular father figure. A sort of cuddly old grandad whose shoulder I could cry on."

"Not too much of the 'avuncular, cuddly and old'," I say.

"Sorry." She throws her tissue into the fireplace. It flares up briefly and dies down. She reaches across the small gap between our chairs and puts her hand on mine.

"You're a lovely chap, Dave. You really are. Your warning saved me from a major disaster and I'll never ever be able to thank you enough for that. I hope that I may one day be able to repay you in some way, but I gave you completely the wrong idea. I'm so sorry. What must you have thought of me? Did you tell Sheila? Did you tell her there was a desperate widow trying to take you away from her?"

"Not quite."

"But she knows that you're here with me now?"

I nod.

"That's so nice," she says. She pauses and looks around the bar. "She's not here now watching is she? I'm not going to have to be looking over my shoulder on the way home?"

"No. She's at home getting the dinner ready."

"Well, when you get home you can tell your Sheila she's got nothing to worry about from me. She's a very lucky woman."

"I'm not sure she'd agree with that. But I'm lucky to have her."

"I'll drink to that," Angela raises her glass and drains her wine. "Perhaps I could meet her one day?"

"I think she'd like that. She'd love your clothes."

I drain my beer glass and put it back down. I look at my watch and stand up.

"I'm so glad that we had this conversation." I say.

Angela stands and puts her arms around me. She pecks me again on both cheeks.

"Me too. Why don't me meet here again – the three of us?"

"That would be good."

Chapter Sixty-Two

Dave

It's spring when Martin Hetherington makes his appearance in the High Court. Life has quietened down following our exciting winter. After our initial worries that things weren't well between them, Simon and Maria are going strong and we've become very fond of his Spanish companion. She makes us stonking paellas when he invites her round and we've had fun with impromptu Spanish lessons. Simon is good at languages and we often find the two of them whispering Catalonian sweet nothings. Sheila and I appear to be getting over our midlife crisis - or *my* midlife crisis - and we are enjoying the freedom we get once or twice a week when Simon sleeps over at Maria's place.

The trial has been running for eight days and it's drawing towards the end when I take the stand. Martin hasn't spared a penny on his legal team and there are two silks and an assistant on his side. As far as he's concerned they'll have done a wonderful job so far, as vulnerable woman after vulnerable woman has had her evidence torn to shreds under cross-examination. None of them ever met him and, as far as his barrister is concerned, there's no motive. Why would a wealthy man like Martin con women out of such trifling sums? There's nothing to connect him with the scores of desperate, conniving, charming and deceitful emails.

As a witness I haven't been able to listen to any of this but Sheila and Angela have been in court every day. The two met for a coffee at my suggestion and they got on like a house on fire. So, as Sheila says, at least *one* good thing came from my dodgy bladder. They are now firm friends and they've been sitting together in the public gallery. They've told me everything that's gone on, about all the evidence including the photos that accompanied some of his more salacious emails and were screened in court much to the amusement of the jury who were told, in no uncertain manner, by the judge to behave themselves. The photos were simply dismissed by his legal team by one word 'circumcision'. The public and the jury fortunately didn't have to experience Martin waving anything around in court to prove this point as the judge accepted a signed affidavit by an independent doctor.

The only solid piece of evidence against Hetherington has been his fingerprint on Angela's cheque. I feel confident that that piece of key evidence will convince the jury that he is behind all of the offences.

It's my turn to give evidence on behalf of the prosecution. I swear on the bible even though I don't believe in any of it, and I wonder if that's a bit like keeping your fingers crossed as a child when you tell the teacher that the cat ate your homework.

The first few questions go well.

The barrister asks me to recall my meeting with Martin at the gym and our subsequent journey to and from the hospital. I recount it in detail. I tell the court all about Margarita and the handbag.

"And did the accused mention his financial situation at all during this conversation?"

I hesitate.

"Not really," I pause, "Well, yes, he did in fact - in a roundabout way."

"A roundabout way?"

"Well, he said that his ex-wife had taken him to the cleaners in the divorce. He lost his Chelsea Mews house and his Bentley."

There's a ripple of unsympathetic laughter in court.

"But," I continue, "he got to keep his Porsche and Mercedes...and bought a penthouse."

More laughter.

"Did he mention the *significant* holdings of shares in Lehman Brothers that he insisted on keeping as part of the divorce settlement?"

"He did not. Martin likes to speak of his successes - not of his failures."

I'm feeling rather smug when his barrister stands to cross-examine me.

"Good morning, Mr Prendergast"

"Good morning, sir."

"This won't take long."

"So you say that my client told you that his *modus operandi* as you put it was to send *expensive* handbags costing" he looks down at his notes, "one thousand, five hundred pounds to young women he met on, what you described as, a Sugar Daddy website. Is that correct?"

"It is."

He holds up one of the handbags that have been used as exhibits.

"One of these handbags?"

"Yes."

He looks at the jury as he asks me his next question.

"But this isn't an expensive handbag is it? This is a cheap fake."

"It might be a cheap fake but it is the one that he sent to the waitress at Casa Nuestra."

"You say that it was him that sent the bag, Mr Prendergast but we only have your word for it. We have already heard from Miss Simonez and she could not identify my client. How many years have you known my client."

I think for a second.

"Around forty years."

"Forty years?"

"Yes, sir."

"And where did you first meet him?"

"We met when I started work at the bank. He was working as a junior. I was a cashier."

"And you stayed with the bank for your whole career?"

"That's right."

"And you retired when?"

"A couple of years ago now."

"And what position did you hold when you retired, Mr Prendergast."

"I was Head Of Securities Desk."

"My. That sounds a *very* important position. Where does *Head of Securities Desk* come within the bank hierarchy? Is it a directorial position?"

"No."

"But surely *Head Of Securities,*" he spits the words out as if he's just bitten on a lemon, "is an *executive* post?"

"No."

"So, it's not an executive position. But it *is* a senior managerial post?"

"No."

"Junior management then?"

"No. It is a senior clerical post."

"I see," he pauses, "A senior *clerical* post?" Another pause. "Are you jealous of Martin Hetherington, Mr. Prendergast?"

"No. Why should I be jealous?"

"My highly successful client soared to the highest echelons of the bank; a senior executive who left you trailing behind in his wake. Weren't you just a little envious of his success while you went from menial clerical post to menial clerical post? I put it to you, Mr Prendergast that your hearsay tale of your conversation with my client is born out of simple jealousy of Martin Hetherington - a jealousy compounded by a belief that your wife, how should I say, *admired* him."

"That's utter..." I pause as the right word might get me in trouble with the judge "rubbish. I have no reason to be jealous of Martin Hetherington and my wife married me. Not him."

"I'm sure, Mr Prendergast that the jury will decide upon whether you had cause to be jealous of Mr Hetherington and whether or not that envy led you to make up your preposterous tale in order to incriminate him."

The prosecuting barrister leaps up to object at this but whether the judge overrules or not, the jury has heard the suggestion. I'm not at all jealous of the bastard but I can imagine how easy it might be to think that I am.

I'm hardly listening as the eminent silk tells me that

he's got no further questions. I look for Sheila and Angela in the public gallery and give them an apologetic shrug. Now that my moment on the stand is over I am allowed to join them. I leave court, wearily climb the stairs to the gallery and squeeze onto the end of a packed bench.

There's excitement around the court as Martin takes the stand. I'm surprised that he didn't accept his right to remain silent, but he always was a cocky bugger. The prosecution lash into him with a harsh line of questioning but he simply denies everything. This email? It wasn't him. And this one? It wasn't him. His tracks are well and truly covered but at least we've got his fingerprint.

His own defence brings up the cheque and I am initially puzzled at their line of questioning.

"Mr Hetherington, are you familiar with this cheque which the prosecution exhibited as Exhibit F?" The barrister holds the cheque in its sealed polythene bag in front of the witness box.

"I am."

"And can you offer any explanation why this cheque may bear your fingerprint?"

"I can."

"You can?"

"Yes. As you can see, the cheque is one of *my* bank's cheques."

"It is indeed. But it is not the practice of senior executives to come into contact with cheques is it, Mr Hetherington? And even if it were, you were retired when this cheque arrived at your bank."

"Yes, I was retired and yes handling cheques is a *clerical* job." He looks up at me in the public gallery.

"So you could not possibly have handled this cheque when it was being processed.'

"Absolutely. But I certainly could have handled the cheque."

"How is that?"

"If you look at it you will see that it is printed with a highly decorative and unusual background."

"Indeed it is." The silk shows the jury the modern art design on the cheque.

"That was an innovation we offered to our high-worth customers. We liked to give them a personal and exclusive service. In fact it was an innovation that I, being an art lover, suggested to the bank."

"I see. But surely, Mr Hetherington you, a very senior executive, would not have had any further involvement after initiating the idea."

"No, I would not but, because of my interest, our stationery people brought me ten or so of the first cheque books when they arrived so that I could see how they looked. Being a Picasso lover, I particularly liked this design and I spent a while looking through the books my stationery people brought me."

"But it was several years ago when these books were produced and you, forgive me, *checked* them over."

"It was, but as you probably know from your own financial affairs, with Internet banking, direct debits and credit cards, very few cheques are written nowadays. It is quite possible for a book of thirty cheques to last for five years."

"I can see that, in these circumstances it is very possible that *this,*" he holds the cheque up again in front of the jury, "is one of *the* cheques that you approved for your stationery department."

"Yes, sir."

"No further questions."

We adjourn for lunch and I walk down the road with Angela and Sheila to a small coffee shop for a sandwich and a coffee. There's a general air of despondency.

"The judge is going to throw this out for lack of evidence," I say to nobody in particular. We all shuffle silently on our seats. After everything that Angela and those other poor women have gone through he's going to get away with it. Typical. He'd fall in a cesspit and come up smelling of roses.

When we get back into the public gallery the judge tells

us that there is a final prosecution witness who has been delayed but has now arrived back in the country. I smile to myself. Good old MacIntosh. She's been to all the way to Africa. My spirits are lifted. I whisper to Sheila and Angela, "It will be one of the handbag boys."

The prosecution lawyer stands up. She's a fine, elegant woman who has done her very best with a difficult case.

"My Lord, I would like to call my final witness, Mr Akash Ahmed."

The court door opens and a slight, wiry Asian man of about forty with Bollywood looks, dressed in an elegant pale blue suit smoulders into the room. An assortment of appreciative noises erupt from the public gallery. He goes to the witness box and recites his oath before taking a seat.

"Mr Ahmed, thank you for joining us after a long and arduous journey."

"It is my pleasure, madam."

"What is your occupation, Mr Ahmed?"

"I run a motorcycle courier business."

"And what is this business called?"

"Triple A Couriers."

"And how many motorcyclists do you employ at Triple A Couriers?"

"Just me."

"Was Triple A Couriers approached to deliver a number of handbags to various ladies throughout London and the South East over the past two years?"

"We were, madam."

"And would these addresses be familiar with you as addresses to which you delivered these bags?" she hands the witness a list. He looks over it carefully.

"Yes."

"And how would you know that?"

"The police officers showed me this list and I checked through all of them with my records."

"And do you see in court today the man who gave you these instructions to deliver these bags?"

"No, madam. I never saw the person who arranged the

deliveries. Everything was done by Internet and phone. I was given a number of bags and packing materials in advance and was told to await instructions."

"How many handbags were you given, Mr Ahmed?"

"It was about twenty or possibly twenty five."

"And who gave you these?"

"My client arranged for them all to be delivered to my home. They arrived on my doorstep at an agreed time. There was a knock on the door. I never saw who delivered them to me."

"And you simply awaited instructions from your client?"

'Yes he would email or text me the delivery details and a message that he wanted to accompany the package."

"And you would giftwrap the bag and write out the message on a card?"

"Yes."

The prosecution lawyer shows the witness a number of cards like the one addressed to Margarita. "So this is your handwriting?"

"It is."

"Thank you, Mr Ahmed. Did the same client ever ask you to deliver or collect any other items?"

"Yes, madam. I was once asked to collect an envelope from the local health centre."

"And you collected that envelope from a Mrs Angela Clemence?"

"Yes."

"And who did you deliver the envelope to?"

"I was told that it was very urgent so I was asked to take it to a café and meet the client there.

"And how would you know him?"

"He instructed me to wear something with my Triple A Couriers logo on and he would approach me."

"And he did approach you?"

"Yes, madam. He stood up as soon as I entered the café and took me to a table in a quiet corner."

"And do you recognise the client here in court today?"

"No madam. I believe that he may have been wearing a disguise. He had a dark bushy beard and long black hair. He also wore a pair of dark glasses that covered much of his face and he was dressed in a heavy overcoat with the collar turned up. I could not see enough of his features for me identify him."

"Did you not think his bizarre appearance unusual?"

"I did. *Very* unusual. Not only was his beard and hair unnatural, I was also surprised that he did not remove his coat. It was a cold day and I could understand him wearing the coat but the café was extremely hot and most people would have taken it off."

"And what happened when you got to the table?"

"We sat down and I gave him the envelope."

"And did you ask for a receipt for the envelope?"

"I did. I always get signed paperwork."

"And do you still have the receipt?"

"No. The police have it."

"Yes. That's right isn't it? This is the receipt." She holds up another sealed polythene bag and shows it to the witness."

"Yes it is. The signature is a mess because he was wearing gloves."

"So there will be none of your client's fingerprints or DNA on this document."

"No madam. But I did think of something that might help."

"And what is that?"

"I said that the client was dressed in a heavy overcoat."

"Yes."

"It made him sweat."

"Are you saying that he perspired onto the form? This form has been checked and none of his DNA was found on it."

"No. Not on that form. But when I tore it off my pad after he signed, he was perspiring so much that a lot of sweat dripped off his forehead and spoiled my next form."

"And what happened to that ruined form? Did you destroy it?"

"No. My accountant is very strict. I have to account for every numbered job. I have to keep all the forms, ruined or otherwise, so that he can audit them." Ahmed reaches into his pocket and pulls out a small plastic folder with a form in it. "I only thought of this yesterday so I brought it with me to court today. As you can see, the print is very smudged." He holds the folder out to the lawyer.

Before the prosecution can speak, the leading defence barrister leaps up from his seat.

"Objection, My Lord. This evidence is totally inadmissible. Defence Counsel has not been notified of its submission and I ask that the jury is instructed to ignore it and that any mention of it is struck from the record."

The whole place buzzes with excitement. The judge calls the court to order but pandemonium has broken out.

The judge summons both leading lawyers to the bench and after a few moments of whispering he declares that the case will be adjourned for two hours and calls for the court to be cleared.

Chapter Sixty-Three

Dave

We go back to the café and order ourselves some coffees. We should be going to the pub for a stiff drink after the day we've all had.

We animatedly debate the new evidence. Since *Making A Murderer* on Netflix we all fancy ourselves as amateur sleuths. Angela reckons that they'll struggle to get enough DNA off the form and she's a medic, but Sheila reckons that Martin is a heavy sweater and the form could have had a good soaking.

I know that he can sweat profusely as I've seen him at a spinning class but I still feel I need to ask Sheila when we get home how she knows this particular aspect of Martin's physiology.

We drink our coffees and get back to the court early so that we can get a seat. The public gallery fills up very quickly and the court officials have to direct people to a standing only row at the back of the gallery.

The judge enters and we all stand. He gestures us all to be seated and we sit back down.

As soon as the court is in session Martin's lawyer stands. "My Lord. My client would like to change his pleas."

"Indeed?"

The judge begins. "Mr Hetherington, please rise."

Martin stands up in the dock. He's his usual immaculate self. He's wearing a Saville Row suit, a crisp, white shirt and a pink, silk tie with matching, silk handkerchief in his suit breast pocket. He takes the silk handkerchief and dabs at his forehead with it.

The judge starts to read all the charges against him. It takes forever as each charge names the victim, a list of dates, a place and the amount he conned them out of. At the end of each charge the judge asks, "How do you plead?"

And every time the judge asks that question an almost silent mumble comes from the dock, "Guilty."

The public gallery erupts in a fractured Mexican wave as, after each guilty plea, a different woman and her friends and family leap from their seats and cheer. The judge's warnings have little effect and when the final charge is dealt with the public gallery rises as one in a frenzy of hugging and back-slapping.

When the court finally returns to order the judge says that he will be giving Hetherington a custodial sentence but the length of sentence will be decided in due course and at a later hearing. He asks Martin if he has anything to say before adjourning the court.

"Will I be able to go home tonight, My Lord?"

"You will not, sir. One usually uses this opportunity to address the court. Why do you ask?"

"My c...." he looks up at the courtroom clock and lowers his voice. "Oh it doesn't matter."

There's a jubilant throng on the steps of the court. It's like a middle-aged hen party as the groups of wronged women bond together and answer questions from the waiting press. Angela is interviewed by a crew from Sky News.

"Are you happy with the outcome of the trial?"

"Yes and no. I'm happy with the guilty pleas but wish that he had made them at the start of the trial and saved all of us," she gestures around to our new hen party friends "from having all our private correspondence and some of our most intimate thoughts dragged into the public domain."

As she speaks, a slight figure in a motorcycle helmet begins to walk down the steps. Angela breaks away from the interview as he is swamped by the crowd. A few seconds later he's being held shoulder high like a triumphant football captain parading the FA Cup.

Triple A Couriers has a rosy future I think.

Sheila, Angela and I decide that a celebration is called for and agree on dinner at a nearby hotel. As we walk along the road towards the hotel restaurant a lorry passes us and draws to a halt. We can't get past so we stand and watch as the council team hoists a large silver Mercedes onto their vehicle.

"Oh dear. How much is that going to cost the poor driver?" says Angela.

One of the council men overhears her. "They'll be paying two hundred pound flat charge and forty pounds a day storage for every day it remains unclaimed."

I smile at the lorry driver. "I hope you're on commission."

Angela looks at me inquisitively. Sheila laughs.

"You don't know whose car that is do you, Angela?" she says.

"No. Should I?" She pauses and thinks for a moment. "It isn't?" She opens her eyes wide and puts her hand to her mouth, "Oh my God! It is, isn't it?"

I nod. "At forty pounds a day it could be sixty thousand pounds by the time he comes to collect it."

Chapter Sixty-Four

Dave

I have to hand it to the Lenhams'. The sale has been very well publicised and, although the pre-sale press releases about the Yabu Meizan vases were not taken up by any of the national papers, there's been a photo and a few paragraphs in *The Antiques Trade Gazette* and I've had a call from our local press after Matsuko asked me if I was prepared to speak to them. It's a few days before the sale when a local reporter phones and I agree that she can pop round.

There's a sharp rap on the front door. I open it to a young woman of around twenty with cropped black hair. She's wearing a donkey jacket over a denim skirt, thick black leggings and a pair of Doc Marten boots.

"Is the bell not working?" I say tetchily.

"Sorry. I'm used to knocking," she says. "Half the time they've got their music on so loud a bell is next to useless even on the odd occasions there's a battery in it. Are you Dave Prendergast?"

"I am. You must be Margie Mitchell."

"That's me." She smiles and offers her hand.

I can't help but warm to her winning and intelligent smile. I shake her hand briefly and invite her inside.

"Sorry if I was a bit off " I say pointing her to one of the sofas in the lounge. She sits down and I sit opposite on the other sofa. "I've had a difficult few days. We've been in court."

"Anything interesting?"

"An Internet fraudster."

"The bank executive?"

"That's the one."

"One of my bosses was covering that story. I only started a few months ago, after I got my degree. I'm still on golden wedding anniversaries, bicycle thieves, amateur dramatics and er..." she looks down at the Lenhams' press release "old pottery."

"Hey, go easy on the 'old pottery'. Those aren't any old pots they're the finest Japanese Satsuma."

"But they *are* old pots. Do you think our readers will be interested? *Local resident puts old vases in auction* is hardly going to win me Junior Reporter Of The Year."

"Maybe not but what if it was *Local Resident Finds Fortune On eBay.*"

She leans forward in her chair.

"Now that's a bit more like it." She takes a notepad and ballpoint out of her donkey jacket.

I know I've already said too much and try to backtrack. I've told nobody outside the family about eBay and, as far as the auction house is concerned the vases were simply *The Property Of A Gentleman.*

"But your readers won't want to hear about that will they?"

"I think they will. A bit of a lucky streak, you know, a small lottery win, they love that sort of stuff. A guy found a stash of Roman coins on a building site and we put it on a two-page spread after the Treasure inquest."

"Well, perhaps we are a bit early you know. What if the vases don't sell? It will be a bit of a non event."

"You may be right but if they do sell and sell for what?" he emphasises her question by throwing her palms open.

"Lenhams have put a reserve of thirty grand on them"

She gives a small whistle, "And you bought them on eBay for how much?"

"I'd rather not say."

"It's up to you," she says, "but I can just spend a few hours on eBay looking. What's your eBay user name?"

"No comment."

"I'm not the police. Don't you want your name in the papers? Most people love to have their names and pictures in the papers."

"I don't want burglars knowing I've come into money."

"We won't print your address and there'll be no photo if

you don't want one. What will you do with the money?"

I shrug. "Treat my wife and me to a decent holiday I suppose."

"That will be some holiday. You could get a world cruise for that."

"Sheila's always fancied a world cruise."

"So how about it? Can I print your name or not?"

"Look," I say, "I need to check it out with my family and a few others. Let me get back to you. It might be a big story after the sale but it might just be a damp squib. *Old Man Fails To Sell Old Pots* won't sell you any papers."

"You probably *are* right," she says. My MacBook Pro is open on the coffee table in front of her. She brushes the mousepad as she moves to put her notebook back in her pocket. The screen springs into life.

"Sorry," she says, "Clumsy me." I stand up aiming to move the laptop out of her view. I can feel my face flushing. She looks at the screen. "Oh, I see you've been back on eBay." She picks the MacBook up and turns it towards me. "Any more luck?"

"No," I shake my head. "The vases were a one off." I push the screen closed and show her back to the door.

I open the door. She stops on the doorstep and turns back towards me. We shake hands again.

"Good luck on Thursday then." she says.

Chapter Sixty-Five

Dave

The catalogue is more than an inch thick and weighs a ton. I sit on the tube with it on my lap. I flick through it. Three hundred and seventy pages and six hundred lots but there's only one lot on the front cover. There, beneath the auctioneer's logo embossed in gold and above the words *Fine Japanese Art,* the Bond Street address and today's date also embossed in gold, are my vases - I mean *our* vases - with the most charismatic of the frogs winking out from the page to captivate and engage the bidders.

I feel like holding the catalogue up to the mixed assembly of tourists, shoppers and commuters in the carriage, pointing at the cover and then at myself and mouthing "Mine." I'm too English to do that but perhaps, when I've turned to the page towards the back of the catalogue where a close up of one of the vase's panels heralds the next section of the sale *Satsuma earthenware & other ceramics Lots 502 - 541,* I can nudge the bloke sitting next to me who is looking over my shoulder and appears to be interested, and casually start a conversation with "They're beautiful aren't they?" When he responds I can turn the page and run my finger across the estimate thirty thousand - forty thousand pounds. And when he raises his eyebrows I can run my finger across the words that caused such hilarity in the Prendergast household - *Property of a gentleman* - and point to myself.

But sadly, although he's looking over my shoulder, the guy next to me - nodding to the tinny beat of his headphones - appears to be more interested in the pair of legs opposite me and firmly attached to Maria so "They're beautiful aren't they?" might be inappropriate, although I have to say they are pretty fabulous legs. Nobody else seems interested in the old guy with the glossy catalogue. They are all too engrossed in *Metro* and someone from *Big*

Brother's 'Three-In-A-Bed Sex Romp.' I'm now sixty-three and I haven't had a three-in-a-bed romp since I bounced on my mum and dad when I was a toddler.

Simon is sitting opposite me squashed between Sheila and Maria. He too has a catalogue, but it's simply resting on his knee and he's busy whispering into Maria's ear. Sheila is reading *Metro* but she turned over the scandal pages with a disparaging shrug and now appears to be engrossed in the financial page no doubt working out how best to deal with our imminent windfall.

I spoke to Matsuko a few days ago. I visited the saleroom for the viewing. The room that had been so beautifully filled with Chinese works of art was now full of Japanese pieces. There was still a museum-like quality to the display but, instead of porcelains and ceramics, the room was adorned with fearsome Samurai armour known as *tosei gusoko,* amazing swords like those used to bloody effect by Uma Thurman in *Kill Bill* and display cabinets filled with tiny ivory netsuke and okimono. There, in the middle of the room, standing on their own in a glass display case and illuminated perfectly were the frog vases. She began by asking me if I liked the display and the catalogue and then she said that she had a question for me.

"Fire away," I said.

"I have been asked by one of our clients, one of the world's biggest collectors of Yabu Meizan pieces if you could come to an arrangement over the payment."

"How do you mean? Come to an arrangement?"

"It happens quite often with high value lots," she said, "The buyer simply asks for an extra month's credit on top of our usual terms and conditions which require almost immediate payment."

"Oh."

"You are not happy with this?"

"I'm just worried if he docsn't pay."

"There is little question of non-payment. We have known this client for fifteen years."

"So, what's in it for me?'

"You have the world's most serious collector bidding for your vases. One month of waiting is a small price to pay if he bids the lot up."

"I see." Sheila was not with me. She was not going to be happy but I had to take an executive decision and told Matsuko that we we'd go along with her suggestion.

We alight at Bond Street and take the escalator up. All the electronic advertising panels beside the escalator are showing the catalogue cover. Maria is behind me.

"What would your Grandad think of this?" I ask.

"I think he would think it was very funny."

"Funny?"

"Yes. He had very little money. He would have laughed at anyone prepared to spend thirty thousand pounds on some pottery. I do not think he earned thirty thousand pounds in his whole life."

We leave the station and walk in the direction of Bond Street. I point out the saleroom to Simon and tell him that we will meet him there for the afternoon session which starts at half past two. He tells us that he's booked a pedicure and spa treatment for Maria while he has to go and collect something he's ordered.

I leave the young lovers and link arms with Sheila. We walk along Oxford Street and cross over to Selfridges. We spend a while looking at the handbags.

"Do you want a real one?" I say picking up a Mulberry bag.

"Thirteen hundred pounds for a bag," she says inspecting the ticket, "We're not made of money."

"Not yet. But by five o'clock."

"By five o'clock we'll know how much they've sold for but if it's the big bidder who gets them we couldn't buy anything here today. We won't be able to pay the credit card bill in time."

"We can always throw caution to the wind, live dangerously and pay interest on the credit card."

"Something we *never* do."

"Go on. Let me treat you."

"If you want to treat me don't buy a handbag at that price, take me to Next and buy me two for under two hundred pounds. Theirs are just as nice."

"But they don't have a label."

"Stuff the label. I'd rather have the extra thousand pounds."

We have similar conversations at the perfume counters, the make up kiosks, the shoes and the designer clothing and I can see that the money is not going to change Sheila. We've toured the ground, first and second floors and we've spent the grand sum of nine pounds ninety nine on mascara. I am itching to get downstairs to the home entertainment department. We take escalators from the top of the store to the bottom but Sheila steers me well away from the computers and home cinemas into the small wine bar in the lower ground floor where we enjoy an excellent lunch of tapas with a small carafe of delicious chilled rosé wine.

When we get back to Bond Street Simon and Maria are waiting outside the saleroom looking very pleased with themselves.

"You two look like the cats who got the cream," I say.

"I'm the one who got the cream, Dad." Simon hugs Maria tightly as she holds out a hand to me and Sheila.

Sheila instantly throws her arms around Maria and begins to cry. The manicurist has done a lovely job on her nails, but I'm not going to get emotional about it. At least I wasn't going to get emotional but then I notice the thin gold band with the single, tiny diamond and I find myself welling up as my head fills with thoughts of reduced Waitrose bills, a drastic drop in the ironing and getting to choose what's on the telly.

There's a lot of hugging going on between Maria and Sheila, and Sheila and Simon. It gets infectious and I join in.

"It's wonderful news," I say. "Where are you going to live?"

"I thought I might ask you if Maria could move in with us."

I'm not a hundred percent sure that the wink that accompanies Simon's remark is telling me he's winding me up.

I look at my watch. I tell everyone to pull themselves together as it's almost time to begin.

We go in through the revolving door. The room is now filled with chairs and the lots have been moved from the middle of the floor.

The saleroom is almost full and we find four seats together near the back of the room and settle down for the sale. As we stand to let the bidders squeeze past us for seats further along our row, I'm brushed by exotic couture and megabuck handbags. Each time I avoid being skewered by a stiletto Sheila whispers in my ear. I hear 'Jimmy Choo', 'Manolo Blahnik', 'Louis Vuitton', 'Louboutin' and 'Gucci'. I nudge Sheila, point down at my feet and whisper to her, "Marks and Spencer."

I see Matsuko come into the saleroom. She spots me, smiles and gives a little wave before heading to sit at a long table running along the room to the right of the rostrum: the table is manned by nine or ten of her colleagues including those who I met when I first visited.

The guy from *Antiques Roadshow* is busy chatting to a couple in the front row. He checks his watch then pats the man on the shoulder and gives the man's partner a brief peck on the cheek, before turning away and stepping onto a dais. He gives a couple of knocks with the gavel on his pulpit-like rostrum and the audience takes on a hushed silence. I half expect him to start with "Dearly Beloved" but he runs through a few items of procedure, points out the fire exits and then he starts the sale.

Two mischievous eyes smile out from his crinkled and suntanned face. His scarecrow hair and Frank Zappa moustache contrast with his expensive suit and he looks as if he might start to hold forth on the theory of relativity rather than flog Japanese artworks. He has a polished technique. He charms and teases the audience; he cajoles them to go the extra yard and not to let their lots get away.

There's an air of one-upmanship as the well-heeled punters ostentatiously wave their paddles in an 'I've got a bigger wad than you' sort of way. I know that selling here was the right decision. If anybody is going to be determined not to be outbid or, more importantly, not be *seen* to be outbid, it is this crowd.

The Lenhams staff on Matsuko's table are taking telephone bids. Some lots have three or four telephone bidders battling it out but when bidding gets underway for Lot 534 there's a flurry of activity as Matsuko and all ten at the table start to dial their clients. I see them relax one by one as their call is answered and they settle into their seats to chat animatedly with the bidders. There's a bit of a panic on one of the young floppy haired men's face as he dials again and again and clearly gets no response. Matsuko takes the phone off him. She looks down at the screen in front of him, dials a number and speaks to someone who answers immediately. She passes the phone back to her colleague with an almost imperceptible eye roll.

And then, it begins. Lot 535. Mr Roadshow reads out the description in full. He tells us how much he covets the vases for himself. He says that they are possibly the finest pieces ever made by Yabu Meizan and points out that he is not alone in his desire for them as he gestures to the ten telephones ready to go.

"As you can see. We've had rather a lot of interest in these," he smiles and looks down at his screen, "and I have to start the bidding at..." - a very long and dramatic pause - "sixty thousand pounds."

There's a real buzz in the room. Sheila gives my hand a squeeze. Four of the telephone staff look at the rostrum and shake their heads but Matsuko nods and indicates that her caller is ready to bid on. A paddle goes up several rows ahead of us. A dark skinned hand is holding it. I can't see who it is but who cares? There's a hand holding it aloft and that's all that matters to me. And it stays aloft as the bidding passes sixty-five, seventy, seventy-five, eighty, eighty-five, ninety, ninety-five, a *hundred* thousand. Most of the telephone bidders are clearly out, but the clients have remained on the line, no doubt fascinated to hear the final outcome. The Lenhams personnel appear relaxed and happy to be politely filling them in with the details.

It only takes a minute before the price hits a hundred and twenty thousand. Unless a late bidder jumps in at the close, there is now only Mitsuko's phone bidder and the paddle waver left. Bidding is going up in increments of five thousand pounds and each phone bid is taking longer and longer to coax whilst the paddle has simple stayed up throughout.

Matsuko finally shakes her head after her client declines to bid a staggering one hundred and forty five thousand. No amount of cajoling from the rostrum or from Matsuko can raise another bid on the phone or in the room.

"Going once. Going twice." The hammer goes down. "Sold to Paddle 287 for one hundred and forty thousand pounds."

A polite round of applause ripples around the room and a less polite cheer goes up from our row. The holder of the paddle stands. He is a bespectacled old Asian gentleman with smartly trimmed silver hair and a silver moustache. He is wearing a finely cut light grey suit. He bows politely to the applauding bidders. Sheila and I hug. Simon and Maria do the same. The auctioneer waits to let the excitement of the moment die down as the saleroom partially empties.

I catch Matsuko's eye again as we join the unsuccessful departing bidders and head for the exit. I'm about to wave to her but resist the urge just in time to stop me from bidding eight thousand pounds for lot number 536. I simply smile and she returns my smile with a warmth that belies her usual poker faced expression.

Once we are back out in the street we share a group hug like a football team before kick off.

"Oh ye of little faith. What did I tell you? A hundred... and... forty... thousand," I say to the huddle.

"Before commission," Sheila adds.

"Okay, but it's still going to be way over a hundred and thirty. Let's go and celebrate."

The group hug breaks up and Simon says "I'm up for that Dad. Where to? The Ritz?"

Sheila and Maria both speak as one "The *Ritz*?"

"We aren't millionaires," Sheila adds.

"We're only talking about a couple of glasses of champagne," says Simon.

"Before we start getting ideas above our station and frittering it all away they do a very decent Prosecco in Pizza Express," says Sheila, "There's one in Dean Street. It's not far away."

"Simon might have some Tesco vouchers," Maria says, giving him a knowing glance.

So it's Pizza Express where we toast our success with Prosecco and four American Hots.

As our glasses chink together Simon says, "Hope we can afford this, Dad. The Clubcard vouchers can't be used on drinks you know."

"And we might not be paid for two months," Sheila adds.

Chapter Sixty-Six

Dave

We're back home from our celebration at Pizza Express by eight o'clock. We left Simon and Maria in London. They picked up some late tickets and went to a show The sale result was more of an aphrodisiac than a plateful of oysters so we open the bottle of champagne that I put in the fridge in the morning before we left home and decide to make it an early night.

When I wake up in the morning, Sheila is not in bed. I hear her shout from downstairs.

"You better come and have a look at this."

I put on my dressing gown and run down the stairs.

"What?"

Sheila is holding the local paper. She turns it towards me.

"You're front page news."

LOCAL MAN'S EBAY TREASURE

I snatch the paper from Sheila. Beneath and partially alongside the headline is Lenhams' PR photo of the vases.

A tagline follows;-

£50 VASES SOAR TO £160,000

I read out loud. "A local resident struck it rich yesterday, Margie Mitchell writes, when two Japanese vases that he bought on eBay for just £50 soared at leading Bond St Auctioneers Lenhams' sale of Japanese Works Of Art to £160,000. Bidders gasped as the delicately painted ceramics produced by renowned potter Yabu Meizan left the estimate of £30-£40,000 trailing in their wake, as a fierce bidding war broke out between a telephone bidder and another in the room.

The seller, who has lived in the area all his life and currently wishes to remain anonymous, told *The Mercury* exclusively that he would be treating his wife to a world cruise with the proceeds."

'Where did they get one hundred and sixty thousand from?" Sheila asks.

"That'll be Lenhams. They always add the buyer's premium and VAT to the hammer price to show what the bidder paid."

"And when do we start our world cruise?"

"Dunno. When we get Lenhams' cheque and when we've sorted out Maria."

"And Simon. And Susie."

"There'll still be enough left. Don't worry."

Sheila picks the paper back up and reads the front page again. "You know this is not the last you'll hear of this don't you?"

"It's only the local rag."

"It is today. Your Margie Mitchell got her scoop, but this story is big enough for the national press now you've let it slip that you bought them for fifty pounds. How did she find out?"

"She's an ambitious young reporter. They have their ways of finding things out."

"Well, if a junior reporter on the local rag has found it, it won't be long before *The Mirror* and *The Sun* turn up on the doorstep.

"I can make it more difficult for them."

"How?"

"I can get Maria to delete the photos from the listing and they'll never find them."

"Do it then. Right away."

I check my watch. Simon should still be in the staff room sipping a cup of coffee with his fellow teachers. I dial his number.

"Hi, mate."

"Dad. I wondered when I'd hear from you. Your story is the talk of the staff room. Don't worry. I haven't let on that I know anything about it."

"Good. Can you do me a favour?"

"Sure. What can I do?"

"Get in touch with Maria and ask her to delete the photos from the listing."

"No point."

"Why?"

"The listing is over six months old. It will have gone by now."

"Of course. So how did our sleuth on *The Mercury* find it?"

"She'll probably have searched very thoroughly and spotted it in cached results."

"Does that mean that any journalist can do the same?"

"Pretty much. I'll expect a scrum at the front door when I get home."

"Shit. But hang on. I only authorised Lenhams to give *The Mercury* my details Nobody else."

"You may be okay then. You used the Kinkozanfan account too and there's nothing on the About Me page so you might get away with it." I hear a bell ring in the background. "See you later, Dad. Got to rush."

"See you, son."

I press end call and put the phone down. "No luck I'm afraid, love. Unless Margie is a lot cleverer or luckier than the rest of Fleet Street, we may get some more attention from the press."

No sooner have I spoken than my phone rings. I don't recognise the number. I pick it up and slide the answer button across the screen.

"Hello?"

"Hi, Mr Prendergast? It's Margie. Have you seen today's *Mercury*?"

"I have. Well done, Mazher Mahmood."

"Is that supposed to be a compliment?"

"Okay Bob Woodward then."

"That's better. So? What do you think? Can I do a follow up piece with a photo? The National Press haven't been off the phone to my editor this morning trying to pump him for your details. The story's only got a couple of days life in it. If I can get a follow up in *The Mercury* tomorrow the nationals will only put a small paragraph around page eight and your moment of fame will be over."

"Let me think about it. I'll phone you back."

"You've got my number?"

"Yes. It came up on my screen."

I end the call and speak to Sheila. I reckon that with all the technology at their fingertips any journalists worth their salt will track me down without too much difficulty in an hour or two and, once my name is in a major paper, I might even get inundated by begging letters and worse. On the other hand if Margie runs the story tomorrow I'll get some local publicity but it will blow over.

Sheila agrees that if it's going to be inevitable we might as well take the local route. I phone Margie back and it only feels like ten minutes before she's back rapping on the front door accompanied by her photographer - an old guy weary from a lifetime of snapping happy octogenarian couples and school football teams.

I invite them both in and offer them a hot drink. The offer perks up the photographer, Jerry, who asks for black coffee with three spoons of Nescafe and four of sugar. While I'm making the drinks Sheila shows Jerry around the ground floor so that he can choose the best spot for his picture. He spots the sale catalogue on the coffee table and picks it up.

"So, this is what it's all about then?"

"That's right," says Sheila.

"Someone paid a hundred and sixty grand for that?"

"There *were* two," says Sheila opening the catalogue at the lot and showing it to Jerry.

"I should bloody hope so, pardon my French. I'd expect two dozen for that price. "

Jerry decides that the dining room is the best place for the shot. He positions Sheila at the table with the catalogue open in front of her and asks me to stand leaning over her with my hand touching the page and facing the camera.

"Christ, Jerry. You've done too many weddings. They're not signing the register. We need to make it more sexy than that," says Margie, looking around the room. She fixes on the display shelves in the corner.

"Did you buy any of the stuff on your shelves on eBay Dave?" she asks.

"Most of it yeah. There's still a gap where the vases were."

"Great. Let's get you in front of that. You don't want to be in the picture do you, Sheila?"

"Certainly not. I don't need my mug splashed across *The Mercury.*"

Margie positions me in front of the display. She moves me slightly aside so that the teapots, plates and other bits and pieces are in view.

"Any special bargains there, Dave?"

"Not really. This plate," I point to a beautifully painted floral porcelain plate with a heraldic crest, "I got it for twenty."

"And what's it worth?"

"Oh. About a hundred maybe." I hear Sheila splutter into her coffee. "Seventy perhaps."

"It's nice. Can I move it?" I nod. Margie moves the plate on its stand so that it is next to my face. "There we go. Jerry, can you get a good close up of Dave and get the plate in too. The colours make it a nice picture."

Jerry does the business. I take off my glasses. I smile for a couple of shots and look serious for a few more. He photographs me full length and in close up.

Jerry hands the camera to Margie. She looks at the screen on the back and scrolls through the photos. She nods appreciatively. "Good. We've got what we need there, Jerry. Thanks. See you back at the office." She hands the camera back to him.

Jerry finishes his coffee and Sheila shows him out.

Margie suggests we sit at the dining table while she takes just a few more notes. She asks me about Yabu Meizan, eBay and all the bargains I have found. Sheila points out that it should be just one real bargain and lots of misses. She stands up and heads towards the disasters cupboard but I manage to persuade her that Margie won't be interested in a cupboard full of tat. Margie *is* interested but we manage to avoid opening the cupboard. She chats with Sheila about the kids and about the grandchildren.

In the middle of our friendly conversation, Margie suddenly bowls us a googly.

"So how do you feel about the seller, Muchachabonita?"

"How do you mean?" I ask.

"Well. You bought her vases for fifty pounds and sold them for a hundred and sixty thousand."

Sheila corrects her, "A hundred and forty. And we've got to pay commission on that."

"It's still a lot of money."

"It is," I say. "But don't worry about Muchachabonita. We're going to see her right."

"Honestly?"

"Yes."

"Wow. This story gets better and better. How are you going to see her right?"

"We've agreed to pay her half the proceeds."

"Half? That's brilliant. Can I have her details to check that out?"

"I'd rather not without her permission but, trust me, we've really done the right thing."

Margie whistles. "How many people would have done that?"

We talk some more before Margie looks at her watch and tells us that she needs to get back to the office to file the story in good time. "Look out for tomorrow's front page. And thanks a lot. This story might be my first big break."

Chapter Sixty-Seven

Dave

I don't sleep well. I check the alarm clock every half hour from three onwards and eventually give up and get out of bed. I tiptoe to the wardrobe and take out some jeans and a shirt and jumper. I take my socks and pants from the drawer and carry the bundle out of the bedroom, onto the landing and into the family bathroom where I have a pee and a wash and shave before dragging my clothes on.

The papers won't be delivered for a few hours so I decide to walk down to the local shops and buy an extra copy. I reach News & Booze and head straight to the counter where Mr Ali is still marking up papers for the daily rounds. I pick up a folded copy of *The Mercury* and take out some change from my pocket. Mr Ali doesn't look up and takes the coins. And then he does look up.

"Mr Prendergast."

"Good morning, Mr Ali."

Mr Ali gestures towards the back of the shop where his son is stacking shelves.

"Mohammed," he beckons his son, "Look who is here. Our local hero Mr David Prendergast or *Honest Dave* as they call him in the paper."

Mohammed stops stacking and joins his dad behind the counter. He holds out his hand. "Nice one, Mr Prendergast."

Mr Ali takes another copy of the newspaper and I get a look at it for the first time. My photo - quite a nice one I must add -   fills a third of the page alongside a block headline.

Honest Dave Prendergast's Fantastic eBay Find

Beneath the headline is Margie's byline followed by the tagline

eBAY BIDDER TO GIVE HALF HIS
WINDFALL TO SELLER

Mr Ali is holding a felt tipped pen towards me. He asks me "Can you sign 'To All At News & Booze?'"

I write as he wishes and sign with a flourish. Mr Ali takes the paper back.

"You missed something."

"What?"

"Honest."

I take the paper back and add a small 'honest' above my signature in inverted commas together with a smiley face to indicate that I'm trying to be ironic.

Mr Ali thanks me and I take my paper and head back towards home.

As I walk along the street I look at the faces passing me for signs of recognition. I'm disappointed when there is none but at the same time I sense an air of relief that this will be the end of the publicity.

I get home and go inside and start to prepare breakfast for Sheila and Simon. While I'm cooking I look closely at my photo. I'm pleased with it and the heraldic plate looks really nice in full colour. The photo is captioned *Dave Prendergast at home with another eBay bargain*

I read Margie's article.

Spotting an item on eBay for peanuts and selling it for £160,000 is every bargain hunter's dream but local resident Dave Prendergast wasn't dreaming when two rare vases popped up on his screen for just £50. As we reported yesterday the vases were sold in the West End this week for a world record price for the Japanese potter Yabu Meizan.

Retired bank employee Dave (63), agreed to give up his anonymity for The Mercury and, when asked what he intended to do with his windfall, he told us that, before spending a penny on himself or his wife Sheila (61) and their family, his first priority would be to give half of the sale proceeds to the eBay seller.

We at The Mercury think that Dave's honest gesture makes him worthy of our Mercury Citizen

Of The Month, but what do you think? Would you have done the same? We're running a phone and Internet poll.

I plate up the breakfasts and call upstairs to Simon and Sheila.

After several reminders, there are signs of activity and first Simon and then Sheila walk blearily into the kitchen.

"It's Saturday morning, Dad. What time do you call this?"

"I've been up for hours. Thought you both might like to see this." I hold up the paper.

Chapter Sixty-Eight

Dave

The next two days are a whirl as I am inundated by journalists wanting to ask about my decision to split the sale proceeds. They're contrasting my story with another that's been in the news this week. Two old friends went out like they did most weekends with their metal detectors. They had been going out together for over thirty years. On the day in question one of them uncovered a rare medieval jewel. By a stroke of luck for the reporters, the finder's share, after allowing for half for the landowner, was valued by the Treasure inquest at precisely a hundred and forty thousand. The finder refused to share any of his hundred and forty thousand with his old friend and an acrimonious court case ensued in which one friend said that they had always agreed to split fifty-fifty if anything worth more than five hundred turned up. Needless to say, the two are not friends anymore.

The two stories sparked up a debate online and in the media on honesty and morality. I had a call from the *Today* programme and their mobile studio was parked outside the house all lined up for a Monday morning interview when a catastrophe in Syria knocked my story out of the frame.

I scroll through the comments on various online polls in which I'm hailed in some as a hero and others as a complete tosser - and much worse.

It's late on Monday night when I get another call from Margie.

"Hi Dave. This is just a friendly warning. You'd better check out *The Mirror* in the morning."

"Why."

"They've got hold of a story that you're not going to like. I know my story was bang-on so we're not running this update but I just wanted to give you a heads up."

"Tell me more."

"Well. It seems that..." her voice becomes choppy as the line breaks up I can hear only odd words "Mirror. eBay. Lies."

"You're breaking up," I say, "Hello? Hello? Margie? Can you hear me?"

The line goes dead. I ring back but it goes straight through to voicemail. I send a text but it reads *not delivered.*

I tell Sheila and Simon about the call. I'm facing another sleepless night but Simon points out that the first editions can turn up on railway concourses in the very early hours and offers to drive me into town.

"Hang on," Sheila says

"Later love," I say, "We won't be long."

"But wait—"

"See you later."

We arrive outside Euston at just after midnight. Simon finds a parking space and I jump out of the car and run onto the concourse. Most of the shops are closed but I find a twenty-four hour news and coffee shop where a young man is snipping the tight strapping on huge bundles of newspapers.

"Have you done *The Mirror* yet?" I ask.

He nods in the direction of one of the bundles that he's already cut open and I take a copy. I throw down a pound coin onto the counter and leave the shop. I run to the car and open the door. Simon turns on the reading lights and we look at the front page. They're leading on the crisis in Syria. At least I am not big news.

We turn to page two and three and there's still nothing to worry me. We keep turning frantically and, with each page turned, I relax a little more. Maybe Margie jumped the gun and *The Mirror* pulled the story. It's only when we reach the middle of the newspaper that my heart sinks.

There's a photograph of me walking along our street. Somebody sitting in a car obviously took it but I don't remember it being taken. I can see from the clothes that I am wearing in the picture that it was taken yesterday.

We read the headline together.

NOT SO HONEST DAVE

'Honest' Dave Prendergast the man who sparked a nationwide debate on ethics when he claimed to be sharing half of a £140,000 windfall with an anonymous eBay seller, may not be so honest after all.

The Mirror has been contacted by an independent Diabetes care charity shop worker who identified Prendergast as the man who, posing as a scruffy and unshaven homeless person, donated a bagful of bondage implements and erotica before buying the now famous vases for around forty pounds. His story of making the find on eBay was a complete fabrication and The Mirror now challenges him to live up to his 'Honest Dave' nickname and donate the proceeds to the charity that missed out on a huge payday.

Mavis Edwards who started the charity when her two-year-old daughter was diagnosed with the critical Type 1 strain of the life threatening disease said "The proceeds of the vases could have provided insulin pumps for scores of infants with Type 1 making a huge improvement in their health and saving them from multiple daily injections."

When The Mirror tried to contact Prendergast at his million pound home in a leafy London suburb he was unavailable for comment.

My photograph is captioned 'Honest Dave or Kinky Dave perhaps?'

I put my head in my hands. "Unavailable for comment? What's that about?"

"You told me to say you weren't available. You know you did."

"But not about the charity shop."

"Nobody mentioned the charity shop."

"What's your mum going to say? I've gone from Honest

Dave to Kinky Dave in twenty-four hours."

"You never know, Dad. She might quite like Kinky Dave."

"I've known your Mum for forty odd years and the kinkiest thing she's ever done is eaten a 99 cornet with a twinkle in her eye."

"You sure it wasn't a sprinkle?"

"Ha bloody ha. Come on. We better get home and face the music."

It's two when we get home but the lights are still on. As we open the door Sheila is standing in her dressing gown in the hall. "Welcome home Mr Kinky" she says.

"How do you know? I was going to break it to you gently."

"*The Mirror* website. Duh! I was trying to tell you to check it but, as always, you didn't listen. You just got it into your head to find a paper copy and off you went ignoring me again."

I apologise and promise to listen in future. Sheila reminds me that this is the twentieth time I have promised to listen in the last week alone. I make a mental note to make more effort.

I suggest that we talk strategy over a cup of tea but we're all shattered and decide to try and catch a few hours sleep instead and regroup over breakfast.

Our sleep is ended by a familiar rap on the door. I check the bedside alarm clock. Seven a.m. She's certainly keen. I throw on my dressing gown and shuffle downstairs and open the door.

"Good morning, Dave. Or do we call you Kinky now?" Margie laughs.

"Why are you so cheerful? I've got nothing to laugh about."

"Maybe not, but I've got the chance of another exclusive and, rest assured, it's an exclusive that's going to clear your name."

"Come in," I say opening the door wider and beckoning her over the threshold.

I shout upstairs, "Margie from *The Mercury's* here."

We go into the lounge and Margie sits where she sat

before while I go and make us all some tea.

When I bring the tea back through, Simon and Sheila have joined Margie in the lounge.

"Right," Margie says getting her notebook and ballpoint out of her pocket and sitting on the edge of her seat, "Let's get down to business. You know that you could sue *The Mirror* for libel."

"We can't."

"Why?"

"Because it's true."

Margie drops her pen. Her face contorts into a frown.

"But it can't be true. I did all the research. I found the vases. You bought them on eBay." I see her confidence ebb as her hopes of National Awards evaporate into the possibility of a career-ending mistake. She goes from confident junior reporter to vulnerable child with a quivering lip.

"That was true too."

She perks up.

"I just don't get it. You either bought them on eBay or you bought them in a charity shop. You can't have done both."

"Oh, yes I could."

By the end of our conversation, Margie has filled pages of her notebook. She describes my story as fantastic. She gets up and prepares to leave.

"It's going to take some editing to get this down to the few paragraphs they'll give me," she says.

"Well, do your best," says Sheila.

Margie leaves. Simon rushes off to work and Sheila and I go upstairs to shower and dress. We switch off our iPhones and unplug the landline. It's time to batten down the hatches and wait for Margie to absolve us.

"I'm sorry you've had all this hassle," I say to Sheila. "None of it would have happened if I hadn't messed up with the holdall..Thanks for putting up with me. I can't tell you how much I love you."

"Don't tell me how much you love me," she says, "just *show* me sometimes."

Chapter Sixty-Nine

Dave

Margie does a brilliant job and my yo-yo existence of the past week is over. The true story is out and I can walk the streets again without embarrassment.

More good news arrives with the morning post as a crisp white envelope bearing the Lenhams logo drops onto the doormat.

"It's probably just final details of the sale," I say opening the envelope. I slide a printed document out of the envelope. The top half details the sale together with the commission, photography charges and VAT and a final sum of one hundred and thirty two thousand, one hundred pounds. There's a perforation two thirds of the way down and my hands shake as I realise that beneath it is a cheque for the full amount.

"It wasn't the guy who wanted an extra month then," I say as I carefully detach the cheque. I kiss it before passing it across to Sheila.

"All's well that ends well," she says.

We decide to go straight out and pay the cheque into the bank. I half expect the bank's version of The Spanish Inquisition when I pay it in. I know that money-laundering rules mean that they have to make enquiries on any unusual amounts but the young cashier simply smiles as I make the deposit.

"We all wondered when you might bring this in," he says, "would you like me to make an appointment for you with our investments people?"

"No need. It's all accounted for," I say. "When do you reckon it will be cleared?"

"Technically it's three working days but I'd give it a week if I were you."

I check the Internet banking every day. The balance is one hundred and thirty two thousand, five hundred but the available balance is just four hundred pounds on day one, three hundred pounds on day two, one thousand two hundred on day three when my Bank Pension comes in and two hundred on day four when most of it goes out again but then on day five it's there: Available balance one hundred and thirty two thousand, two hundred and twenty five pounds and sixty-five pence. I take a screen shot and decide to keep it for posterity. Maybe I'll put it in a frame with the title 'The Day That Dave And Sheila Prendergast Were Rich'

I shout Sheila to tell her that it's clear.

"We're rich," I say as she joins me and I show her the screen. She takes the cheque book out of a drawer and we get to work on making us poor again. I write a cheque to Maria for sixty-six thousand, two hundred and fifty pounds.

"That leaves sixty-six thousand, two hundred and fifty for us," says Sheila.

Although we've discussed and agreed upon what we are going to do with the balance so many times, it still isn't easy when it comes to actually doing it.

"Okay," I say turning back to the chequebook, "Here goes."

I write a cheque for twenty-two thousand payable to Simon. I write another for twenty- two thousand payable to Susie.

"Are you sure about this?" I ask Sheila, as I start to write the next one.

"Quite sure."

The next cheque is twenty-two thousand for the diabetes charity.

"So that leaves us er...the grand sum of two hundred and fifty pounds," I say.

"It'll get us that weekend at Butlins," Sheila says.

"But not with a sea view."

We laugh and stand together.

"That didn't last long. We're poor," I say. We embrace and hug each other tightly.

The telephone rings.

"Leave it," says Sheila before kissing me sexily.

I break away.

"Better not. Might be important."

I rush to the hall and pick up the home phone.

"Hello."

"Hello. Is that Mr Prendergast?"

"Yes. It's Lenhams here. Cecil Johnson-Smyth of the European ceramics department."

"Yes?"

"I've been reading about your escapades in the press. Most amusing. A wonderful tale. Anyway, I couldn't help noticing a photo of you in front of a striking porcelain plate."

"Oh, that old thing."

"Not exactly Mr Prendergast. I have a feeling that the plate is from a service that was made in around 1750 for the King Of Prussia."

"Oh, that's what I thought when I bought it but it's a Samson copy."

"Why do you think that?"

"The coat of arms is not quite right. The lion is facing the wrong way."

"Yes I noticed that. That's why I'm phoning. When the king took delivery he was furious that the lions on some pieces were not correct. In fact he was so furious that he personally smashed the offending pieces. But he missed one and we sold it in our Berlin saleroom two years ago."

"You think he might have missed another then?"

"Yes, I do."

"It might be quite valuable then?"

"Yes indeed. The one we sold in our Berlin saleroom was badly cracked but still sold for—"

I drop the phone.

"Sheila!" I shout.

"What?"

"We're rich again."

Epilogue

Dave

The plate *was* the real McCoy and my delight at its discovery by Lenhams' expert was only slightly dampened by the noticeable dent to my ego that came with getting it wrong. Simon started going through the disaster drawer to make sure that there were no other priceless heirlooms mouldering away and Sheila reminded me for months that while I was wasting hours on eBay discovering a pile of tat we could have been on the world cruise, that we've just returned from, years ago.

I ticked the no publicity box this time and we sold in Sheila's name so that she could see 'The Property of a Lady' in the catalogue. It soared above its estimate and, as well as paying for the world cruise, and another lump sum towards a deposit on a flat, it paid for Simon and Maria to have a lovely low-key wedding at the Town Hall followed by a reception at Casa Nuestra.

I don't have a pang of conscience about it at all. The eBay seller has over twenty thousand feedbacks and describes himself as one of Europe's leading experts on antique pottery and porcelain. I didn't rub it in by emailing him the details of the sale. If he's the expert he claims to be he will have seen it in the *Antiques Trade Gazette*.

As we finish unpacking from the cruise, or rather as Sheila finishes the unpacking, I open the pile of post that has accumulated over the past three months.

"There's an invite to Angela's house warming here," I shout up to Sheila.

"That's nice. So everything went through okay then?"

"Looks like it. Martin will be fuming. I wonder if they raised enough to compensate everyone in full."

"Hope so. When's the party?"

"This Sunday. Late afternoon."

"Great. I'll be able to show off my tan. Let's hope the

weather's fine and she can hold it on the roof terrace."

We take a taxi down to the river on Sunday and enjoy a stroll along the towpath before walking to the apartment block. We arrive at the gates just as an immaculate BMWK1600GT glides through them. We walk towards reception and the bike's rider follows us through the revolving doors.

Sheila nudges me.

"I knew it," she says, "Angela told me that she's been seeing him."

As we spill into the atrium, our Bollywood hero strides in after us. The security man immediately acknowledges him with an air of deference. There's a sign on a stand that reads 'Clemence Party' together with an arrow pointing towards the glass lift. Mr Ahmed heads in the direction of the arrow with us trailing a few steps behind. He stops and turns

"Is it Sheila?" he asks. Sheila almost curtseys and holds out a hand. I don't know if she's expecting him to shake it or kiss it. He shakes it and says to me "And you must be Dave."

"That's me," I shake his hand. "How do you know us?"

"Angela's guest list isn't very long and I know everyone else that's on it so by a matter of—"

"Elementary, my dear Watson," I interrupt.

He smiles and gestures around the cavernous leafy space.

"Welcome to Angela's not too humble abode."

"We've been here before," Sheila says it as if we spend half our time in millionaire company. In honesty she doesn't look at all out of place with her hair perfectly styled and wearing an outfit that we bought on the liner and certainly wasn't part of the all-inclusive deal. You can't say the same for me as I'm still in my M&S, Blue Harbour casuals although I've had to go down several sizes after keeping up the exercise.

"The penthouse?"

"Yes," Says Sheila.

"Long story," I say as we approach the lift. Akash swipes his card at the controls and soon we are enjoying the sunny views across the city as we speed skywards.

Angela welcomes us to her new home. It has not changed a great deal since our last visit but Hetherington's art has been displaced by some finer pieces that make the place more homely.

As soon as Sheila has been given a glass of champagne and introduced to some of Angela's friends on the roof terrace, Angela takes my arm and guides me away.

"I've been waiting a long time to show you this Dave. I had these done specially." She leads me into the main living area. Hand made glass shelves that appear to float suspended in air, line the south facing glass wall. Each holds an object of exquisite beauty highlighted by the setting sun; a Lalique glass figure; a Tiffany lamp and, in the focal point of the display, two very familiar pieces of oriental ceramics.

"I told you that I would repay you," she smiles, "There was no way that I was going to let them get away. I wanted you and Sheila to get the best possible price so I bid them up. If I hadn't, the bidding might have stopped a lot lower – although I doubt it. They are very special."

"But it was an old Asian bloke waving the paddle."

"That's right. He was waving it on my behalf. I wanted to keep out of the spotlight."

I shake my head. "Incredible. I never thought I would see them again. I hope you like them."

"Of course I do. I adore them. I wasn't going to bid that price for something I didn't like. Now, I'd better go and circulate."

She leaves me to study once more the wonderful artistry that had such an impact on our lives. After a few minutes of wonder, I leave the living area for the roof terrace.

I find Sheila busy chatting with Akash. I wait for a break in their conversation to interrupt politely, "You'll never guess what Angela's been showing me."

"The Yabu Meizan vases."

"You knew?"

"Yes. I just found out in a very interesting conversation with Akash and his mum and dad..." Sheila pauses and gestures with her champagne glass across the perfectly trimmed plants and greenery towards a woman wearing a beautiful silk sari. She stands alongside the very smart bespectacled elderly Indian gentleman with immaculate silver hair who I last saw bowing in Lenhams' saleroom. "It was Mr Ahmed's lifelong ambition to bid in an auction and, as Angela wanted to keep her bid secret, Akash volunteered his dad to go and bid on Angela's behalf."

I'm not very good at party small talk. I take a glass of champagne from one of the young men holding silver salvers and start to look around the terrace for a familiar face. There isn't one. I think about going across to introduce myself to the elderly Indian couple but they seem busy talking to two other couples.

I cradle my champagne and step back inside. I take a little tour of the penthouse. I admire the beautiful artworks and objet d'art that are displayed to blend harmoniously with the décor. I push open doors and peek inside. One door swings open to reveal half a dozen luxurious leather armchairs in front of a gigantic screen that has to be sixteen feet across. I walk to an armchair and sit myself down. I lean back in comfort and rest my arms on the armrests.

My fingers alight on a series of buttons. I lift the remote from the padded armrest and flick at its screen. The TV bursts into life. I get out of the seat and walk to the door. I close the door and walk back to the seat and sit down. I scroll through the Sky TV Guide. *Antiques Roadshow* is showing. I press select and settle down. I've missed the introduction but they're in the garden of Osterley Park in Middlesex. My Lenhams favourite is sitting at a table beneath a gazebo in glorious sunshine. He's holding items he's just valued at over fifty thousand pounds.

"Oh, and which charity shop was that?" he says.

The camera pans to a character in a navy blue blazer and stripy tie, "Oh it was in London. Diabetes I think."

"Well I am sure that the diabetes charity will be *delighted* to hear about your windfall. How much do you think you'll be donating?"

I punch the air. The shot cuts away from a quivering white moustache.

Fiona Bruce's bum fills six feet of the screen.

And a very nice bum it is too.

Some of the 5* reviews from readers:

'Writing full of warmth and understanding'
'A really beautifully written story'
'Being a child of the 1950s and 60s this was truly a trip down memory lane'
'A lovely story'

A compelling story set in 1969 against the background of the Apollo Moon missions and filled with sunshine, fireworks and pop music, Give Me Your Tomorrow is funny, romantic and moving. Maggie Johnson and her son Alfie arrive on the beautiful Greek island of Symos. She's aiming to save Alfie from an oppressive existence in their home city of Liverpool and to develop a holiday business in the fledgling tourism industry . A family tragedy has confined Nicos Karteras to a lonely life on the island. When Maggie rents his idyllic cottage Nico sees a possible opportunity for friendship and perhaps an end to his loneliness but a simple misunderstanding threatens to blow everything off course.

Available as a paperback and Kindle edition from Amazon stores

Acknowledgements

With sincere thanks to Scott Pack for his tremendous guidance and input when carrying out his edit and to Caroline Goldsmith of Goldsmith Publishing Consultancy for completing an extremely thorough copy edit and providing me with plenty more very sound and helpful advice. Thanks too to Spiffing Covers for providing another excellent cover that perfectly captures the feel of *Mr Prendergast's Fantastic Find*.

I must also thank my test readers Wendy Hewitt, Hazel Hawkins and my sister Julie for the constructive criticism that led to a number of revisions. More thanks to Julie too for correcting my Spanish and giving me the term *viejo verde* to add to my limited Spanish vocabulary.

Finally I must thank my wonderful wife Marion for putting up with my hours spent tapping away at a keyboard and for agreeing to me spending our hard earned cash on perfecting this novel. She would like me to point out that she bears no resemblance whatsoever to Sheila (apart from being extremely attractive of course).

About the Author

John Brassey was born in Heswall in 1953 and grew up in the Lancashire seaside resort of Southport where he attended King George V Grammar School. He left school after completing his A' Levels and joined one of the high street banks working in many branches and offices throughout Merseyside before moving to London as a secondee to the Department Of Trade And Industry. After his secondment he switched careers and used his banking and DTI experience to join Instanta Ltd, his parents' catering equipment manufacturing business in Southport, which he ran initially with his brother Peter and then with his wife Marion after Peter retired. He and Marion sold the business in 2010 and retired to Framlingham in Suffolk in 2013.

John is an avid reader who has always enjoyed writing. He wrote a regular blog for the Instanta website and, upon retirement continued blogging in "Notes From Retirement...Where Did The Years Go?" (johnbrassey.blogspot.co.uk) in which he has charted the adventures of moving to a completely new and unknown area. When not reading or writing he is a regular cinema and gym goer, a cyclist and he also enjoys searching local farms with his metal detector. He is also a voluntary business mentor for Suffolk Chamber Of Commerce and a volunteer for the Framlingham Hour Community. He has two children, Sarah who is a yoga instructor living in St Andrews and Paul who heads a TV Development team and lives in Kent. Since retirement John and Marion have been blessed with three granddaughters, Rose, Catherine and Melody and one grandson, Teddy. A lot of their time is now spent traveling to Kent and to Fife where they have bought a caravan to make it easier to visit the family.

Made in the USA
Columbia, SC
28 April 2017